KC KEAN

Ruthless Riot
Ruthless Brothers MC #3
Copyright © 2023 KC Kean

www.authorkckean.com
Published by Featherstone Publishing Ltd

Cover Design: BellaLuna
Editing: Zainab M. - Heart Full of Edits
Proofreader: Sassi's Editing Services
Interior Formatting & Design: Wild Elegance Formatting

Ruthless Riot/KC Kean– 1st ed.
ISBN-13 - 978-1-915203-39-7

To Maxinne,
Happy Birthday!
To meeting readers at book signings and becoming
addicted to their fabulousness.

.

Families who slay together stay together.

ONE

Scarlett

My heart hammers against my chest despite my cool exterior. As if life couldn't get any worse, I find the man who trained me to be the killer I am, and his son—the first sexual mistake I ever made—standing before me on the steps of the place I was sure to call home.

They were invited here because of their ties to the Ruthless Brothers. I didn't think my life could become any more twisted, but here I am, wound up in another knot of my past, smiling in the face of my present.

With Gray's arm draped around my shoulders in a silent form of protection, he steers me inside, but when he moves toward Church, I quickly edge toward the back of the clubhouse instead.

"Your room," I murmur the second we're out of the bar area, and he leads the way without a word. Only when the door closes behind us do I release the breath lodged in my throat.

Gray's arm drops from my shoulders as I start to pace at the bottom of his bed. I can feel him tracing my every move, but he doesn't push even though he's practically bouncing on the tips of his toes.

My mind is going a mile a minute. I'm drenched in blood. The blood of a Devil's Brute after I was taken from the mall and the memory of Duffer's lifeless body threatens to crumble me to my knees. I can't break. I can't fall. Not now, not ever.

I want to scream, but instead, I settle for tensing every inch of my body in anger before relaxing every muscle from head to toe with a big exhale.

I want to sleep for a week, bathe for a month, and fuck my problems away for the rest of eternity. With the new arrivals, that's not a possibility, though.

"Sweet Cheeks?" Gray murmurs in concern, and I glance up at him. "Let me in."

It's like he can see the walls rising around me, the need to bury myself away and hide from *everything* so I can compartmentalize the loss of Duffer and the entire fuckery that was today. But for the first time in my life, I have someone pleading with me not to.

"I don't know how." My lids close as the truth falls from my lips, and in the next breath his hands wrap around my arms, his breath at my ear.

"You do, Scar. You know exactly how to. You've just never done it before, and that's scaring the shit out of you." My chest clenches as his words claw into my soul and settle in.

"I'm feeling too much all at once, Gray. I was born cold and raised to be lethal, but my chest hurts. The fear I felt today, the loss of an old friend, the danger Emily was in, and the blast from the past waiting out there—it's just too fucking much." He crushes me to his chest, holding me and taking the weight from my limbs as I focus on breathing.

He strokes my hair like he's consoling me, but not a tear leaks from my lids. Numbness drapes over my mind, body, and soul as my survival instincts take over. Just like they always do.

It may be cold, but it's familiar and will help me get through this.

As if sensing my thoughts once again, Gray leans back, grips my shoulders, and shakes his head. "Don't do it, Scar." He grips my chin and tilts my head up, giving me the sternest look I've ever seen on his face. "For me. *Please*."

Fuck.

I lift my hands to his chest, a move I've made a hundred times before, but this time, I slip beneath the leather of his cut and feel the intense beating of his heart. It vibrates through me, grounding me and opening me up all at once. I focus on every beat as I take deep breaths in time with it.

Pa-dum.

Inhale.

Pa-dum.

Exhale.

Pa-dum.

Inhale.

Pa-dum.

Exhale.

"I love you, Scarlett. My heart beats for you. I'm here for you. My entire fucking world revolves around you. Ever since I saw you through the window at the Reapers', I knew you were going to be important to me, my life, and my world. I just didn't imagine it would be this fucking deep, but it is, and I wouldn't change it for the world."

Light-headed, I get lost in his eyes, clinging to the words before I cut the remaining distance between us by fusing our lips together. I don't know how to say those three simple words so effortlessly like he does, but my body refuses to ignore him, opting to *show* him how I feel instead.

He bands his arms tightly around my waist, lifting my feet off the ground as we devour one another, my fingers clawing at his hair. Teeth clash, tongues tangle, and ecstasy tingles through my veins.

"Of all the times for you to be fucking each other, I don't think now is the one. Do you?"

Fuck.

The way Gray blinks his eyes open at me matches mine. We were so caught up in each other, we didn't even hear the door open. But that's definitely Emmett, Ryker, and Axel standing in the doorway with exasperated looks on their faces.

I stroke my fingers through Gray's blond hair before pressing a final chaste kiss on his lips. Slowly, he lowers me to the floor with a soft smile and a pleased gleam in his eyes. Not at all what you would expect from someone who was just denied some fun, but my brain can't decipher what it is that is making him happy.

The others move into the room and shut the door behind them as I reluctantly take a step back from Gray. Catching sight of my hands, I instantly remember the blood coating my skin, but instead of sinking in my emotions again, I stand taller with my shoulders rolled back and my chin raised.

"That's my girl," Axel murmurs. He's the first of the new arrivals to approach me with a smile, despite the tension radiating from him. He stops right in front of me and tucks a loose tendril of hair behind my ear, his eyes attempting to say so much despite the silence coming from him.

My cheeks feel warm under his intense gaze, but he steps away, letting Emmett take his spot.

"You don't know how relieved I am to be standing in front of you right now, Snowflake," Emmett says, his hand capturing my throat as he rests his forehead on mine. It's like they're now taking a moment to feel the relief of my return since we were interrupted outside.

I breathe Emmett in, just as he does me, before his lips ghost my cheek in a delicate kiss. Ryker quickly replaces him, dragging his eyes over every inch of me as if he's committing every mark on my skin and stain on my clothes to memory.

"We will retaliate for this, Scarlett." Ryker's tone is clipped, angry, and his brows furrow in a swarm of emotions. "I will burn every inch of this damn town to the ground to find where they're located then slaughter every single one of them. Devil's Brutes be damned; they don't know the true strength of the Ruthless."

My adrenaline pounds ferociously through my veins as I absorb his words. The promise of blood and chaos is just another way of giving me those three particular words that Gray murmured. I was definitely made for them.

"It sounds like a date." The corner of my mouth tips up as he musters a half grin in response before capturing my lips with his. It's over far too quickly as he leans back, and the four of them form a circle with me.

"Before we get you cleaned up and taken care of, we need to discuss the absolute mind fuck that's outside," Emmett states, tainting the moment with the reality of life, and I sigh.

"Did they say anything after I left with Gray?" I ask, instantly beginning to calculate my next move as I always do.

"Declan grinned like the Cheshire fucking cat, and Graham acted confused. Asked us what you meant by teaching you everything you know."

Fucker, of course he did. "What did you say?"

Axel shrugs. "I said I had no idea what you were talking about either."

Relieved, I sigh. "Good, that's good. We can use this to our advantage if they think you don't know who I truly am."

"What are you saying?" Gray asks, shuffling his feet so they're shoulder-width apart as he stares intently at me.

"Graham taught me how to kill until my eighth birthday, then my father deemed me worthy and took over my training himself. He knows who I am, but I don't think he ever learned I was the Grim Reaper, just like Kincaid."

Axel paces while Emmett's nostrils flare angrily at the reminder of my past.

"How do you know he doesn't think you're the Grim Reaper?" Ryker asks, hands on his hips as the wheels turn in his head, the leader in him considering the facts from every angle.

"Because only two people knew, other than those dead at my hands—my father Freddie, and his bestie..." I say mockingly before wetting my parched lips and dropping the name that I know will cause problems. "Billy. Billy Weaver."

All sets of eyes whirl in my direction, but there's a hint of expectation and understanding from Axel after our heart to heart.

"That's why you took him out at the same time as Banner," Ryker pieces it together.

Axel clears his throat, sensing my internal stress as he responds, "There's more to it than that, Brother, but he fucking deserved it regardless of the details."

I want to kiss him. I want to throw myself at him once more and feel his arms around me, but I'm unsure whether it was a one time thing or not, so I remain rooted to the spot instead, mouthing my thanks as the others accept that small snippet of information.

I'm sure they would love to know more, their hearts and minds demanding it, but respectfully and surprisingly they redirect the conversation.

"So, we need to figure out how we want to play this shit

with Graham, Declan, and their chapter," Emmett grunts, and Gray waves his hand in the air enthusiastically.

"I vote we kill them."

Axel nods eagerly along with him, but I halt that idea. "No, no way. Well… not yet, at least," I amend, but Axel and Gray still glare at me like stubborn toddlers who just had their favorite toy taken away.

"I didn't know they were connected with you, but the fact remains the same. Freddie was clearly fucking close with them in some way. Which means—"

"They might actually be familiar with the Brutes," Emmett finishes, and I nod.

Fuck.

"That only makes me want to kill them more, Reaper." Axel folds his arms over his chest, a pointed look on his face as I smile at him.

"They either have information we need or are linked to them. Once we figure that out, you can do with them as you please, but I really think we can use them to our advantage a little first." All eyes shoot to Ryker, the prez, for a final answer, but there's another detail we need to add before we confirm or deny anything. "I also think we should push the fact I'm a club whore here too."

"Fuck no," Gray grunts, wagging his finger in my direction as Axel growls, Emmett shakes his head, and Ryker glares at me.

"They need to see me as nothing here. Inconsequential. They'll either realize my abilities or my importance to…" I trail off, almost embarrassed and diffident to finish the sentence, but Ryker happily takes over.

"Or your importance to us." Silence drapes over the room as the words settle and he reluctantly sighs. "She's right."

"Of course she is," Axel grumbles, and I smirk. Fucker. "Then it's settled."

"Not a single other man lays a hand on you, Snowflake. Not one. I will give up the secret before I allow that," Emmett bites, and fuck does it make my core clench.

"I'm yours and yours alone," I breathe, my heart soaring at the fact. "Now please, let me fucking shower the blood off of me and let me see Emily with my own damn eyes."

"Whatever you need, Rebel."

TWO

Emmett

Anger burns through my veins at the pain that still lingers in Emily's eyes when I look at her, at the distress that drapes over Scarlett, and the loss of another life at the hands of the motherfucking Brutes.

I'm done with all this bullshit, just like I'm sure my brothers are too. Action needs to be taken, but it can't be any more small moves. It needs to be nuclear, and if that means biding my time for a moment or two, then I'll persevere.

My heart ached at every word that fell from Emily's mouth, the panic that Scarlett was gone for good weighing heavy on me until she careened up the club drive as crazed as ever. We shouldn't have expected anything less from her. She's a survivor, through and through. Those fuckers didn't stand a chance against her.

I find Maggie behind the bar. Her gaze flickers to the Church doors, indicating that's where our guests are. She's the most vital part of the Ruthless Brothers, without actually being a damn member. She holds us together like glue, the heart of our leathers. Like Scarlett does.

I have to get my thoughts and emotions under control before I step in there, though. They can't see the core of our problems shining in my eyes, not now that we know the paths they have chosen.

"Shift is with Emily. We'll catch him up on everything afterward," Ryker murmurs, tucking his cell phone away. The last thing I want or need is for my sister to be unattended right now. She might give me hell and rage about being a grown-ass woman, but I lost ten years of my life today. It's going to take me more than a minute to get over that.

"Please remind me why we just agreed to act casual as shit in there?" Gray grunts, pointing at the Church doors that sit slightly ajar, offering a peek at the unwanted men inside. "We called them for help, not more bullshit."

"It's going to serve us in the long run, Brother," Ryker murmurs, walking in line with the three of us as every single person here watches our every move.

"I don't like it," Gray grouches back, and I can't help but agree with him.

"Me either, but I trust Scarlett and I trust her judgment. Do you?" He glances at Axel to his left first before casting his eyes over Gray and me, and the two of us nod reluctantly.

"With my life," Axel bites, making my steps falter and my eyes widen.

Well, fuck.

It was something else entirely when I watched Scarlett run straight into his arms. The shock almost dropped me to my knees, but hearing him admit that he trusts her, a woman, with his life, is ground-altering.

He doesn't slow his pace, like the three of us gaping at him; instead, he cuts the remaining steps to the Church with determination, giving us no time to push on his thoughts and feelings. Which is a good thing because we need our game faces on to deal with these assholes.

Ryker and Gray step inside before me, and I kick the door shut as the last in, trying like hell not to glare at the three fuckers already warming the seats in our Church. Graham sits at the opposite end of the table to Ryker, Declan to his left, and a guy with a patch that reads 'Oakley' to his right.

Nobody speaks a word until we're all seated. I take my usual VP spot beside Ryker, with Gray to my left, leaving Axel to sit across from me.

Graham's gray beard straggles down to his chest, the skull bandana wrapped around his head like it always is as his bulbous nose twitches. Declan must get his looks from his mother because he doesn't look a thing like his father. But the sinister glimmer in his eyes is one I'm only just noticing. He looks like a fuckboy with his swept hair, chiseled jaw, and tattoos covering him from head to toe. Oakley is the only one wearing a half smile and an unfazed expression. He either doesn't know shit, or he's high. Maybe the latter, maybe both.

"What's going on, Ryker?" Graham asks, cocking a brow as my best friend relaxes back in his seat. "You didn't give much away on our call, just something about a kidnapping and retribution. Here we are."

I'm itching to answer, but it has to be Ryker. Old schoolers like this don't see equality in a club. Just them, their thoughts, their ideas, and everyone else falls in line or pays the price in blood.

"We've lost a lot of lives the past few weeks. Emmett's dad, Eric, being one of them."

Graham's tongue flicks out as he assesses me. "Sorry for your loss, Brother." I want to tell him to go fuck himself, yet I nod instead. "What happened today that made you reach out, though?"

"We lost another life, a prospect protecting Emmett's younger sister. An attempt at kidnapping one of our women also took place, but they didn't succeed."

"Who didn't?"

"The Devil's Brutes."

I observe all three of them for a sign, a signal, anything

to hint that they are familiar with who we're talking about. It's a slight twitch to Declan's left eye that gives him away.

Motherfuckers.

Inside, I want to reach across the table, tear them apart limb by limb until the anger is satiated. I wish Scarlett had never been in the same room as either of them and I wish she didn't have to continue now, but Ryker is right. We trust her completely, and this is her call.

If we didn't already have a president we would blindly follow into the darkness that lurks in this town, I'd be nominating her next and she's another unpatched member.

"And the girl, is she okay?"

"She's fine." The bite to Axel's tone is clear he doesn't have his feelings under control, but I don't glance at him. That would only draw attention to his vulnerability right now. *Our* vulnerability.

"It wasn't little Scarlett Reeves, was it? I remember her father. God forbid if anyone hurt her. She's all alone now that the Reapers are gone." I glare at Declan and his choice of words.

Scarlett was alone where she was, but she isn't any longer. She isn't little either, but that's just another way to demean her as a woman, as a person. I keep my mouth shut though, letting them continue to underestimate her, and I'll be sure to let her be the one to pull the trigger to end their lives.

They fucking deserve it.

"So, the Brutes. Is this an ongoing issue?" Graham asks, not waiting for a response about Scarlett. Either that, or he knows he won't get one.

"It seems so," Ryker grumbles, swiping a hand down his face. "We refuse to give into their demands which has put a ticking bomb on the situation." Graham hums in understanding as Ryker leans forward and braces his elbows on the table, making eye contact with the president. "That being said, we need numbers. If you can offer your aid, it would truly be appreciated, Brother."

Graham's gaze slowly travels from Axel, to Ryker, over me, before glancing at Gray. I hate letting them know we need their help. Even before Scarlett's bombshell, being vulnerable is not something I offer to anyone. Especially not another chapter.

When he's sure he's dragged the silence out for long enough, Graham finally sits forward in his seat, mirroring Ryker's posture. "Then we're at your command, President Ryker."

I don't like the undertone of how he said that, but I settle for clenching my hands tightly in my lap instead of lashing out. He pisses me off as much as Kincaid, the president of the Devil's Brutes, who has his eyes now firmly set on Scarlett.

It's official. I hate people. Anyone that isn't a loyal

Ruthless Brother, my sister, Maggie, or Scarlett—I hate them. Ruthless Bitches included. I can't *people* any longer, not when I hear Ryker murmur his thanks, knock the gavel on the table, and call time on the meeting.

All we've achieved right now is extending their unwanted stay, but there's nothing we can do about it. *Slow and steady.*

"We'll set you up in the—"

"Put us as close to the whores as possible. You know that's where we'll be spending most of our time anyway," Declan interjects with a grin on his lips that I want to erase with my fists.

"Of course," Gray replies, clapping his hands as he stands, and I follow suit.

It makes me realize that we never placed Scarlett in a room near the Ruthless Bitches. Ever. Not even from the moment she stepped through the doors. This guy knew long before the rest of us how important she would be. It may not have been intentional, but it was subconsciously pieced together.

Gray leads the three men from the room, his stance tight and his shoulders bunched together. The second they're out of earshot, Axel slams his fist into the table in anger. "Keep it together, Ax," Ryker mutters, tension lining his face as he, too, feels the strain.

"We can do this for her, for us, for the club. We lay this

all to rest once and for all. We just have to bide our time." I don't know if I'm trying to soothe them with my words or myself, but as true as it may be, it's not working.

"She was almost gone. Did you see the state she was in when she hightailed it in here in that SUV with two dead fucking bodies in the back? Scarlett's been through enough. Enough." Axel's chest heaves as he looks at his hands. There are smears of blood across his palms and fingertips, and seeing them there only confirms what he did earlier.

Moving around the table, I come to a stop beside him. "Are you okay?"

Three words that hold no real value for what I'm asking. He held her in his arms, almost squeezed the life from her lungs as she held him back. When he doesn't respond immediately, Ryker breathes his name, concern etched in every letter. "Axel…"

The man in question doesn't lift his gaze from his hands, but he leans back in his seat. "I… It's… I don't even know where to begin or process it. I thought she was gone, pain ripped through every cell in my body with the panic of her being in their grasp. Only for her to be back on our doorstep before we could even make a move to help her." He gulps, blinking up as his eyes slowly travel from Ryker to me and back again. "I didn't think. I didn't do anything but feel, and fuck, man… it was everything. Her arms wrapped around me, and I felt like…"

Ryker pats his shoulder and finishes the sentence for him. "You felt like you were home."

He nods, one small sharp move, and my chest fucking swells, understanding the feeling Ryker is explaining.

We're nomads. Home isn't something we look for, yet it somehow found us. In the form of a dark-haired, porcelain-skinned beauty who wields our hearts as well as she wields any weapon.

"We'll figure this all out, Ax. But for now, you need to shower and take a second to feel these emotions. We're here if you need us." Ryker smiles, his words making the corner of Axel's mouth tip up too as he stands.

"I'm going to go and check on my sister. If you need me, just holler," I offer, clapping hands with both of them before I head back through the bar area. I keep my head down and gaze diverted so no one gets the idea that they can talk to me right now. I rap my knuckles on my bedroom door and step inside.

Shift darts up from his seat beside the bed, tension thick in his eyes as he juts his chin up. My eyes don't last more than a second on him as I look at my sister's sleeping form and the body lying beside her.

I'm moving before I realize it, rounding the opposite side of the bed as Emily's blonde locks intertwine with black.

Scarlett.

"How long has she been here?" I whisper, desperate to reach out a hand, but fight against it instead.

"As soon as she had showered. Emily didn't stir. If anything, I think she fell deeper into sleep in her presence."

My heart soars, and my chest tightens with raw emotions. Everything she did to defend and protect my sister will never be forgotten. Ever. Scarlett sacrificed herself to the enemy to save Emily. And the first place she winds up afterward is back at her side.

Fuck, I love this woman.

I stroke the back of my finger over her soft skin from her temple to her chin, and that's when I see it. A lone tear, tracking down her face.

My love for her blossoms into anger at the enemy. Fury descending over me as I promise her here and now. I will make this right. I will protect her from the storm ahead, and more than anything, I will love her to the very end of time.

THREE

Scarlett

Apparently, sleep didn't ease any of the pain from my limbs, and the tension in my neck tells me I didn't doze as soundly as I was hoping.

I wonder what it would be like to spend a day without being trapped inside my head.

Yawning, I slowly blink my eyes open and startle when I come face-to-face with Emily staring at me with a smile.

Fuck.

I forgot where I was for a second, but it all comes rushing back to me in a flash. The elevator. Duffer. The car ride. The blood on my hands. Graham and Declan. Shit. My mind kicks up to a mile a second and any chance of letting the stress pass me by is long gone.

"Hey." Emily's smile grows a little, and I force myself to reciprocate.

"Hey. Are you okay?"

Her eyebrows pinch as she regards me, a snort falling from her mouth. "Am *I* okay? Fuck, Scarlett. *You* were taken. Taken!" Her voice rises as I chuckle.

"I'm aware," I offer with an eye roll. "But as you can see, I'm back." I'm not sure if my words are soothing or overwhelming, likely the latter, as her eyes brim with unshed tears in the next second. "Those better not be tears for me," I balk, my heart stuttering in my chest and threatening to drown me in my own emotions.

"People *can* care about you, Scarlett," she grumbles with a fake glare.

"Sure, just not so directly *at* me. I don't know what to do with myself." I grin, and she relaxes beside me as a cloud of sadness descends over the room, and I remember the thought I had earlier when the mess of yesterday came crashing over me.

Duffer.

"He's really gone, isn't he?" she mumbles, emotion rasping her voice, and I manage a nod.

"Yeah." The pain cocoons us as the reality sets in.

"You knew him?" she asks, and I nod again, struggling to find words. "Things seemed different with you guys after we went to the doctor's office," she adds, nestling closer to me.

"Yeah, he… he explained who he was from when we

were kids. He and his mom offered me a sense of home and comfort among the craziness that was my life. When she died and he was forced to leave, I felt my first drop of true pain and loneliness after being offered a glimpse of an alternate life that wasn't meant for me."

The words are heavy but true, and my heart hurts at the fact that I never got a chance to repay him. For making me whole at a time when I was anything but. I've killed before, many, many times, and watched people die around me more times than I can count, but I've never felt remorse or sadness for it except for Duffer and his mom.

My eyes clench shut. Emily's hand on my arm grounds me in the present and stops me from wallowing in the corner of my mind.

"I'm so sorry, Scar," she whispers, and despite my pain, I force my eyes open.

"I'm sorry too. I'm sorry I couldn't save him as well—"

"No, you can't carry that burden. That wasn't your job and there wasn't a second to consider it. You spent the few seconds we did have protecting me. Not yourself. *Me*. I'm forever going to be grateful for that." My next breath lodges in my chest, her words tearing down my usual thoughts as she forces me to hear them loud and clear.

"Me too."

My neck almost snaps as I whirl around to find Emmett leaning against the door frame. His expression is unreadable as he glances between us, making me gulp as I take in every inch of him. My blond Viking is only wearing a pair of gray shorts. No t-shirt, no cut, no shoes, with his blond hair twisted up on top of his head.

Was Viking the right word to use for him, or should I be leaning more toward a god?

I'm so caught up in watching him that I don't notice the bed shifting beside me until Emily is on her feet, drowned in her brother's t-shirt as she smiles at me.

"I'll be back in a while."

I rise to my elbows, panic kicking in as I blink at her. "Why? Where are you going?"

Her soft smile is disarming as always and relaxes me despite my concern. "I've been awake for a while, and Emmett insisted I get something to eat since it's almost lunchtime, but I refused to leave until you woke up."

Lunchtime? Shit, how long was I out?

"Thank you," I murmur, my heart soaring at her need to stay with me, just like my need forcing me to pass out beside her instead of in my own bed.

When Emily gets to the door, Emmett steps aside but still throws his arm out to offer her a hug. As she leans back, I can see the mischief glimmering in her eyes before she speaks. "Don't fuck her too loudly, you'll put me off my food. And make sure to change the sheets before I get back." She winks and bolts out of the door without

34

another word, leaving me to gape at the space she occupied moments earlier.

"When did she become such a menace?" I ask as Emmett slams the door shut, the frame rattling with the force. Cocking a brow at him, I twist my lips. "Are you okay?"

He doesn't speak a word as he moves toward me. Slowly, measured, predatory. The room fades to darkness around him as he nears me. The muscles in his neck are bunched together, the scar down his chest drawing my eyes as the tension ripples around me.

"Emmett?" I murmur, uncertainty clenching my chest as I grip the sheets beside me, and still, he says nothing.

He goes from slow, calculated moves to pouncing on me all at once. The bed bounces as he clambers up the length of me until we're face-to-face and I'm trapped beneath him. My chest tightens with anticipation as I look up into his gaze, before his mouth consumes mine.

He's a force to be reckoned with as he devours me, his fingers running through my hair as I claw back at him just the same. He steals every kiss, elicits goosebumps with every touch, and drowns me with the raw emotion between us.

When I can no longer breathe, he leans back, the tip of his nose brushing against mine as he wraps his fingers around my throat, holding me in place. There's a new level of urgency between us, one that wasn't there before, or if it was, it's intensified now.

Looking up at him through hooded eyes, I startle at the ferocity I find. "I'll never be able to repay you for what you did back in that elevator to save Emily. Yet, I'll never be able to punish you enough for putting yourself in harm's way."

My mouth dries at his words as his fingers flex along my throat. "That sounds like a win-win situation to me," I say, my core tingling with the sparks between us.

"Fuck, Scar. You're not supposed to say shit like that."

"What *am* I supposed to say, then?"

He wets his bottom lip, his stare only darkening as he assesses me. "You're supposed to fear those words and promise to never do it again." I raise my eyebrows and continue to stare at him. "Fuck. But that wouldn't be you, would it? I can't decide if that makes me angrier or happier," he grumbles, and a smile spreads across my face. "Don't smile, we could have fucking lost you." His fingers flex on my throat, forcing me to bite back a groan.

"But you didn't."

He eases slightly, a sense of calmness washing over him. "But we didn't," he repeats my words, his tone calmer than it was moments ago, until he runs a finger down the side of my face where I know there's a bruise from yesterday's incident. "I'll make them pay for this,

Snowflake," he breathes, determined.

"Agreed, but not now. Right now, it needs to be me and you, no pain, no interruptions, no reality. I need to forget it all for a second, Emmett. I need to get lost in you." I shock myself with how earnest I sound, how desperate, but there's no controlling it at this point.

I mean it. I need him.

"You'll be the death of me, Scarlett."

"That's the first thing I thought about you, too, Mr. Viking. Standing in my room with your gun aimed at me, asking questions I wasn't ready to answer. It would have been one hell of a way to go. But it wasn't my time then, and it isn't ours now. So fuck me, direct *all* of that energy toward me. I want to feel you."

His hand flexes once again while he grips the sheets beside my head with the other. I love nothing more than getting under his skin in the best way possible.

His lips graze the corner of my mouth, teasing me, then he trails his lips down the side of my throat, between his fingers that are wrapped around me. My hips buck up to meet his, my legs eager to wrap around him as I let him consume me, body, mind, soul... and my heart.

I pout when his hand leaves my skin, but it's only to heave me forward, ripping the oversized t-shirt from my body, and placing me back down again. I'm still panty free, and his gaze drops to my core.

"Fuck, Emmett," I gasp, running my hand over his chest and across his scar, but he moves away in the next moment, removing his shorts and letting his huge length spring free.

"*You'll* be the death of *me* with that fucking thing," I mumble, gaping at its beauty.

"It'd be one hell of a way to go," he mimics my words from moments ago and steals my thoughts from me. "Come here, Snowflake," he orders from his spot at the bottom of the bed, crooking his finger at me.

Excited, I slowly shuffle around so I'm on my hands and knees before crawling toward him. His eyes darken, his jaw flexing as he watches my every move, my every breath, until I run my tongue over the underside of his cock. I groan, turned on by every ridge and vein I can feel as he pulses.

"I didn't ask you to touch me yet," he states, cocking a brow at me, attempting to act casual, like I'm not tasting him, but I know better. On my next pass, when I reach the tip of his cock, I don't just run my tongue back down him again; I swallow him whole, taking as much as I can while lifting my hand to hold him.

His eyes roll back, and I grin triumphantly. A hiss from his lips making my thighs press together.

"Do you think you're a good girl when you disobey me like that, Snowflake?" Pausing, I look at him with wide eyes. "Don't you want to be my good girl, Scarlett?" The wicked gleam in his eyes and the way the corner of his mouth tilts up makes it clear he knows he's back to having the upper hand.

Fucker.

Do I want to be his good girl? Fuck yeah.

Was I born good? Hell no.

"I think I need reminding of what a good girl acts like," I breathe, releasing him from my mouth but remaining close enough that my lips brush against his tip as I speak.

A gasp tumbles from my lips as his hand engulfs my throat once more, lifting me up before him until we're chest to chest. "I don't know if you deserve a reminder. You're not listening now, you put yourself in harm's way, you risked yourself, the woman I love, at the hands of the enemy," he says, still rattled by yesterday's incident, and I instantly know what we need right now.

Fuck being a good girl; I just want to be his girl.

Placing my hands on his chest, I rise to my feet, eyes fixed on his as I stand an inch or two taller with the bed beneath me. "Sit down, Emmett."

I step aside and point to the spot beside me when he frowns. He rubs his lips together, searching my eyes for whatever it is I have planned, but I give nothing away, and he eventually sits down.

"Tell me, Emmett. How many times do you feel like

I've defied you?" I say when he finally obeys me.

"Too many times to count," he grumbles, running his hand over his beard as I jump down from the bed.

"Pick a number," I push.

"At least five."

"Do we need to round that up to ten?" My chest heaves with every breath I take as I move to stand between his open legs.

"We probably should," he agrees, still clueless as ever.

I tilt his head up to meet my eyes and smile. Before pressing an open-mouthed kiss to his cheek, taking his hand, and repeating the motion to his palm.

I turn and glance over my shoulder as I slowly lean forward, my hair touching the floor as I brace my hands on my shins, offering my ass to him. "You have ten, Viking. Make them worth it."

He licks his bottom lip, rubs his palms on his knees, and stares at my exposed pussy and the globes of my ass. "Are you sure you want that?" he asks, unable to tear his eyes from me.

"I'm sure that I want you. I'm sure that I want to *feel* like I'm right here with you. Where I'm meant to be, Emmett. And you need the reminder that I'm back in your hands and not theirs."

He doesn't utter a word in response. Instead I feel the sting of his hand on my left cheek, before he soothes the spot with a gentle caress. "Count for me, Snowflake."

It takes a moment for me to release the breath lodged in my throat, and the delay makes him glance at my face as I stare at him. He nods, encouraging me, and I smile. There's my man.

"One."

Smack.

Caress.

"Two," I gasp, my skin prickling at the sting but quickly easing at his touch.

Smack.

Caress.

"Three."

The next five hits come in rapid succession and I don't even get a chance to call them out, too busy relishing in the feel against my skin as my core is rocked.

"What number are we at?" Emmett asks, his voice raspy as I try to catch my breath.

"Eight, we're at eight."

He nods and lands two final smacks on my skin, but this time, they're not on my ass cheeks. He targets my pussy, and I shatter without him even teasing a finger at my entrance. A sob breaks past my lips as euphoria dances over my skin, and I stumble back against him, thankful that he catches me as I try to take a deep breath.

"You're so fucking beautiful, Scarlett," he breathes

against my ear, making me shiver in his hold.

Now to make him mine.

I turn to face him head-on, and his hands instantly go to my waist as I shuffle onto his lap, knees braced on either side of him as his cock twitches beneath me. I place his tip at my entrance, my juices coating him, and my need is evident as I stare deep into his eyes.

"Tell me where I am, Emmett."

He looks at me in confusion for a second before understanding seems to dawn on him.

"You're right here."

Correct answer.

Taking my time, I push down on his length, taking him inch by inch until my walls are clinging to his every ridge.

"Where am I?" I repeat, determined to drive the point home as I join us in the most perfect way possible.

"You're right here with me," he answers, and I rise up on my knees until only his tip remains before slamming back down on his length. "Fuck," he grunts, fingers bruising my waist as he fills me up.

"Where. Am. I. Emmett?" I bite out, short, fast thrusts in-between each word as I bounce on his lap, my nipples brushing against his chest.

"Fuck, Snowflake. You're right here in my arms, where you're supposed to be," he growls, grabbing my waist in a punishing hold as he controls my movements, and I let him, sinking my nails into his shoulders and enjoying the ride of my life.

Sweat clings to my skin, trailing down my spine as we fuck, claw, and take from each other until there's nothing left to give.

"Come for me, Scarlett. Mark me as yours. Show me exactly where you are."

My movements become jagged, my limbs screaming with exhaustion as I slam down on him once again, only this time I grind my core, brushing my clit against him for the most exquisite friction, before falling apart.

Head flung back, a slow groan parting my lips as my skin heats from head to toe, I feel every crash of my orgasm as it claims me. Emmett's brutal grip on my waist eases as he holds me in place, his cock pulsing his release inside of me.

Spent, I rest my forehead against his shoulder.

We're nowhere near done with the mess determined to bring us down, but with a moment of solace comes an unwavering and unbreakable connection. Ours.

He's my Viking and I'm his Snowflake.

But above all else, he knows it. I'm his good girl.

FOUR

Scarlett

My entire body aches as I tiptoe out of Emmett's room, not wanting to disturb him after we passed out from fucking so hard. As much as I want to lie with him all day, the grumbles coming from my stomach tell me I've been there long enough. At least the ache between my thighs is for the most worthy reason, everything else is just a reminder of yesterday. Or was it the day before? I can't remember at this point. It's all merging into one.

The coast is clear as I cut across the hall into my room and lock it. Being in one of my men's beds is different than being in my room alone, especially with Declan and Graham here. It's no longer as safe as it was, but as long as I know that, I can be alert and on guard. Forgetting could cost me dearly, and I refuse to lose anything else.

Leaning back against my door for a second, I make sure

no one is in here. I probably should have done that *before* locking the damn door. What does catch my attention, however, makes my heart stop as my spine stiffens.

Bags are placed neatly on my made bed, the brands familiar as I recall my shopping trip with Emily and Duffer in tow. Taking cautious steps toward them like they're a ticking time bomb, I catch a glimpse of the items inside. T-shirts from the first store Emily dragged me into, and piles upon piles of lingerie in every color, material, design, and fit.

Someone must have retrieved them from the back of the SUV I brought home.

Fuck.

Swiping a hand down my face, I feel a pang in my chest. A loss so profound it catches me completely unaware. He's the one good memory from my childhood and I had to watch him die.

My stomach grumbles, irritating me as my mind saddens, but I exhale and reach for the first bag, trying to get through the overwhelming emotions attacking me.

Eyeing the new options I purchased, I pick the charcoal-gray frayed tee. The big decision will be my underwear, but as I flick through the bags, my attention is pulled once more to what happened to Duffer as I take in the specks of dried blood splatter on the bag.

Despite myself, I reach out and run my thumb over the

dried crimson stains, my heart aching for it all to stop. A lump forms in my throat, my emotions cloud my vision with unshed tears, and I take a step back.

I'm not doing this. I'm not breaking. Not now or ever. But most definitely not when there are people around here that I don't trust.

He wouldn't want me to crumble, he would want vengeance. Duffer didn't die for nothing. I refuse for that to be the case. I refuse to forget him.

Taking a deep, calming breath, with my mind fixated on determination and food, I get dressed in a lilac lingerie set, my new tee, and a pair of cut-off shorts from my duffel bag. Raking my fingers through my hair, I pile it into a bun.

Once my combat boots are laced up my ankles, I head for the door, my stomach playing an orchestra in my gut as I unlock the latch and step out into the hall. My pace and stride is halted as I bump into a hard chest, but the whiskey barrel scent that envelops me instantly tells me it's not one of my Ruthless Brothers.

"Hey, Scar, I've been looking everywhere for you."

My teeth clench at the sound of Declan's voice. I keep my facial expression neutral as he reaches around me to try and grab my door handle but I click it shut behind me. One swift move, though, and he has me caged in.

Fucker.

"I'm here. You've seen me. Now you can fuck off," I

grumble, and he leers down at me. It makes my skin crawl, but I refuse to give him the satisfaction of knowing he gets under my skin. There's no good way or bad way with him. Either way, it gives him the attention he wants.

"I got the Ruthless Brothers to place me near the whores so I could be close to you, only to find that you're not there," he breathes, planting his palms on either side of my head as he leans down, bringing his face far too close to mine for comfort.

"Back off, Declan." My voice is monotone, bored from his proximity as my hands desperately itch to punch him in the throat, face, or stomach. I'm not fussy either way, as long as I hear him scream.

He moves in closer so our noses are nearly touching and strokes a finger down my throat. "I took you once before, I can take you again, Scarlett. I don't usually fuck the same whore twice, but I can make an exception for you. Look how much you've grown. Perky tits, peachy ass, and hips for me to bruise as I pound into you."

Those words from anyone else's mouth might excite me, yet I'm quite sure my vagina curls in on itself in fear. He's still as clueless as he was the first time I met him. When I decided it would be freeing to hand my virginity over to someone I would never have to see again. I was wrong, real fucking wrong, and now that bout of spontaneity is biting me in the ass.

I hate the old me right now.

Does he know what his father taught me? Do either of them understand their impact on my life and the things I can and will do? Surely not, because he wouldn't be trying his fucking luck right now. Not unless he thought he could still 'handle' me, take me down. But he didn't know any of those things when I bled for him seven years ago, when I didn't realize *who* his father was, so I'm going to hope and assume he doesn't know now.

Tilting my head to the side, I quirk an eyebrow at him. "I'm only going to tell you *one* time. Get your hands off me."

He smirks, his sneer running from ear to ear as he pushes me further against the door, wrapping his hand around my throat in the exact same hold Emmett did earlier. Only this time, it's not for my pleasure.

Before I can retaliate, a hand darts out between us, locking around Declan's wrist at my throat, tearing him away from me. It takes a second for Declan to release his grip, yanking at me, but a moment later, he releases his hold and my head flies back against the door.

Gasping, I turn to my left. Axel's grip on Declan's wrist is deathly, the snarl on his lips haunting as he all but growls at the man who dared to touch me.

"Move, before I make you," Axel bites out, and I'm sure the floor fucking rumbles with his boom. His grip on

Declan's wrist slackens, and the asshole quickly raises his hands in surrender as he takes a step back.

"It's all good, man. I just thought this merchandise was available to sample," he says with a grin, sweeping his tongue along his bottom lip as he rakes his eyes over me.

"Not to you. Not to *anyone*. Not ever." Axel sidesteps to place himself between Declan and me, blocking me from his leery gaze.

Instinctively, I lift my hand to soothe him, but stop myself before I touch the fabric of his t-shirt. Pinning my arms at my sides, I hold my breath, scared I'll make the situation worse if I spook him.

"If that ever changes, Axel, which I'm sure it will, just let me know." Declan chuckles and retreats. Axel inches closer so his back is touching my front. I'm too scared to move, my mind flipped upside down.

I've gone from pain over the loss of Duffer, anger over Declan's sudden appearance and the reminder of my past mistakes, to fear of making one wrong move and fucking everything up with Axel.

Axel slowly turns to face me, putting a little more distance between us, but not much. He's closer than he usually is, but not as close as yesterday when I was in his arms. I long to feel that again, more than I care to admit.

We stare at each other for what feels like an eternity before I clear my throat. "I'm supposed to be of no importance, remember?"

He shakes his head, eyes blazing into mine as he sighs. "I really couldn't give a shit when your safety is at risk."

It feels like he has thrust his hand into my chest, encasing my heart with his palm as he squeezes raw emotion from me. When I'm sure my knees are going to give out with how close he is, he shocks me even more by raising a hand to my face, but stopping a breath away from touching me.

The hesitation is clear and my body stills. His eyes search mine, but it's not because he's searching for permission. I'm not entirely sure *what* he is looking for, but he must find it, because he ever so slowly cuts the remaining distance and *cups* my cheek. My skin tingles, goosebumps flaring under his palm as I involuntarily lean into his touch.

His eyebrows pinch for the briefest moment before he relaxes, rubbing his lips together as I remain locked in place. "Are you okay?" He's raspy and uncertain in his actions.

I want to lift my hand to his, feel his hand beneath mine, but this is dangerous territory with no map, and I refuse to step on a landmine right now. This is too important. *He* is too important.

"I'm okay," I murmur, which earns me another shake of his head.

"It's cute that you're pacifying me, but I can see right through you." His thumb dusts over my cheek, setting me alight. "You can't hide from me, not even if you try. So, tell me what's going through that pretty head of yours."

I feel like a teenager with a fucking crush or something because my knees just got weaker at him saying I have a pretty head. Fuck.

Write me off now and call me done. I'm a killer, a survivor, a fucking warrior, but I'm nothing but putty in his hands and he fucking knows it.

He doesn't rush me as I take a few moments to calm my breathing, but every time I think I have it under control, he strokes his thumb again and I'm right back at the beginning.

"I can't think straight with you this close," I admit, gaping up at him.

"You and me both, Reaper." He smirks. I fucking hate that word in every sense, except when it falls from his lips.

"Are *you* okay?" I ask, hoping to distract him, but he cocks a brow at me and waits some more.

Attempting to organize the mess inside my head is futile, so I opt to just blurt it all out since he wants to hear it so much. "I'm hurting. Duffer is dead, like *dead* dead, and I've never felt sad about anything like I do about this. I'm fucking furious that Declan was out here looking for me, and mad that he got a rise out of you. But most of all,

I'm obsessed with you, but I'm scared to move or fucking breathe because I don't want to trigger you and risk you pulling away. You're making me fall, Axel. Hard. I don't care if it's never mutual, if this is all it can ever be, but I can't deny that you mean more to me than I ever thought would be possible since you've been a major asshole to me from day one."

His eyes widen with every word, his nostrils flaring, but it doesn't feel like anger. "We'll figure this shit out in the order you just spewed it," he murmurs, and I roll my eyes. He knows he's leaving me on the edge, unsure of what else is to come for us, but I still hold on for dear life as he sweeps his fucking thumb over my skin again. "Let's start with Duffer," he offers, and I gulp, squeezing my eyes shut for a brief moment as I try to focus on his words and not his proximity.

When I'm sure I'm not going to leap at him, I open my eyes again, finding the determination I had before I stepped out of my room. "I want to see him."

FIVE

Scarlett

Numbness coats every fiber of my being as I stare at Duffer, or as my younger self remembers him, Dylan. The second I laid eyes on him here, it came rushing back to me. His skin's already graying as blood blotches taint it.

Dead.

Four letters making up a single word that is such a part of life, especially mine, but for the first time, it stings like a bitch. The closest I've ever come to hurting like this was with his mom, but I was too young, too confused, and this is entirely different. She took her life, but this... Duffer was shot.

I can feel Axel's eyes on me from the corner of the storage room, which is tucked away at the back of the compound, where they've kept him in a huge fridge. Since when was it even there? Now, he's lying across a decorating table like it's fucking normal or something.

"What will happen with him?" I ask, not tearing my eyes from him.

Axel takes a step forward. "He should be gone already, Scar. It's the Ruthless Brothers' way, but something told me you needed to see him first."

My gaze flicks to his, and I struggle to find the words to explain how important that was for me. "So what does that mean for him?"

Axel rubs the back of his neck as he replies, "We get rid of the body."

My gut knew that was what he was going to say, but I wasn't ready for it, not at all. My chest clenches with irritation. "He deserves more than that."

"I know." His words are gentle, probably the softest I've ever heard from his lips.

I turn to face him, nostrils flaring as tears threaten the back of my eyelids. "He can't die in vain, Axel. He can't."

"And he won't, Scarlett. I swear it."

But he's still going to get rid of the body, just like they always do, and it doesn't sit well in my stomach. "I want to bury him."

He shakes his head, his gaze downcast.

"That's not the—"

"I don't give a shit whose way it is or isn't. You can't just get rid of him like that, he can't just be forgotten."

"He wouldn't, Scar, he—"

"That man died for me." I point a finger at Duffer's body, my chest squeezing so tight I can barely spit out the words. "He died for me, for Emily, for this fucking club. I. Want. Him. Buried." My breaths come in short, sharp bursts as I try to keep my emotions in check, but it's pointless.

"Scar," he breathes, taking another step toward me, and I know he's trying to let me down gently. "That's not possible. Not without the risk of him being found."

Dragging my fingers through my hair, I want to scream, but the second my fingers lock around my loose ends, it comes to me. "I have a spot."

"It's not—"

"I. Have. A. Spot. Axel," I interrupt, a bite to my tone. It's not aimed at him, and the gentleness in his eyes tells me he knows that too, but it still leaves an essence of guilt inside me. Yet I can't find the words to apologize, not until I get what I want like a spoiled princess, but I don't care. This is important to me. Duffer—*Dylan*—was important to me.

Axel gapes at me, trying to find the words to talk me down, but it's settled in my mind now, there's no turning away from it. With resolution in my veins, I exhale hard, a calmness clinging to me as I turn to look back at Duffer.

"Before anything else, Axel, that guy was my first

friend. At a time when I had nothing but men showing me things no child should see, hearing threats no child should hear, he was a glimmer of hope. Small bursts of carefree moments in an otherwise torturous dungeon." I reach out, touching his cold hand as my body racks with the threatening onslaught of emotion, but I bite it back. "He was never a Reaper; he was a prospect for the Ruthless, but he was *always* my family."

My heart thunders in my chest, my pulse ringing in my ears as I slowly look back at the man holding my world in his hands right now.

Axel rubs his lips together.

Shuffles from foot to foot.

Dips his shoulders.

Finally, defeat takes over his features, but not with anger; with a kindness I've never seen before in my life.

"Show me where."

Water hits the pool below, calming me in a way only *it* can as I stand on the boulder Emmett fucked me on. It feels like a lifetime ago. It felt like I had all of the problems in the world. If only I had been able to fast forward to now, then I would see the difference.

Axel, Emmett, Ryker, and Gray work tirelessly, digging

and digging and digging. It feels like it's never ending, but more than that, I know it's for me. I don't know how to display my gratitude.

The moon shines above us, shadowing what we're doing here as portable lanterns line the ground around us. This is supposed to be a moment of peace, a farewell so deserved, but I can't tear my eyes from the four shirtless men as they shovel the dirt.

Watching their muscles and the sweat beading along their skin as they move is mesmerizing, and the way Gray keeps smirking at me tells me he fucking knows it too. Asshole.

Tearing my gaze from them, I turn to Emily, who is sitting in the bed of the truck parked behind me. She's got a blanket thrown around her shoulders and a little pink nose, but she doesn't complain. The second I told her what was happening, she burst into tears, thanking me repeatedly as she quickly dressed.

Now that we're here though, it feels so final, but my heart knows that just getting rid of his body would have left our feelings and emotions exposed for an eternity. There would have been no closure, not like this. Not that I expect it to magically make me feel okay, I know that won't be the case, but it offers me something at least.

"How are you holding up?" I ask, dropping off the boulder and moving toward the truck.

She smiles as I take the spot next to her. "I'm doing okay. It hurts, and it's not easy, but it's a relief to be doing it." She leans into my side, resting her head on my shoulder.

"We're going to make them pay for this, Emily. We know we have to be calculated and ruthless, but their time is coming, and I'll have their blood on my hands all in his name."

Emily hums, not moving from her spot as she nestles closer. "It's weird hearing you say that. Like my instinct is to say leave it to the guys, keep yourself safe and protected, but a deeper part of me knows that it's you I'm talking to. And you aren't just any woman. You're Scarlett fucking Reeves, the crazy-ass woman who stood toe-to-toe with my brother when you first met me, protecting me without even knowing the details. You stand for family, even though you've never truly known one until now." She lifts her head and smiles. "So I'll let you keep that promise. His retribution is yours, and I'll make you a promise of my own."

Wetting my lips, I try to clear the lump in my throat, but my voice is still hoarse as I speak. "And what's that?"

"I promise you a family with me, no matter what."

Is she purposely trying to make me cry right now? I'm sitting here, struggling to keep my emotions on lock, and she's saying shit like that. Shit that matters to me even when I don't realize it.

I swallow back the overwhelming emotions the best I can and fix my eyes on her. "I promise you a family with me too."

Her eyes glisten with unshed tears. "The crazy thing is, Scarlett, that's all you've ever shown me already." She floors me once again, but if she knows it, she doesn't show it as she drops her head back to my shoulder. "My mom told me something before she passed, something I never truly knew or understood until now. Do you want to know what it is?"

"It's cute that you offer it out there as a choice," I murmur, and she chuckles.

"Families who slay together, stay together."

"Wise woman," I murmur, feeling those words deep in my soul as she rubs my arm.

We sit in comfortable silence for a little while, the combination of trickling water and heaving shovels our only background noise until Ryker calls my name.

"It's time, Rebel."

My mouth dries instantly as Emily rises beside me. "It's time to say goodbye," she whispers, emotion clogging her voice as I nod silently in response.

Axel and Emmett gather Duffer from the other truck parked beside us and lower him into the hole they've spent hours digging. He's thankfully wrapped so we can't see him anymore, but it still hurts my heart when he's lowered into the soil.

Overwhelmed with emotion, I start to question if this was actually a good idea. But as much as it hurts, and it does, like a fucking bitch, I need to feel it. He deserves this.

I take Emily's hand in mine and we join the four of them, but the second we come to a stop, she rips her hand away and darts to the left, confusing everyone until she spins around with two freshly plucked flowers in her hand. Tears glide down her cheeks as she offers me one, and I offer her a wobbly smile back in response as Ryker clears his throat.

"We lost a good man in Duffer, a loyal friend to the very end. He was a carefree guy that wanted to belong, and he did. To Scarlett, to Emily, to us, he was the member you always search for, a diamond in the rough, and he'll forever be remembered."

I frown, fully aware that Duffer wasn't a member but a prospect. When I turn my attention to Ryker, I find him holding up a patch, a member's patch, and my heart breaks as a sob parts my lips. He lifts the emblem to his lips for the briefest of seconds before dropping it into the hole, and my heart soars.

I know I've only spoken with Axel about all of this, but that doesn't mean the others haven't been on hand to wordlessly help. Without thanks, without validation, they've just been there. Like a club, like a family, just as I needed, and just as Duffer deserved.

Lifting the flower to my nose, I inhale its scent, committing it to memory before murmuring my goodbye and adding it to the hole. I move to wrap my arms around myself as Gray drapes his arm over my shoulder and pulls me into his side.

Emily follows the same motion, and Emmett is there to catch her as her legs threaten to give out. The four of us watch in silence as Axel and Ryker start the tiring task of adding the soil.

My body thrums with pain and love all at once, so much so that I'm sure it could kill me. But it doesn't; it just adds another layer to my armor, another purpose to my step, and another breath to my lungs.

Emily was right, families who slay together, stay together, and I've found mine.

SIX

Scarlett

I'm not surprised to see Emily's sleeping face beside me this morning. I remember her being there from last night. I could tell the guys wanted to battle it out among themselves where I slept, but one look at her face and I knew where I needed to be.

She passed out quicker than I expected, which was a relief. This is hard as hell on me, but she spent a lot more time with him than I did, especially this past year, and after just losing her father too, it's wiping her out.

He's been laid to rest. It makes my heart ache and my soul feel warm all at once. Today is a new day, and all I can hope is that it doesn't consume me when I slink from the bed.

Slipping from under the sheets as quietly as I can, I startle when I find a sleeping form against my bedroom door. My chest clenches, not with fear or annoyance, but with… happiness? Fuck, I don't know.

"Morning," he rasps, blinking his eyes open.

When I first arrived here, if I found Axel in my room unannounced, I would have assumed I was about to meet my maker. Over the past two weeks, it would have felt like he needed me, his pain and triggers getting the better of him, but this morning, it almost feels romantic.

"What are you doing in here?" I whisper, moving toward him but still keeping enough distance between us. Not as much as usual, but I'm also not pushing him against his will.

"Declan," he grunts, and it takes a second for me to piece it together. He's sitting here because of that fucker catching me outside yesterday.

Yup. Definitely romantic.

Crouching down in front of him, I quirk a brow. "I could have handled him."

He smirks, sweeping a hand over his face as he sits straighter. "I know. This was more for my peace of mind than anything else," he admits.

A swarm of butterflies takes flight in my stomach at his confession. "I'm sorry I'm adding more bullshit to your plate when you've already got enough to handle," I murmur, feeling odd being at someone else's mercy. But he quickly shakes his head dismissively.

"This is nothing."

His eyes darken and his jaw clenches, making me squint at him. "Why do I get the feeling there's a lot more to that statement I don't know about?"

"Because you're smart, Reaper," he breathes, a ghost of a smile on his lips, and my legs nearly give out.

I'm a sucker for his nickname for me, even though it reminds me of my past, and I don't know why. I can feel my cheeks heat, but if he notices, he doesn't say a word. I want him to expand on what he means, but a giggle sounds from behind me.

"Are you two fucking? I'm scared to open my eyes." Emily chuckles again, making me laugh. Axel grins from ear to ear.

"She wishes," he replies, winking at me as he slowly stands.

I gape at him from my crouched position, and his eyes darken even further, but this time, it's with a level of heat and hunger I've never seen there before.

She really fucking does. I can't say it out loud though, the fear of scaring him off is too great inside of me.

Emily continues to laugh from the bed as I rise to my feet, eyes still locked on Axel until he glances down the length of me. I know my nipples are pebbled, brushing against the material of my t-shirt, and they've got his attention too.

My next breath lodges in my throat as he extends his arm out, ghosting his thumb over my left taut peak for the briefest second, before a cell phone chimes.

I'm a stick of dynamite ready to explode from one simple touch, only to be interrupted by the one noise I'd rather not hear right now.

"Was that—"

"Euro's cell," I finish, hearing Emily's harsh gulp ringing in my ears as Axel's jaw tightens. He glances over my shoulder to where the cell phone is, and I turn to face it.

I know whatever pops up on that screen is going to ruin my moment with Axel, and I know it's going to be from someone I loathe. Which means I'm only going to want to kill them more.

I step away from the bubble forming between Axel and I and open the message on the screen. My annoyance only rises as anger instantly rushes to the surface.

That motherfucker…

What a motherfucking ballsack.

"What does it say?" Axel asks, thick tension radiating from him as I turn to him with a sympathetic smile. Already hating that I'm being given more shit to put on the club.

"It's from Kincaid."

"And…"

I exhale harshly through my nose as I prepare myself to read it out. "I want Scarlett Reeves on a platter. You have a twenty-four hour window."

Staring at my reflection in the mirror, the slinky red dress makes my porcelain skin appear even brighter. It accentuates my breasts, curls in at my waist, and barely covers my ass. Paired with glittery sandals, hair piled on top of my head with tendrils framing my face, and smoking hot makeup, I look like I've been Emily'd again.

I feel hot as hell, but that's not the purpose of tonight. It's not what I've spent all day preparing for, and it's likely not the best outfit of choice for the occasion. But there's a show we must put on. The other chapter is still here, and to them, I'm nothing more than a whore.

I grab the purse Emily gave me that matches the shoes and step out into the hallway. There's no Emily tonight. Even *she* agreed not to be present. She's no longer just a risk against Emmett, she's a weakness for me, and the way I defended her the last time the Devil's Brutes came calling only proves it. But to them, she's supposed to be dead.

She's been placed under Shift's watchful gaze for the evening. I'm sure if you asked that man to miss out on this for anything else, he'd tell you a straight up 'hell no', but for her… everything is different. I heard them murmuring over some chick flicks to watch together, and he was willing to give her whatever she wanted, so I know I shouldn't worry about them.

As I approach the end of the hall, Maggie peeks her head out from the kitchen, her smile widening when she sees me. "Come on, girlie, Duffer deserves a celebration, and you deserve some food. Maybe a stiff drink or two," she adds, holding out a tray of meat for me to carry.

Duffer does deserve a celebration. I just wish we were getting an uninterrupted one.

"Do you need me to get anything else?" I offer, but she shakes her head and waves me off.

The bar area is empty, but the second I step outside, everyone comes into view. The scene before me is all too familiar. Picnic benches are spaced out around the grassy area, music plays from the sound system somewhere, and the smell of the barbecue floats through the air.

The Ruthless Bitches are to the far right, laughing, joking, and eyeing up the new men on offer from the other chapter, *Declan's* chapter. Declan sits with his men across two tables on either side of the bitches, leaving the Ruthless Brothers to hold up the rest of the seats. *My* Ruthless Brothers sit in the same spot they always do— Ryker, with a view of the entire space; Emmett and Axel flanking either side of him. While Gray sits across from him, a beer poised in his hand, but not a sip has been taken.

We're all on high alert, but there's a reason there are no

old ladies or kids here tonight. It's simple.

Draw this fucker out of hiding and kill him.

Why does my stomach swarm with uncertainty if it really is that easy?

Sweeping my tongue over my bottom lip, I carry the tray toward the grill, feeling eyes on my every step. Not just from the table I want it from though; Declan's too, and when I glance at Axel, he's glaring at the fucker without a care.

Maybe co-existing and acting dumb around them is going to be a lot harder than I expected.

Maggie appears behind me, taking the food from my hands and waving me off toward the guys. My purse feels heavy over my shoulder, the weight of the gun spiking my veins with adrenaline, and I place it on the table beside Ryker as a heavy rock song starts.

Maybe I should have taken Maggie's advice and had a shot or two on the way out here. That might have taken the edge off. It also has the chance to knock my focus too, and that takes priority right now.

I'm used to making my hits from a distance most of the time. That's what my paid jobs were, but up close and on the line like this is an entirely different feeling.

Emmett sweeps his tongue over his bottom lip as he eyes me. Gray adjusts himself through his jeans, making a show of it as my thighs clench, while Ryker's hand palms the globes of my ass, and Axel glares over my shoulder.

What—

"Boys, you sure make Scarlett come out of herself, don't you? I don't think I've seen her in anything other than a band tee and shorts. Well, unless we count the time I took her—"

Axel slams a dagger down into the wooden table with force, rattling the bottles on top and making my heart skip a beat. "Choose your next words wisely. I've already warned you, Declan. Keep pushing, you're not going to get far."

"Woah, man. I asked one of the Bitches, and they said Scarlett's fair game."

I want to glare in their direction, Molly's more specifically, but instead I keep my features bored as I stare at him. None of that matters when Ryker pulls me down into his lap in the next second, pinning me to his chest as he breathes against my ear.

"The bitches don't run this club, Declan. I do. If I say a whore is just for me and my closest, then that's what she is."

Goosebumps prickle over my neck from his lips and my thighs from his hands. They're not supposed to be turning me on right now, but it's clear I don't have a say in it.

Revving of engines rumble.

It's time.

In the driveway, three bikes draw closer, and the late evening glimmer of sun shines down on the Devil's Brutes' patches. They take their time, playing this out just as I expected. The guy at the front rises from his seat once he's come to a stop, taking his helmet off to reveal one of the men from the shopping mall.

My nails dig into Ryker's thighs, anger heating my limbs as I hold myself back.

It takes a moment for me to confirm it, but there's no Kincaid here. He's sent his men instead.

"Celebration?" the Brute asks, staring around at everyone as the music dies down.

"What the fuck do you want?" Gray bites, his anger aimed at the Brute, but it's rising inside him for the exact same reason as mine is.

"Kincaid sent us here to tell you he fucking *knows* Euro isn't here, and you're going to pay for thinking you can outmatch him."

Out of the corner of my eye, I spy Declan's hand resting on his gun at his hip, but tilting slightly to see beyond him, I watch the open surprise on Graham's face.

That's all we needed to know.

"Do you have anything in response to that?" the Brute asks, grinning like he's the man with all of the power, but he has none and knows nothing.

Just. Like. Kincaid.

"Yeah," Axel replies, leaning back in his seat with a grin so manic even I'm caught off guard. "You can tell him this is for Duffer," he bites. My heart lurches as Ryker bands his arm tightly around my waist. "All the way from hell."

In slow motion I watch in complete awe as Axel takes him out with a gunshot to the head at the same time Gray and Emmett lift their weapons and take out the other two Brutes with precision.

Holy fuck.

In sync, three prospects rush forward, checking over the dead bodies before organizing their removal, but my attention drifts to Ryker as he shifts beneath me.

"Did you want anything else, Declan?" he offers, noting the fucker that still lingers at our side. There's a tinge of distrust in his voice that is warranted but goes unheard by the fucker in question.

"Nah, man. I'm good." He steps back without a word, but he's already shown his hand. I wait until he's out of earshot before leaning into Ryker.

"His hand was poised on his gun, but Graham looked shocked as fuck by the interruption."

"He has no clue."

"None, but we were right. When we replied to Kincaid that the other chapter is here, his response never came because he got his answer from somewhere else."

"Declan."

SEVEN

Scarlett

This week's top podcast plays from the Bluetooth speaker in the garage that I've linked up to my cell phone. The usual drawl of the presenter soothes me the best it can as I polish the chrome detailing on my motorcycle. I know I'm stressed when I need the podcast *and* the labor of cleaning my Harley Davidson.

Yesterday may have had some positive outcomes, in the sense that we know what side both Declan and Graham are on in this war, especially since it's not technically the same, but that doesn't make their betrayal any easier for the guys. It also makes me want to rip their goddamn heads off. Fuck being incognito, it's not worth it if they're still breathing; Declan more so than Graham.

I've been out here for almost two hours already this morning, completely alone, and it's calming and exhausting all at once. I ran out of water about thirty minutes ago and I've been slowly melting from the heat ever since.

Axel and Ryker are out on a job somewhere, and Emmett and Gray are inside doing whatever it is they do to relax, giving me a moment to think about just myself. It's so easy to get swept up in every single moment of the club that you can forget how to survive without the adrenaline coursing through your veins. So here I am—grounding myself.

Refusing to leave until I'm done, I run my cloth over the final chrome panel before taking a step back and wiping the sweat from my brow. Pleased with my handiwork, I head back to the main building to get a drink or two. Once I get back, I can shift my focus to the wheels, anything to keep me busy.

There are a few members and prospects in the yard, chatting among themselves and smoking, and they offer a nod or murmur of acknowledgement as I walk past. It's still weird to me, to be acknowledged above all the clubhouse craziness. At the Reapers, I was their most powerful asset, yet treated like shit, and my self-doubt allowed it. Here, everything is different.

Stepping inside, I sigh with relief at the blow of the AC and slow my steps toward the kitchen to appreciate it fully. Thankfully, I make it all the way to the fridge without a run-in with a Ruthless Bitch or anyone from the other chapter, and I make sure to grab a few bottles of water to keep me going.

It's not until I'm at the doorway, ready to head back out again, when I hear raised voices come from down the hall.

Who the fuck is that?

Curious, I follow the sound of the commotion. Two steps away from the lounge and I've narrowed it down to Emily and Emmett, but when I step into the room, I find Shift and Gray there with them.

"That's not fair, Emmett. You're being an asshole," Emily shouts, arms folded over her chest. Her eyes are puffy, cheeks red, and her bottom lip is a little wobbly.

"I can live with being an asshole if it keeps you safe, Emily," he says, matching her stance. Despite his harsh words, regret and disappointment shine in his eyes, but he clearly believes in whatever he's saying enough to push past it. That doesn't make it okay for me to see her so worked up though.

"What's going on?" The pair of them whip around to glance at me. Even Gray and Shift glance at me with relief. Emmett dips his head, while Emily swipes at her face. Both moves only irritate me more as I watch Emily suffer. "Emmett, I'm going to need you to start talking," I push, taking a step toward them, but it's Emily who sighs.

"He's pulling me from college."

Did she just say what I think she just said? The guilt on

Emmett's face tells me all I need to know.

"You can't do that, Emmett."

He cringes at my words, but shakes his head all the same. "I can, and I will."

I scoff, taking another step toward him as I wag my finger. "No, you fucking can't," I bite, hating the disappointment written all over Emily's face. But Emmett only stands taller, doubling down on his decision.

"There's no one to protect her when she's there, Scarlett. I don't trust any of the prospects enough yet, and we can't risk being a man down at the moment, which leaves her completely exposed, and I can't do that." His chest heaves, his arms moving animatedly with each word as he tries to get me to see it from his point of view. And I do.

He loves his sister more than anything, but caging her in isn't the answer to this. Stripping her independence and prospects for the future is going to have the opposite effect on her than what he wants. As much as we all want to keep her safe, it can't come at the cost of her freedom.

Looking at my best friend, *my* sister, all I see is loss and frustration in her eyes, and I can't bear it. I turn back to Emmett on the balls of my feet, shoulders rolled back as I brace for impact.

"I can do it."

"No, you can't," they respond in sync as the White brothers remain quiet on the sofa, neither agreeing nor dismissing my offer. At least it wasn't a full house like I anticipated. That tells me I've got a chance to help her here. Emmett just needs to listen.

"Why is that?" I ask, glancing between them, my fingers flexing around the water bottles at my side as I wait for a viable response, and it's Emmett who tries first.

"For safety reasons." His gruff words hit me hard, my hand flying to my chest in surprise as I squint at him.

"Did I not keep her safe last time?" My emotions are high, my hurt noticeable in the croak of my words. His eyes widen as he takes a step toward me, but I quickly take one back.

Raising his hands in surrender, he takes another step, and I hold my position. "That's not what I'm saying, Snowflake. What I mean is, there's no one there to protect *you*."

Oh.

My heart races at his words, but it doesn't change my mind on the offer. My thoughts whirl a mile a second trying to piece together a solution, when Shift clears his throat.

"If needed, I could drive them to and from campus and Scarlett could take the classes with Emily," he offers.

"She would have to be enrolled for that," Emily mutters, and he shrugs in response.

"If she wants that, then I can make it happen."

I gape between them, mind blown as I process what

he's saying, what he's offering.

College?

Me?

Is that even fucking possible?

Even the word feels strange on my tongue, but it's not out of the realm of possibility. Not when I have all of the documents he set up for me in my duffel bag.

"Snowflake, it's an amazing offer, but it's not something you have to do," Emmett murmurs, but my gaze is locked on Gray's as he smiles at me.

"You do you, Sweet Cheeks, we're here to support you no matter what," he says, making me smile. I slowly turn my attention back to Emily to find hope in her eyes, and I know the decision without even having to consider it.

"Sign me up."

I quickly learned it's not as simple as that. There are hoops, jumps, and an entire assault course to get through, but Shift takes it all in his stride. I don't know who is more excited; him or Emily. I'm sure it's supposed to be me, but I'm more apprehensive than anything. I've spent my entire life hiding, too scared to really live in fear of the unknown, to all of a sudden be thrust into the real world.

Enraptured, I continue to watch every step of the

process from my spot in Gray's lap. A variety of pizzas are sprawled across the coffee table, and as every hour passes, another Ruthless Brother joins us. Emmett sits beside us with Emily to his left. Ryker takes the chair with Axel propped on the arm, while Shift paces back and forth in front of the television, much to Gray's annoyance.

"Yes, that's correct, sir. Uh-huh… Yes… I understand… It's greatly appreciated…"

Nestling deeper into Gray's lap, his hand strokes leisurely over my back, making me yawn. It's been hours now, and I still have no clue what's going on, until Shift suddenly stops in his tracks, back to us, as he speaks again. "That's correct, no dormitory is required for the transfer."

Does that mean we're a step closer? Fuck if I know.

I do know that the dorms are no longer needed at all, Emily included. Part of our agreement with Emmett for this to continue is that Emily moves into the compound with us. She didn't even bat an eyelash at the demand, willingly agreeing with her gaze flicking to Shift a time or two. It does mean she's going to take over my room though, and I'm— "You're all mine tonight, Sweet Cheeks," Gray mutters against my ear and tightens his arm around my waist as I hum in agreement. I'm being divided between the guys.

Completely and utterly worth it. I wholeheartedly agree that it's the right thing for Emily to be closer where she can be better protected, but as fun as it is having our little sleepovers, waking up in a pair of thick arms against a hard chest is just superior in every way.

"Thank you for your time, sir," Shift murmurs and ends the call.

He remains with his back to us for what feels like a lifetime until he finally turns to me. I can't read his facial expression, which leaves my stomach churning with uncertainty.

"What did he say?" Ryker asks, breaking the silence as Shift shrugs.

"He said he would see your pretty face Monday morning," he replies, gaze locked on me as a grin spreads across his cheeks.

Emily squeals, Gray squeezes me tight, and sighs of relief echo around the room.

"How do you feel?" Emmett asks, rubbing my thigh as he leans in close.

"I don't have a clue."

That's the truth. I'm bewildered and completely swept up in the entire situation, but as much as it's for Emily, I'm also excited for myself. I'm going to need to up my reading and writing lessons with her, but it will be worth it.

There's a chance for me to be more than who I already am, more than a killer, more than a tool or a weapon. There's an opportunity for me to be a person. Living and breathing, not just surviving.

"Thank you," Emily says, cheeks stretched with her infectious smile.

"You're welcome."

"I'm going to go and tell Maggie," she announces, buzzing with excitement as she darts from her seat. Emmett rushes after her to catch up while Shift moves to stand in front of me.

"I have a few final pieces of paperwork to arrange with them. I'm going to get it taken care of now," he says.

"Thank you."

"No, thank you."

I don't try to correct him and he leaves without a backward glance as Ryker stands and stretches. "I'll go and check in on everyone." He doesn't walk straight to the door though, he rounds the coffee table and stops in front of me. Butterflies swarm in my stomach as he leans forward, pressing a soft kiss to my lips before heading out. He leaves me desperate for more, as always, and the way Gray shifts beneath me tells me he knows it too.

Then there were three. Looking over at Axel, I frown. His elbows are braced on his thighs, chin resting on his fists as he stares off into the distance. With the madness that was going on around us, I didn't notice him getting quieter and quieter. I instantly don't like it.

"Axel, what's wrong?"

He blinks a few times, then focuses on me. "There's enough going on around here for you to worry about without me adding issues into the mix as well."

Gray doesn't hold me back as I take a few steps toward Axel before stopping shorter than I want to. "Whatever is going on with you is just as important as everything else. If you don't want to let me in, *us* in, then that's okay, but don't think I don't want to help when that's all I want to offer."

It feels like he stares into my soul until he's seen every inch of it, and the last glimmer of uncertainty dissolves in his eyes.

"I need to leave."

RUTHLESS BROTHERS MC

EIGHT

Axel

Scarlett's eyebrows furrow. "What? I don't understand. I—"

"I don't know what the hell he's on about, but it's probably more to do with the fact that he's really not explaining properly," Gray grumbles, glaring at me.

He's right, I need to explain.

Exhaling, I glance between the two of them. My mind has been overwhelmed with worry and stress for Scarlett, but it's still niggling at the back of my mind that Shift gave me the details for the final woman on my hit list. I can't ignore it any longer. I need to speak about it to someone, or more specifically… *her*.

Shift doesn't really know the extent of who he's been hunting down for me, but he knows better than to ask. He *only* knows because his tech skills are next level. Gray, on the other hand, knows nothing.

"Shift has been helping me," I start, hoping I can keep the momentum going so I can explain.

"How?" Gray asks.

Pinching the bridge of my nose, I take a deep breath before looking at Scarlett. "He's helped me track down every woman that—"

"Fuck." The curse is a whisper on her lips as she drops to her knees in front of me. My heart aches and soars all at once. The pain in her eyes looks exactly like how I feel, and I know she gets this on some level that no one else can.

She flattens her palms between her thighs, waiting patiently for me to continue while Gray proceeds to keep his mouth shut for a change.

"He found the last one."

Scarlett's eyes flare with a mixture of surprise and excitement. She's back on her feet in the next moment, hands planted on her hips. "I'm coming with you. Let's go."

I startle in surprise at her order, remaining where I am as she moves toward the door. "Scar, I'm not telling you this for you to be the hitman. I've honestly never spoken about this to anyone, but I found out where she was just before I learned you were taken…" She smiles then. "Now, I just need to figure out the how and when, since everything is up in the air—"

"Now and in a vehicle of your choice. It's that simple," she interjects, raising her eyebrow at me in question, and I grin despite the turmoil inside of me.

Feelings and emotions swarm in my head, fighting to explode past the walls I've built around myself, and it's all because of her. I don't know how much longer I can deny myself. She's shown me time and time again that she cares, that what you see is what you get when it comes to her, and I'm obsessed with every inch.

I just don't know how to show any of that without my past rearing its ugly head and ruining everything I touch.

"Where the hell did you come from?" I breathe, looking at her like she hung the fucking moon for me. She blinks, rubbing her lips together in confusion. I've caught her off guard. That's a rare occasion.

"What?" she finally asks, and I stand, cutting the distance between us in a single beat.

I don't stop until we're toe-to-toe, my chest rattling with shallow breaths as my dick stirs to life. Tentatively, I tuck a loose tendril of hair behind her ear, looking deep into her wide eyes as she waits for a response. I know this woman doesn't have much patience most of the time, but when it comes to me, she has all of the time in the world.

"You make my heart race, my breath catch, and my dick come to life."

She grins at me, tilting her head to the side. "Those

sound like good things, Axel. So, why do you sound mad?"

"Because I don't know how to give you more than this." The room spins into darkness; the only thing I can see is her, the only smell I inhale is her, the only thing I can touch is her.

"I'm not asking for more," she whispers.

"But you want it." I can see the signs, the twitch to her fingers when she wants to reach for me, the way she moves an extra inch closer every time we're in close proximity. All of it.

"I'm not going to stand here and lie. Of course I do. I want all of you, but I'm crazy enough to take whatever you offer. You're a part of me just as much as Ryker, Gray, and Emmett. I don't think this is a dynamic any of us ever saw coming, especially you and me, but I want it. Whatever *it* is."

Who knew perfection was spelled: S.C.A.R.L.E.T.T.

It sure as fuck wasn't me, but now, it all makes flawless sense.

Brushing my thumb over her cheek, I inch a little closer. It's a mixture of fear and need, and it stops me from cutting the remaining distance and taking her mouth with mine.

"I love and hate that you don't touch me back, Reaper." Her pupils dilate. "I've never felt like this. Ever. I don't know what is and isn't a trigger, and I'm scared as hell that one wrong move might fuck it all up and I'll end up hurting you."

"Ax."

I blink. Gray's voice cuts through the fog as I remember he's still in the room. He runs his palms over his jeans before waving me closer.

I don't want to step away from her, but the look in his eyes has me moving nonetheless. Stepping toward him, I instantly miss Scarlett's closeness, but then he whispers in my ear and my world stops spinning as his words sink in.

Fuck.

"What's going on?"

I turn from Gray to Scarlett. "Gray has an idea," I rasp, my body ablaze with need at the proposal.

"That's ominous as shit," she says with a grin, eyes flicking between us.

"Do you trust him?" I ask, needing her to believe in him far more than me for this to work. She nods without pause, intrigue flashing in her eyes. "Good, then follow me."

NINE

Scarlett

Axel leads the way, and Gray laces his fingers with mine as we follow after him. I don't know what's going on, but I'm eager to find out. I can't imagine what he must be going through, knowing he has the location of the last woman who hurt him. It's clear what's happened to the others, but I'm here to be whatever he needs to get through it.

He turns into his bedroom, and Gray guides me inside, kicking the door shut behind him.

I want to ask what's going on, plead to know what Gray whispered to him, but I'm more intrigued to see whatever it is as it unfolds before me. There's no hesitation in what the next step is though as Gray runs his hand down my spine and moves to stand flush against my back. His cock presses against my ass, and I shiver with anticipation.

"Look how pretty she is, Ax. Her pouty lips, her soft skin, her flushed neck," Gray murmurs, and I preen. He's remained quiet since Axel started talking, but it seems he's found his tongue again.

"I'd look even prettier with my nipples on display," I say with a grin, getting caught up in the attention they're giving me. Axel's eyes darken, his tongue sweeping out across his bottom lip as Gray's hands find their way under my t-shirt.

His fingers trail over my skin, lifting the material as he goes. He takes his sweet-ass time, leaving me wound tight when he finally lifts it over my head. I'm not wearing a bra, so the vision I wanted to give Axel is instantly on display, and when he grabs his dick through his jeans, I feel accomplished.

"Shall we show him a glimpse of your pretty pussy too, Sweet Cheeks?" Gray whispers against the shell of my ear, and I nod eagerly.

Yeah, we definitely should.

Gray's hands drop to my waist, and I throw my arms back over my head, running my fingers through his hair as he finishes undressing me completely. If his idea was to put on a show for Axel and get him all worked up, then it's working, and I like it. A lot.

Standing bare, I part my legs a little as Gray runs his hands over my thighs. Axel watches every move, every detail, as my body heats from Gray's touch and his intense stare.

"I want to see her chest flush with desire, her pupils blown with need, and her pussy glistening with cum," Axel mutters huskily, and my thighs clench together at his indirect order.

"That would be a sight to fucking see," Gray murmurs, shuffling me over to the bed. I take a seat as he strips out of his clothes, revealing his hard length as he prowls toward me once more.

Leaning back onto my elbows, I spread my thighs and put my core on display for them to see. My heart races as Axel shakes off his cut, draping it over the chair in the corner, before slowly removing his boots.

Please, if any god is fucking listening, make him tug at his cock at the sight of Gray taking me. I'd die a blissfully happy woman.

A thud echoes around the room as Gray drops to his knees at the foot of the bed, grabbing my thighs and hauling me closer before closing his lips around my clit.

"Fuck," I groan, head falling back as pleasure courses through my veins.

His lips vibrate against my pussy as he hums. Goosebumps flare up across my body, highly aware that I've got an audience as I feel Axel's eyes on me. I'm already strung tight, desperate between them when Gray thrusts two fingers deep into my center as he laps at my clit.

"Oh my God," I gasp, drowning in desire as his hold on my thigh tightens. I can't wait to see the little bruises dotted along my pale skin when we're done.

"Imagine me tasting your tight nipples, Reaper," Axel grunts, making me moan as they seem to grow tighter with need. "You'd like that, wouldn't you?" I nod, lazily glancing in his direction as I writhe against Gray's hold.

"Her pussy's clenching so hard, man. She definitely would," Gray murmurs, making me even hotter as he explains my body's reaction to Axel.

"Imagine my hands gripping the globes of your ass as I keep you spread out wide for Gray. My lips along your neck, down your back, and between your thighs, just like Gray's," he grunts, tugging at his cock.

My core tightens as a small glimmer of my orgasm begins to form. I rock against Gray's hand, and when he rakes his teeth over my clit, I climax. Crying out with ecstasy, wave after wave of pleasure consumes me as Gray coaxes every inch of it from my lips.

When I lock eyes with him, he slowly pulls his fingers from my pussy and sweeps my essence over his lips. My teeth sink into my bottom lip as heat radiates through me. *That's hot as fuck,* and he knows it.

He stands, fingers glistening, and I expect him to hover

over me, his cock at my entrance, ready to paint his dick with my release, but he turns away from me. He cuts the distance between him and Axel and brings his fingers to our spectator's lips.

Holy. Fucking. Shit.

Mesmerized, I watch as Axel laps at Gray's fingers, taking them all the way to the back of his throat. His eyes darken as he glances in my direction, and Gray groans at the movement. When the fingers are pulled from his mouth, his nostrils flare and he grabs Gray's chin before running his tongue over the remains of my cum on his lips.

Slay me dead right now. That is the hottest fucking shit I've ever seen.

I'm too scared to move or even breathe, watching it unfold before me like a vision from a wet dream.

The slip of his tongue leads into a kiss, and their tongues tangle, a moan falling from Gray's mouth in time with my own.

"An exhibitionist *and* a spectator. She really is perfect, Ax," Gray murmurs, leaning back from Axel, who grins at me with raw, primal need.

"And she thinks this is the idea you were talking about," Axel replies, pointing at me.

"She hasn't seen anything yet."

I haven't?

"Show me," I plead, desperate to know what could

possibly top this, when Gray moves toward the bed and drops to his hands and knees beside me.

My next breath lodges in my throat as Axel grabs a small bottle from his drawer and joins us by the bed. I'm too scared to blink as he drizzles lube into his hands and over Gray's ass. My fingers dart to my folds.

With my pulse ringing in my ears, I gape with need as Axel teases at Gray's entrance, a groan sounding from beside me as he leans back into Axel's touch.

"She's fucking touching herself, man. How am I supposed to survive this?"

Axel's gaze darts to me, and his pupils widen. "Bite down on her nipple so I can try and speed this up," he rasps, making my core clench.

Gray leans back, and I silently slip beneath him so he can wrap his lips around my breast, while giving myself enough space to draw soft circles around my clit.

"Fuck," Gray grunts, before lapping at my nipples, and I groan from the touch as Axel works his body from above.

I don't understand what's happening, but I'm obsessed with it anyway. I wasn't joking when I said I would take whatever it is he has to offer, especially when they lay it out for me like this. Watching him fall apart is hot as hell, and I enjoy it just as much as the orgasm that Gray gave me.

"I'm ready, man. I'm ready. Just let me get inside her,"

Gray pleads, cheeks reddening as he looks at me with desire swirling in his eyes.

"Ready for what?" I ask, dipping my fingers inside my core as they shift slightly above me.

Neither of them bothers to respond with words. Gray pulls my wrist and replaces my fingers with his cock, nudging inside without missing a beat, and I moan at the stretch in comparison. When he's deep inside of me, he pauses, shifting a little so his hands are planted on either side of my face.

"Are you ready, Sweet Cheeks?"

"Ready for what?"

A deep groan vibrates from his lips. My hands lift to his face, confused, until he jolts a little inside of me, and my eyes widen in disbelief.

Axel comes into view, as naked as the two of us, with his hips flush against Gray.

"Are you... Is he..."

I can't bring myself to say it in case it's a lie, but the light chuckle from Gray and the flex of Axel's hips answers my question.

He's fucking Gray as he takes me.

He's... Oh my fucking God.

Looking back at Gray, I'm in awe at the delight on his face as he pants with each breath. "This is about me, you, and Axel, Sweet Cheeks. He might not be ready right now, but I'm here to glue you together. Are you happy with that?"

My fingers tighten around his face, an overwhelming sense of love flooding my veins as I stare in wonder at the man who does nothing but offer the best version of himself time and time again.

"You complete me," I breathe. "All of you do." Tears prick the back of my eyelids as Axel juts into Gray slightly, creating a ripple effect as Gray flexes inside of me. "Please make me yours," I beg, looking at Axel, who nods.

"You always have been."

With that, he leans back, letting Gray do the same before he thrusts deep inside of him, and I cry out as the domino effect fills my core. I clench around Gray's cock as he gasps, eyes rolling to the back of his head. His cock is drenched in my heat, and his hole is filled with Axel's.

"This is too fucking good, Ax. You're going to need to speed this up because I'm about to last five fucking seconds and I want to feel her come on my cock one more time before I die from my own climax," Gray grunts, a ghost of a smile touching his lips as he winks down at me.

Axel doesn't need another word as he does just that. I move my hands to Gray's chest as Axel holds his hips, and any caution evaporates as he pounds into him hard, fast, and completely feral.

Our moans morph into one another's, perspiration

clinging to every inch of us as we get lost in the moment. Gray's cock fills me over and over again, at the pace Axel sets, and just like he said, he glues us all together.

I can't take it any longer, slipping my hand between us just enough to graze my fingers over my clit. The friction's light, but enough to get me exactly where I want to be.

"Fuck, I'm going to come. She's clenching too hard around me. Fuck, fuck, fuck," Gray chants, and I scream with satisfaction as every inch of my body shatters apart at their hands.

Gray pulses inside of me as he sinks his teeth into my shoulder, joining me over the edge of ecstasy, before a ferocious growl parts Axel's lips, and he explodes along with us.

Every limb feels like jelly as I slowly come down from the most surreal moment of my life.

Nothing has ever given me hope more than this second, and I'll cherish it forever.

TEN

Scarlett

G ray carries me to the bathroom when he's sure the coast is clear, helping me clean off as he keeps a smile plastered on his face. "Are you okay?" I ask as he places me down on the vanity.

Somehow, his grin grows as he nods. "That was the hottest fucking sex of my life," he admits, and I shiver.

"Watching you both together… Fuck, it's unreal."

He steps between my thighs and trails his calloused fingers over my skin. "Watching you watch me and feeling your core clench around my cock in response is indescribable, but definitely my new favorite thing."

I press my lips to his, and he instantly takes control, taking my every breath in the slowest, most tantalizing way.

"I love you." He rears back, eyes wide, and I say it

again, "I. Love. You."

I mean it, with every fiber of my being; it's all-consuming and he needs to hear it. His hand lifts to my cheek. "You do?"

Nodding, I raise my hands to his shoulders. "I wanted to say it in there, but I didn't want you to think it was because I was in a sex-induced haze. I want you to know I mean it."

Our lips crash together, harsher this time as we take and give to each other effortlessly.

"I fucking love you, Scarlett. The way you effortlessly fell into sync with us, or us with you, who the hell knows at this stage, but it only proves this is meant to be."

Gray wraps his arms around me, pinning me to his chest, and I bask in his warmth, smiling like a fool as my heart swells.

"There's something I want to do," I breathe, needing to get my thoughts out to someone. He leans back, and I force my eyes open to see a knowing smile on his face.

"Let's get dressed and then I'll help you."

"You don't even know what it is yet," I reply, eyebrows raised as I let him lower me to the ground. We both clean off as quickly as possible, but he doesn't respond to me until we both have towels wrapped around us.

"Of course I do." I cock a brow at him as we step out into the hallway and he leads me down the hall. He slows at Axel's door, and I'm shocked to see him passed out on top of the sheets. Wordlessly, Gray closes the door and ushers me inside his room instead.

My duffel bag is now in the corner of his room since Emily has taken mine, and I quickly get dressed. This guy thinks he has a clue as to what's going on in my mind, but he has no idea. Opting for my combat pants, black vest top, and combat boots, I tie my hair in a slick ponytail before pulling on my leather jacket.

Nervous, I turn to Gray to find him dressed in his usual jeans, tee, and cut, putting his gun into the holster at his waist.

"I think Shift is in the kitchen with Emily."

My eyebrows knit as I still, staring at him in confusion. "Okay?"

"That's who you want to speak to, right?" The longer I stare, the wider his smirk goes. He cuts the distance between us, one hand falling to my waist as the other lifts to my chin, propping my face back a little as he stares into my eyes. "What you want to do is find Shift, hound him for the details on the woman Axel told us about, and get ready to wreak havoc at his side. Because you know as well as I do that Axel's not going to hand that information over."

Well, fuck.

"How…"

He presses a kiss to both corners of my mouth before

looking deep into my eyes. "I know you, Scarlett. And you operate just like we do. If I'm thinking it, I know you're thinking it even harder."

I don't know how he manages to blow me away again and again, but here I am once more, floored by his understanding of me.

"That bitch needs to pay, and he needs to see that he's not in this alone," I state, trying to swallow past the lump in my throat.

"And he will. Now, let's go."

I reach for Gray's hand, squeezing his fingers with my own as we head to the kitchen. Shift and Emily are sitting side by side at the table, sipping hot cocoa from big mugs as they smile at each other. Clearing my throat, I startle their little stare off, making Emily blush as Shift glares at the interruption before he plasters on a tight smile.

I glance at Gray from the corner of my eye, expecting a reaction from him, but it seems to go over his head as he moves to take a seat at the table. Consumed with anticipation, I can't sit still, instead, I brace my palms on the end of the table and turn my attention straight to Shift.

He sits up in his seat, confusion flickering across his face as I sense Emily leaning back in her spot. "I need something from you."

"Whatever you need, Scarlett. I told you that," he says.

"I need the woman's address that you gave to Axel."

Surprise widens his eyes as he instantly shakes his head. "I can't do that."

Wow. This is going to be harder than I thought.

"Let me rephrase. Give me the address of the woman you gave to Axel."

His nose scrunches as he looks at his brother before coming back to me. "I'm sorry, Scarlett, I can't."

"I know you can, I know you have it. So it's not a case of *can't*; it's a case of *won't*. Why?"

Frustration vibrates through my veins instantly. The last thing I need right now is someone making this harder than it needs to be.

"Because Axel made me promise to keep this between the two of us. It's his decision if you two know. If *he* wants you to have the address, then *he* can be the one to give it to you."

Shit.

I wasn't expecting this to be a loyalty thing.

"This is for Axel, Shift." The soft smile he offers me in response tells me that means nothing to him and he stands by his words. Fucker. Admittedly, this is exactly the level of loyalty and care Axel deserves from his family, but these are different circumstances. "I can do this the hard way too. I was hoping to avoid it, but this is important to me. *He* is important to me."

He glances from me to Gray, but this time, I look to his

brother as well. He shrugs. "She's the boss, big bro. I'm just here for the entertainment of watching her put you in your place."

I almost smile in appreciation, but I manage to hold it back. Emily remains quiet in her seat, nervously nibbling on her bottom lip as she places her mug down on the table and Shift does the same.

"There is no hard way here, Scar. There's just all of us respecting Axel's privacy," he says like he's trying to calm me down, but there was no stopping the inevitable once he denied me.

"I'm really sorry about this, Shift," I offer, smiling weakly at him as his chair scrapes across the floor in an attempt to put some distance between us. He doesn't get very far though as I reach for the collar of his tee and yank him back toward me.

He doesn't make a move to get me off him though. "You're not going to hurt me, Scar, just like I'm not going to hurt you."

"You're hurting me by not giving me what I need. The second he wakes up, I want to go take him, don't spoil that. He's going to go on his own otherwise, just like he has every other time, but it's different now."

My chest heaves as the truth slips from my lips, but I can tell by the stricken look in his eyes that he's still not seeing this from my point of view. "You know you were my best friend when I had no one else in the world, right?" He nods in acknowledgment. "So you know it pains me to say that I will punch you in the face for this, right?" Shift appears to ponder over it, but the longer he doesn't respond, the more I know he still doesn't see it. "Kronkz," I warn, but he shakes his head.

"You wouldn't—Fuck."

I slam my fist into his face, hating the grunt that falls from his lips, but he really needs to fucking see how serious this is. Blood spills from his nose, I hate it, but don't question how far I'm willing to go.

"What the hell, Scarlett?" he hisses, still not pulling out of the hold I have on the collar of his tee.

"This is important to me. I warned you. Now, are you going to help me or do I need to show you exactly what I'm willing to do?"

His sleeping form is fucking magical. Axel, awake with a scowl, is hot, but in the stillness of his dreams, he's intoxicating. I could watch him forever, like a creep, unabashed and addicted. My addictions are shifting seamlessly like his. I don't want just anyone to fuck me hard and brutally, only them.

They're mine, I'm theirs. In every way possible. The

lines blurred before I even got here, and denying it now feels ridiculous.

Gray offered to wake Axel, but I left him in the kitchen with Shift and Emily. I don't want to pull him from his sleep though, so instead I sit here, lost in him. But it's like he can sense me or something because it's only a few minutes before he stirs and I'm left looking like a total creeper.

Clearing my throat, I make it clear he's not alone before I speak. "Ready to go?"

He lifts to his elbow in surprise and his gaze turns my way. When his eyes land on mine, his pupils dilate and he sighs in relief. "Do you always lurk in guys' bedrooms, Reaper?"

"Only the hot ones."

A grin ghosts his lips, making me smile along with him. He flings his legs over the side of the bed and straightens. "Where is it we're going?" he asks, and my grin widens.

"Out."

"Out where?"

"Does it matter?" His brows furrow, clearly not into the whole surprise thing like me, so I relent. Not wanting to waste any more precious time when we've got a drive on our hands. "Fine, we're going to Xenia Springs, Florida."

He rushes to his feet. He's only wearing his boxers and it's distracting as hell. So much so that it takes me an eternity to meet his gaze. When I finally find his narrowed eyes, I know he knows what I'm talking about.

"How did you get that location?"

"Does it matter?"

"Yes," he bites, but he's not snarling, so we're taking this better than I predicted.

"I asked for it," I offer, which only makes his nostrils flare and jaw tic with annoyance.

"And he just handed it over to you?" he growls, storming for the door before I even get a chance to answer. He's charging down the hall as I chase after him, but when he reaches the kitchen, he stops dead in his tracks. "What the fuck happened?"

The question is aimed at me as he points inside. I know what's got his attention, but I don't answer until he steps inside, and I follow after him, getting another view for myself.

Gray sits closest to the door, a smirk on his lips as he watches Emily hold a cold compress to Shift's bloody face. I rub my lips together to stop a smile from spreading. Axel's questioning gaze is still aimed my way, but it's Shift who answers for me.

"She wouldn't take no for an answer, man."

Axel's eyes bug out as he turns back to me and I lift my hands with a shrug, acting as innocent as possible, but it's bullshit and we both know it.

"She's as crazy as me," Axel murmurs, and my smile widens, pleased with his assessment. Emily chuckles and shakes her head at me, not at all fazed with the fact that I did what I had to do to get the information from Shift. She gets to play nurse and she loves it.

"She just might be, Ax. You should have seen her, it was amazing," Gray states, blowing a kiss at me, and I catch it, putting it in my pocket for later, which only makes Emily laugh louder.

"I'm glad this is fun for everyone," Shift mumbles, pouting, as he glares at the four of us, but it only lasts a few seconds until he's smiling too. "I totally deserved it."

"You really fucking did," I retort, wagging my finger at him.

Axel sighs, turning for the door, and I frown. "Where are you going?" I ask, halting myself from reaching out for him.

"To get dressed. We've got a long drive ahead of us," he concedes, and I bounce on the spot, clapping like a fool.

"This was easier than I was expecting," I admit, and he squints at me again.

"You're making me soft, Reaper, or I'm making you even crazier," he assesses. "Either way, we'll go down together."

ELEVEN

Axel

We barely get two steps out of the door when Ryker appears from nowhere like a damn mugger hiding in the shadows. Only he's standing in front of my pickup truck, which is already loaded up with a duffel bag each for Scarlett and I.

I know this move is crazy as fuck, but the way she pulls at my damn soul leaves me helpless to it. She's a siren out at sea, drawing me out into the darkness, and I'm drenched in fear with every step I take, but I take it anyway.

Scarlett squeaks in surprise as my best friend leans against the driver's door with his arms folded over his chest. News always travels fast around here, but I thought we had time. Clearly, I was wrong.

"I don't know where the fuck you two think you're going on your own. It's cute that you even think I'm going to consider it, but if you want to entertain me with whatever bullshit you've come up with, then I'm all ears."

"Ryker," Scarlett starts, taking a step toward him, but he waves a finger between us before she can continue.

"You're insane." He aims at me. "And you're a maniac." His finger settles on my new partner in crime. I glance at her out of the corner of my eye, expecting to see a glare, but it's a sweet smile we're greeted with instead. She looks like every biker's wet dream. Skinny jeans wrapped around her long legs, a white tee that offers a peek at the pale pink bra underneath, and a leather jacket sitting sharp on her shoulders. Add the combat boots into the mix and I'm surprised any of us can even function around her.

Visions of earlier flash in my head, and I bite back a groan. Gray offered me something I didn't know I could give. To both of them.

"Thankfully, you love us *despite* our finer qualities," she sasses, pulling me from my thoughts as she takes another step toward him, fluttering her eyelashes.

"That's besides the point," Ryker grumbles and widens his stance. "The point is you're not going anywhere."

I'm not really in the mood to argue, but it seems like there's no need for me to get myself stressed over it when Scarlett is invested.

"It will be good for us, Ryker. Axel needs this... closure, and I need time away from your friends in there that really get under my skin." Her reference to Declan and Graham pisses me off more than the mention of the 'closure' she speaks of. Ryker didn't know what Shift had been helping me with over the past few years, but the look in his eyes now tells me someone has caught him up to speed.

My money is on Gray, since with the bloody nose Shift is sporting, it probably wasn't him.

"We're going to talk about this little secret that you've been hiding, Brother, but I still don't think—"

"Ryker, please listen to me," Scarlett interrupts, placing her hand on his chest. She inhales deeply, readying herself. "I'm not saying we're coming home healed, but it's going to be… something."

They stare into each other's eyes for what feels like an eternity. Acting like I'm not even standing here watching, like I'm not part of the topic of conversation, but to my surprise, it's Ryker who sighs in defeat.

"Fine, I want your asses back here in twenty-four hours." His grumble is cut off as he leans forward and presses his lips to hers.

"Forty-eight," Scarlett quickly refutes, smiling against his mouth as she peppers him with a few more kisses. My stomach clenches, wanting to feel that for myself, but I'm not ready yet. Ryker raises his eyebrows in question, leaning his head back, and she smiles wider. "It's a seven hour drive in each direction *without* stopping, and I need my beauty sleep to become a killing machine... *Mr. President*."

My cock twitches at her sultry tone. Ryker's eyes widen, too. He fucking liked that. *I* definitely liked that.

"Fine," he relents, far quicker than I expected, his gaze drawing to mine. "Forty-eight, but don't make me send out a search party for one of you."

Scarlett glances back at me, confusion flickering in her eyes. "What does that mean?"

"He thinks one of us will kill the other," I offer. She gasps, pulling her hand from Ryker's chest to press it against her own.

"I would never," she says, turning back to look at him, but his eyes are settled on me.

"I've definitely thought about it," I admit, slowly cutting the distance between us as Ryker steps away from the door. He pulls Scarlett along with him, wrapping his arms tightly around her for an extra beat as his lips find her temple.

"No, you haven't." Her jaw is slack as she peers at me, and I shrug. "Well, that's not nice. I only ever considered maiming you at most," she insists, her eyes narrowing before she turns to Ryker. She runs her thumb over his bottom lip before kissing him one last time. When he reluctantly releases her, she offers me another pointed stare as she opens the truck door and slides across to the passenger seat.

I don't answer her until I'm seated beside her, seat belt in place, door closed, and engine rumbling beneath us.

"I deserve you maiming me, but if it helps, I haven't even considered your demise since you let me see into your soul."

Darkness is all I can see. The twilight hour swallows me whole as we near our destination. Scarlett sleeps beside me, head lolled to the side so I can see her face, and it's hard as hell to not pull over and watch her.

She's so innocent when she's sleeping. You can't see the way life has tainted her. There's no calculated glare, no scanning for exits, no instant wall that she hides herself behind. I've never met someone so closely resembling myself.

I don't know how to communicate with her past my usual grunts and growls, until it comes to my ropes and a level of intimacy I've never felt with anyone else. I don't want her to think that's all this is though, because it's far from it. I'm addicted to her, just like I said I was. I still have my cigarettes in my pocket, but I haven't even had a drop of liquor since she let me bind her arms that first night.

Cocaine hasn't even been a consideration, because when the urge comes, I think of her, and my needs transform.

I want to give her more, more of me, more of life, more of everything. I want to kill Declan and Graham for her and lay them at her feet, then I want to cut Kincaid's head from his fucking shoulders and box it up as a present for her.

Talking with flowers, sunshine, and sprinkles isn't me, and I get the feeling it isn't her either. Just like she's sitting here, en-route to kill someone who hurt me. I need to give her that too. I will.

My grip on the steering wheel tightens, pent-up anger and energy overflowing. We should be there in about twenty minutes. We stopped once on the way. Scarlett pestered me to let her take over driving, but I wouldn't be able to do anything but get lost in my head if I was sitting shotgun. At least, this way, I'm occupied with the road just as much as I am with my head.

I should probably wake her, I just don't know how.

As if sensing the stress building up inside of me, her eyes peer open, and she smiles lazily at me.

"Hey, Cutie Pie."

My brows knit together as I focus on the road for a moment before glancing back at her. "Cutie Pie?"

She yawns, stretching her arms out and sitting up taller in her seat. "Yup. I have a Viking, Blondie, a newly named

Mr. President, and a Cutie Pie."

"You've never called me that before," I grumble, not sure why my chest is warming at the sentiment.

"I know, I just thought of it now, and I'm sticking with it."

"No, you're not," I grunt, glaring at her while trying to focus on the road.

"Yeah, I am."

"I'm not a cutie pie."

"Yeah, you are. Handsome as shit too, but I wanted something cute and fluffy to catch you off guard. So, cutie pie it is."

I try to find anything to respond with that will work in my defense, but I come up blank. A little giggle sounds from beside me and I know she's pleased with herself. Tilting my head to her, I note the triumph on her face.

"You really are going to be the death of me, Reaper."

"I plan on it, but we've got this bitch to take care of first. How are we looking?" Her lips drop into a thin line, her eyes darkening as she starts to lose her carefree vibe and focuses on... death.

Clearing my throat, I focus on the road. "We're about fifteen minutes out."

"Perfect."

She reaches for the small bag at her feet and starts to meticulously piece her armor together. Tying her hair into a braid, she curls it at the base of her neck and secures a blonde wig over her head. Bright red lipstick comes out next, followed by bright green contact lenses. I keep my mouth shut as I watch in awe as she transforms before me. Black gloves adorn her fingers, then she pulls a Stanley knife from her bag and cuts a few slits into her tee, offering a glimpse at the pink lace beneath.

Shit. I'm not going to be able to participate in any of this with my dick this hard.

Once she's done, she turns to me with a smile, barely recognizable and she knows it. "How do I look, Cutie Pie?"

I gulp, glancing down at her exposed breasts as I will an answer to my lips. "Stunning," I rasp, unable to deny the effect she has on me. Her eyes speak when her mouth doesn't move. Her gaze is warm despite the lenses, her cheekbones lifting with another teasing smile, and this time, I smile right back.

It almost feels foreign on my face, but I like it.

"Are you ready to recap?" she asks, and I nod. "Okay, Shift confirmed that she has no children and lives alone. Works six days a week at the dive bar in town, where she also dances on occasion. It doesn't close until six in the morning, which is an hour from now. She's addicted to prescription drugs, and is in over thirty thousand dollars' worth of debt." Scarlett balks. "Fuck, I think we're doing her a favor here."

I wonder what this woman has been trying to escape, because that's exactly what it sounds like she's trying to do in my opinion. But she's not as wise as she seemingly thought she once was. I learned quickly that there is no running from this pain; there's only surviving it, and that only now seems possible since Scarlett appeared in my life.

"So, how do you want this to go?" she asks, making me frown as I process her words for a few moments.

"You're letting me have a say? I thought you were commandeering this entire thing." I smirk.

"I mean, I'd like to, but I'm also highly aware that this isn't about me. I want to march into that bar and slaughter her in front of everyone, but only if you'd like that too. I want whatever will bring this to an end for you, Axel. You fucking deserve some peace; it may not come today, or even tomorrow, but knowing she is gone will make a difference. Is it savage and barbaric for me to say that? Yeah, but that's who I am, how I was raised, and one of the few things I'm glad I have. This is a dark world, being savage and barbaric is survival, and we're both sitting here because of it."

She's not here to get blood on her hands. Well, she is, but that's not the point of this little trip. The point is I'm not alone. She's here however I need, whenever I need, and it sets my fucking soul on fire.

Nodding, I don't reply for a moment, deciding what I truly want to accomplish here, but first, I should explain some more. "She was the one who paid the most visits," I explain, clenching the steering wheel like my life depends on it as we start to make our way through the derelict town. Scarlett doesn't speak, and I don't turn to glance at her, wanting to focus on getting it off my chest first. "She's the one who took my... virginity, the one who paid extra when I cried, the one who cried out the name of a small boy when she came, playing with her body just like she taught him how to do."

Bile burns the back of my throat, embarrassment heating my cheeks.

"She won't be able to physically touch you ever again after tonight, Axel. Between us, we'll make sure of it. Then with your last abuser gone, hopefully, closure will find you."

Unshed tears line her eyes as her jaw clenches, and I nod. "I don't care how she goes, I just want it done."

The neon lights flicker above Candy's Retreat, and my heart races as I pull the truck over further down the road. When I'm sure we're out of sight, I send a quick message to Shift, confirming we're not visible on any of the cameras, and wait for his response. Once he has everything technically shut down, all the security cameras gone, then we can move.

"Want me to at least go in and lure her out?" Scarlett offers, and I nod at the same time my cell phone vibrates.

"We're all clear," I murmur, confirming Shift's message. Wordlessly, she slips from the truck, leaving her duffel bag in the back, and I frown. Climbing out after her, I whistle to catch her attention. "Aren't you going to load up?" I ask, pointing at the weapons, but she shakes her head.

"This needs to be a quick process for *you*, Axel, not her. Bare hands will make less of a mess and give her some suffering on the way out."

She turns on her heels and struts toward the club. Is there always that much of a sway to her hips when she's walking? Fuck, that's not what I should be focusing on right now. In the blink of an eye, she's sliding between the unmanned open doors, leaving me to wonder where the fuck I should wait.

Keeping to the shadows, I round the back of the building, assuming she will head this way, and wait by the trash. Barely two minutes pass when laughter sounds from the back entrance before the door is swung open and two women stumble out.

"Girl, please, you have to help me get a job here, you're too much fun."

Scarlett. I'd know that voice anywhere, even if the blonde hair is completely throwing me off. She blocks my view of the other woman for a moment, but the sound of her voice pins me in place.

"For sure, hun. You line me up with your dealer and I'll have you in here working like that." She snaps her fingers, hinting at how quickly she can help her out. Her nasally tone shrinks me back down to a child again.

"Girl, my dealer is my boyfriend. He's picking me up. You want a lift?"

They turn to face me. Scarlett's eyes find mine instantly as Carrie fucking Drury grins with excitement. She's already wasted if her stumbling is anything to go by. It almost makes me want to draw this out and wait until she's fully sober to make my move, but that would only cause me more pain.

"Hit me up, hun," Carrie singsongs as Scarlett comes to a stop in front of me. A snarl turns my lip as she slowly raises her eyes to mine, and I'm faced with my abuser after too many years. She doesn't recognize me though; she just beams up at me, hoping for a hit. "Hey, my bestie here says you can help a lady out."

My blood runs cold, memories of her saying those exact same words all those years ago flooding my veins. Her hair is ginger now, but her piercing gray eyes are exactly the same. My chest heaves with every breath, but I can't move, I can't blink, I can't even look at Scarlett. I'm locked in place, held prisoner by my memories and lost to my pain.

I try to gulp, but fail. As if in slow motion, Scarlett wraps her arm around Carrie's throat in a deathly grip. Her knees quickly give out as she thrashes in place, face reddening under the soft glow coming from the club, but Scarlett only yanks at her harder.

"Sorry, Carrie, the only thing he's serving right now is death."

Her moves become lethargic and stilted as she softens in Scarlett's hold until she's nothing but a bundle of limbs. Scarlett slowly lowers her to the ground, checking her pulse to confirm she's dead before digging her cell phone out and making the cleanup call Shift had arranged.

She doesn't even look at me as she goes through the motions, bundling Carrie up and tucking her out of sight, only then does she nod for me to follow her. We wait in the shadows in silence, and Scarlett sighs with relief when someone arrives to collect the remains we left behind.

"Let's go," she whispers, leading the way back to the truck like everything's fine, and I still haven't been able to piece a damn word together.

It's not until the truck doors are closed and we're both locked inside that I'm able to breathe. My body tingles to life, a rush consuming me like I've never felt before.

"I'm sorry, Axel. It looked like you were stuck, so I just kind of took over—"

I wave my hand for her to stop, not wanting her to continue with an unnecessary apology. Looking deep into her eyes, I exhale sharply, and speak the closest and rawest truth I can offer.

"Reaper, I don't know what love is, but what I imagine it to feel like… that's how I feel right now… about you."

TWELVE

Scarlett

A xel's words hang in the air, draped around my shoulders like a delicate shawl. I sink back into my seat, closing my eyes for a second as I repeat his words again, only this time out loud and not just in my head.

"Reaper, I don't know what love is, but what I imagine it feels like... that's how I feel right now... about you." They'll be committed to my memory for as long as I live.

I recognized the sinking look in his eyes when he finally came face-to-face with that bitch, and I knew I had to step in. He was rooted to the spot, unable to even comment on my actions, and when I organized the removal of her body, he was still just as quiet and timid. It was all worth it when his shoulders sagged with relief when we got back in the truck, and after he muttered those words, his limbs seemed to get looser. He tapped his fingers to a beat from his mind on the steering wheel, leg bouncing in tune as the corner of his mouth remained up.

That man was walking on cloud nine, even though it may not feel like that in his head. His body was enjoying the freedom from the tension that had him wound so tight for so long. We pull up to a motel, and he leaps from the car, bounding through the doors of the reception area before diving back into the truck with his grin still firmly intact.

"Reaper, I don't know what love is, but what I imagine it to feel like… that's how I feel right now… about you."

All I can do is watch him in awe as he drives us around to the furthest block and parks. This time, I follow him out of the truck and help with the duffel bags. My wig and contact lenses are long gone, but the tear in my tee and the red lipstick aren't so easy to remove.

"Let's go, Reaper," he murmurs, leading the way toward the building, and I keep within a step of him as he opens the room at the end, sweeping his arm out wide, in a gentlemanly gesture which I would expect from Gray more than Axel. I grin as I step inside.

Two double beds with god-awful brown bedding fill most of the space. There's a nightstand on either side of them, and a door at the back leading to the bathroom. The walls are as grim as the bedding, the carpet worn beneath my feet, but it's dry, warm, and far better than some places

I've stayed.

When the door clicks shut behind me, I startle a little. Axel places his bag down on the bed closest to the door, and I slowly move toward the other. As I clear my throat, Axel glances at me, and I try to find the right words to approach the subject.

"Are you sure you're going to be okay with one room? I can organize another if needed."

He shrugs. "I can protect you better if we stay together."

"I don't want to stress you or trigger you though," I reply mildly, still not dropping my bag down onto the bed.

"You won't."

It's not as simple as that, and we both know it.

"Are you sure? I—"

"Honestly, Reaper, shut the fuck up, you're ruining my good mood." If it wasn't for the grin on his face, I would swear he was pissed. Brushing off my concern and trusting his word, I finally set down my bag and shake off my jacket.

"I got them to order some pizzas. They should be ready in a few minutes from the pizza joint around the corner because it's open twenty-four hours," he explains, and my stomach grumbles at the thought. "Good, you're hungry. Why don't you clean off and I'll go get them. Then we can pig out and pass out before the long drive back."

"Thank you," I breathe, unsure how he's still standing.

I'm exhausted and I napped on the way. I'm sure it's the adrenaline that has him still going, but that will only last so long. A crash is coming his way very soon.

He steps toward me, tucking a loose curl of hair behind my ear, an act he does more and more lately. "I'll be quick," he murmurs and shuts the door behind him.

I exhale heavily. It's been a long day, or night, depending on how you look at it, and I'm ready to rinse it all away. Kicking my boots off, I re-secure my hair in a bun and close the bathroom door. It's dim in here, but it looks clean enough, and that will do. The sound of the water spraying from the shower acts as the perfect background as I strip out of my clothes, and I groan when the steamy droplets hit my skin when I step into the stall.

My skin feels raw by the time I step out, but the feeling of freshness you only get after scalding yourself cascades over me in the best way possible. Not that it was completely by choice, it seems the dial on the shower isn't the best, so it was hot or… hot. When I wrap the threadbare towel around my chest, it falls just below my ass cheeks, and I realize in my excitement to freshen up that I left my change of clothes in the bedroom.

Shit.

Steam billows around me as I open the bathroom door a little, but Axel's not back yet. I rush into the room, grabbing my bag at the exact same time the front door opens.

Of course this shit happens to me.

Instead of hightailing it back to the bathroom, I freeze, caught like a deer in headlights as he saunters into the room with two pizza boxes. He smiles as he meets my eyes… until he trails his gaze lower, his mouth forming a thin line as he takes me in.

"I'm so sorry, I left my bag out here," I mutter, and he slowly brings his gaze back to mine. His pupils are blown, jaw ticcing, and the fingers of his free hand flex at his side. *Fuck.* "Don't look at me like that, Axel."

"Like what?" His eyes are fixed on the towel at the top of my thighs again, making me bite back a groan.

"Like you want to taste me."

"I do."

My thighs clench, nipples pebbling at the rasp in his voice as an overwhelming sense of need washes over me. Like I wasn't being fucked by Gray and Axel less than twenty-four hours ago.

"I will only be a second." I wave the duffel bag meekly, sounding way more breathless than I should, but I need to move before I fuck all of this up with my raging hormones.

I haven't even taken a full step when his gaze snaps to mine. "No."

"Axel," I sigh, pressing my eyes closed for a moment before I look back at him. "You're killing me here, and I really need to gather myself."

"I. Said. No." The challenge in his eyes only heightens everything I'm feeling as he slowly walks toward me and drops a pizza box on my bed. "Eat. You're hungry."

He takes a seat at the foot of his bed, opening his box to reveal a meat feast inside, and I slowly sit on the other bed, releasing my grip on my duffel bag and reaching for my pizza as well.

Half Margherita, half pepperoni.

I barely mumble my thanks as I reach for a slice and sink my teeth into it. I groan with delight as the cheese melts perfectly on my tongue and the pepperoni adds the perfect hit of deliciousness.

"Fuck, Gray warned me about those groans. I thought he was lying."

I peer over at him, raising my eyebrows as I fake innocence. I really need to get a hold of myself and my love for greasy food. "I don't know what you're talking about," I mumble, stuffing my mouth with another bite as he shakes his head at me.

"Of course you don't."

I work really hard not to make a sound as I demolish the pizza. I'm always the most hungry after killing someone, and tonight's no different. Axel watches me the entire time, and I can tell when I let a moan slip because his eyes darken more and more.

When only crumbs remain, I close up the box and

reach for my duffel bag once again.

"Do you understand the meaning of the word *no*?"

He has a pointed look on his face as he glances from me to the bag, and I shrug.

"I just thought you meant…" My words trail off as he rises from his spot, discarding his pizza box and prowling toward me.

My heart hammers like crazy when he stops right in front of me, silence washing over us as he searches my eyes for the longest time. I don't know how I become complete putty in his hands, pliant at his word, when I'm so usually vocal and outspoken. He doesn't just consume my body; it's my mind and soul too. That's the only explanation for it.

"Do you trust me?" he asks, and a smirk forms on my face.

"That's yet to be decided."

"Good… but right now, at this moment… Do you?"

"Yes."

He nods, inching away from me and leaving me needy as he searches his bag for a moment. I barely blink before gaping at him as he holds out a long piece of rope between us.

"You brought your rope?" Every inch of my body tingles, from my toes to my lips. The possibility of passing out is high.

"I hoped, but…"

"Where do you want me?" I interject, not needing him to explain anything to me.

I'm here, I'm willing, and I'm his.

His brows knit as he glances at the rope. "There's no one here as a buffer between us though. No one to tell me to stop."

"I can tell you when to stop."

He shakes his head slightly, like he's thought of that and yet it doesn't make sense to him. "If I don't hear you, then I could—"

"You'll hear me, Axel. I know you will," I interrupt again, needing him to hear me now at this moment, and to my surprise, he does.

"Lie on the bed."

Yes, please.

Knocking my duffel bag to the floor, I keep the towel around me the best I can as I shuffle up the bed, lying on the pillows.

"You're not going to need the towel, Reaper," he states, making no move to join me on the naked side, but I still open up the towel and reveal myself to him.

His teeth sink into his bottom lip as he casts his eyes over me, and a shiver zaps down my spine with anticipation.

"Arms up, Scarlett," he commands, and I do it immediately, relishing the feel of the rope as he drapes it over my skin and intertwines it around my limbs.

For the first time, I'm facing him, and I bask in the view I get, watching the concentration on his face as he weaves his favorite material. How this man thinks he could hurt me, or not hear me, is laughable. No one takes this much care with someone and has the ability to hurt them too. I refuse to believe it.

My jaw grows slacker with every tug, and my back arches as he encourages me to shuffle back down the bed a little so he can tie the top of the rope to the bed above me.

"How does that feel?"

"Perfect," I manage with a gasp, thighs rubbing together in hopes of catching some friction as I stare up at him. His hair has fallen free from his hair tie, tucked gently behind his ears as his pupils remain wide with awe.

"You still trust me?" he asks, and I nod eagerly. "Good. You're going to need that trust in about two seconds. Okay?" My eyebrows pinch with nerves as I weakly nod again.

He grabs his bag and brings the entire thing closer. I watch his every move, hating that I can't see into the bag as he digs around in it, but with every second that passes, my anticipation heightens.

"Please, Ax," I whisper, need clawing at my insides, and he pulls a small package from his bag, tearing it open to reveal a vibrator. "Holy shit."

He's tied me up to play with me. How is this actually my life right now?

Axel flicks the switch, and it comes to life in his hand, a grin forming on his lips as he brings it closer to me. "Don't move an inch, Reaper," he orders, and I mumble my agreement, but it turns to complete gibberish as he presses it against my exposed clit and a scream tears from my lips instead.

Holy. Fucking. Shit.

"Look how wet you already are, Scar. How much you like being at my mercy." The smirk on his lips is wicked, tantalizing, and sexy as fuck. And he knows it. "Do you think you can come from me playing with just your clit like this?" he teases, and I groan as he presses down more firmly with the toy.

"You're about to watch it happen," I gasp, feet planting on the bed as my back arches, but he retreats, taking the toy with him as I cry out in frustration. "Don't be a dick, Axel," I bite, sweat clinging to my temple as I glare at him.

"Remember that trust?"

"Not right now, I don't," I grunt, and he smirks, walking back around to his bag.

"You should. Now, close your eyes."

I stare at him for a beat, trying to read his face, but he gives nothing away, so I give over the remainder of my trust and do as he asks. The second my eyelids close, my anticipation ramps up. Goosebumps dance over my skin as I wait, and wait, and wait, the sound of the vibrator the only noise apart from my panting breaths.

Vibrations ripple at my core as he places the toy at my entrance. He works it back up to my clit, only this time it's coated in my arousal. He keeps the pressure light as something else teases my pussy.

"Axel."

"Trust, Reaper. Trust."

It's solid, cool, and rigid as he teases my entrance, and I fight to keep my eyes closed. I want this moment with him more than I want to know what it is, and he must sense that too because he inches deeper, pressing a little more with the vibrator at my clit.

"So fucking wet, Scarlett. One day, I'm going to feel you on my cock. I swear it."

I sob at his words, my muscles clenching even tighter at the thought as he works deeper into my pussy, filling me completely. I can't distinguish what it is as my hips buck up off the bed, needy for everything he has to offer. His restraint disappears as he fucks me without actually touching me.

It's brutal, claiming, and stretching me with every thrust, leaving me desperate for another and another as the vibrator makes my clit sing and I know I'm close. "Axel! Fuck, I'm so close," I cry out, arms pulling on the restraints as my back arches.

"Open your eyes, Reaper, watch what I'm playing your body with. That will send you over the edge," he croaks, and I blink my eyes open.

My gaze lands on him first, the wild look in his eyes and the sweat between his brows as his arms tense with every thrust inside of my core, adding to the thrill thrumming through my veins. He doesn't relent as I take my time, looking every inch of him over until I look between my thighs.

"Oh. My. God," I whimper, my muscles tightening until there's nothing more I can do but combust at his touch. I gape at the gun he has peeking out of my pussy for the briefest of seconds before he slams it back inside of me.

He claims me again and again, and my orgasm rips through my every vein, my release dripping down my thighs.When my body is completely wrecked, he slows altogether, removing the gun from my core as I watch in shock and awe.

"A gun, Axel? A fucking gun?" I repeat, fucking awestruck at this man and the ideas swarming his head. Anyone else and they'd be running for the hills, but that was… the hottest thing I've ever witnessed, and it was happening to me. That's the shit dreams are made of.

He doesn't respond straight away, but his eyes remain locked on mine as he brings the gun to his face. The remnants of my orgasm glisten over his weapon when he drags his tongue over the metal, tasting me.

My core clenches again, pleasure rippling through me as I watch my ecstasy on his tongue.

"I was right," he breathes, dropping the gun without care and collapsing beside me. I can barely think through the sex-induced haze fogging my brain, but I manage to mutter a single word.

"What?" Once again, he tucks my hair behind my ear.

"You taste like heaven."

THIRTEEN

Ryker

The time on my watch shows only five minutes have passed since I last looked. Which was five minutes before the time before that. Checking it does nothing to stop my leg from bouncing, my eye from twitching, and my heart from skipping every other beat.

I've heard nothing from Scarlett or Axel, but Shift reassures me that the job was done, the cleaners were called in, and the dead body collected had no resemblance to either of them. That doesn't mean they weren't at each other's throats before and after the act.

They've got two hours to reappear in front of me before I start hunting them down. Club matters be damned. That's my best friend and the woman consuming every inch of me. At least when they're mad at each other here, we can attempt to manage them, but Scarlett was so sure this was a trip they needed to do together.

I've clearly been too caught up in club affairs to acknowledge there may have been a shift between them. Shit, he fucking hugged her when she returned.

Swiping a hand down my face, I sigh.

The reality of the situation is that I'm too scared to put hope into them being… more. That would be life changing, for Axel more than anyone, and he deserves the happiness Scarlett offers up without even trying. But he's his own worst enemy, his own destructive force, so he needs to be able to constantly see the light at the end of the tunnel. A task he's never been able to achieve previously.

"You good?" Gray asks from beside me, lifting a bottle of beer to his lips. His eyes are heavy. None of us have slept much without her here, a fact that's far too embarrassing for any of us to actually admit out loud, but we can tell by the state of each other.

"I've been better," I grumble, lifting my drink as Emmett nods at my other side.

"We're all sorry-ass motherfuckers."

Too true.

The slam of a door catches my attention over the low hum of conversation that takes over the bar, and I flick my attention to the source, but it's not them. It's Graham and Declan with a few of the Ruthless Bitches trailing behind them.

Of course that's where they feel most at home.

"Ryker, how is everything going?" Graham asks, sliding into the booth without invitation. He slaps his palm on the table for a beer to present itself and Ruthie quickly rushes off.

Declan takes the other side of the booth, and as much as I want to refuse him out of principle, I maintain silence. His time will come, I just have to bide my own.

"We have some of the prospects on the streets trying to gather any intel they can, but it's like they're God or something. Known by all but never seen unless they want it that way." I don't mention that I *know* Declan has a link, an in, that could lead us right to them, but it was clear the other night that Graham has no idea what his son has been up to. Or if he does, he just doesn't care.

"You want us to send some of our men out, Ryker? Might do a better job," Declan offers with a smirk, pulling Molly onto his lap, and she preens like a fucking peacock. The sparkle in her eyes as she glances my way says enough.

She finally has a spot in the prez's booth.

There's a challenge in her stare for me to make a point of it, but she's not worth the value a conversation would hold or the time and effort behind it. Focusing on Declan, I shake my head. "We're good for now, thanks for the offer, but I need your men ready to fight when the time comes. That's why they get to explore everything we have to offer here instead."

His grin widens at my statement as Ruthie returns with two beers, placing one down in front of Declan before climbing into Graham's lap.

"Is it not worth getting a message out to meet on neutral ground?" Graham asks, and my mind instantly drifts to the diner in town. The last time I was there, I had a run-in with the deputy, followed swiftly by a meeting with Kincaid outside. Was he more civilized? Sure, but that's not what we're going for now.

"This escalated beyond neutral grounds when he killed a prospect defending two women connected to the club. Some moves are just too dirty to come back from," I grunt, checking the time again.

"I'm sure he—"

"It was my fucking sister, man. There's nothing to consider on his end. A line was crossed and there's no backing away from it," Emmett interjects. They glare at each other, and Graham chuckles, slapping his hand on the table again, and it cuts through the tension enough for their stare-off to end.

Gray glances at the time while I reach for my beer. We really are sorry-ass fuckers. I'd much rather be sitting here wallowing in my own pity over the gaping hole I feel at both Axel and Scarlett not being present, but it seems the assholes we wrongly let through our doors have other ideas.

"Not just that, Declan, but they got their hands on their favorite pussy. Can't have that now, can we?" Molly's words are like ice through my veins, and I have to fight against the overwhelming need to pull a Scarlett move and slam her face into the fucking table.

I really should have let my woman end her long before now.

"That pussy must have matured with age then, because when I first met little Scarlett, she was nothing more than a vir—"

"Say one more word, motherfucker, and I will stab you in the throat at the same time as I shoot your fucking cock off," Gray bites, whipping out a damn blade and gun from nowhere and aiming them directly at the cunt beside him.

I want to chant for him to do it, but he just showed his hand to these fuckers.

"See," Molly murmurs, a giggle ripping from her throat as she leans into the enemy. Declan laughs along with her, like Gray's threat means nothing. A fact my brother isn't going to appreciate.

His hand flexes around the handle, ready to follow through on his threat, when Shift bursts in from the back of the clubhouse, with Emily in tow. "They're back."

He doesn't need to explain who or where, we already know.

Gray shoves at Declan to get out of the booth, catching

him by surprise as he stumbles to the floor, Molly dropping with him. "What the fuck?" he grunts, but the three of us clamber over them without a backward glance toward the yard. There are more pressing matters than dealing with his shit.

Emmett somehow gets to the double doors first, nudging them open with his arm as we spill out into the yard with Emily and Shift behind us. Axel's pickup truck rolls down the driveway, slowing to a stop a few feet away from us.

Axel turns to Scarlett in the truck with a frown pulling his brows together. Her head falls back in response, and her laughter echoes around us. I don't know what the conversation is, all I know is she's happy, and what the fuck is that? Is—

"Man, is Axel laughing too or am I tripping out?" Gray asks, rubbing at his eyes dramatically, and Emily chuckles.

"I didn't even know he could do that," she muses, and I mindlessly nod along with her statement. It's a rare fucking sight, that's for sure, but watching his shoulders relax and the tension leave his expression makes my chest clench.

Scarlett was right, they needed this. They needed this journey to maybe have a chance of coming together. Even if it just means they can tolerate being in the same room as each other, but the sparkle in both of their eyes tells me there's more than the opportunity of friendship there.

The door squeaks behind me, but I don't turn to look, enraptured by the pair of them in the truck.

"You need to be careful with that girl, Ryker." I glance back to see Graham lighting a cigarette as he watches her intently.

"What makes you say that?" I ask, my muscles coiling with anger at the mere mention of her from his lips.

"She's damaged goods."

Shaking my head, I gaze at her as she steps out of the truck. "Aren't we all?"

I can barely spit the words out, my throat is so tight, my body working overtime to stop myself from smacking the fuck out of the old man.

"She was raised by wolves, Ryker."

"And now she fucks them." Emmett's words cut through the air as he chuckles, and when I turn to him, I can see the anger floating in his eyes. Someone clearly overheard Graham's snippet of advice.

"Hey, Sweet Cheeks, I missed you," Gray hollers and rushes to our girl's side. He lifts her and twirls her in the air.

"What, no spin for me?" Axel grunts, making me grin as I step toward him. His hand slaps mine like always, and the swift pat on the back seems longer this time. His body is saying what his mouth can't. I don't exactly know what he's trying to express, but I'm here for him no matter what.

"I'm glad to see you both breathing," I joke, leaning back and cocking a brow at him. He glares back at me just like I expected.

"Shut your mouth, Ryker."

I act innocent as I search out Scarlett, desperate to get to her, but she's wrapped up in Emily's arms, so I give her a second before stalking toward her. She must sense me getting closer though, because her gaze finds mine when I'm a few steps away.

"Mr. President," she sings, sending a jolt straight to my dick.

"You're gross," Emily mumbles, fake-gagging, and everyone laughs.

Pulling Scarlett into my arms, I hold her tightly to my chest, relieved to feel her there once again.

Home.

That's where I feel like I am when she's in my arms. It's bizarre as fuck, but I crave it.

"Everything go okay?" I whisper in her ear as she tightens her arms around my neck.

"Better," she offers, like that makes any sense, but she seems calm, and I can always get a good read on a situation from her vibe. So I trust in her statement. "How have things been here?"

"Awful," I grunt, pressing the outline of my cock against her stomach as I lift her off her feet and inhale her floral scent. She hums against my throat.

I should put her down, step away, and make it look like she means nothing to me, but I just… can't.

My arms refuse to release her, my fingers pressing tighter against the leather jacket she's wearing. We're swimming in a clusterfuck right now, and her just being here changes it all. I feel like I can breathe through everything again. The past forty-eight hours reminded me what my life was like without her, and even though it really wasn't that long ago, it's still a complete contrast to now.

Like night and day, she offers me a sense of light I never knew existed, and now, I cling to it, cling to her.

"You're going to have to put her down eventually," Emmett grumbles from somewhere, but I grunt in response, not moving an inch.

"No, for real, I'm going to need her tomorrow, Ryker," Emily states, confusing me as I reluctantly turn to her. Scarlett follows my line of sight too, and Emmett's sister beams. "Because tomorrow, she starts college."

FOURTEEN

Scarlett

"This is so ridiculous," I grumble, huffing as I slouch in my seat.

"What is?" Emily asks from her spot beside me, and I give her a pointed look.

"All of this." I wave my hand at my clothes and the backpack sitting at my feet. "Sure, you can dress me in a pair of cute jeans and a silk top, but my combat boots and leather jacket scream I'm crazy and we all know it." Shift laughs from the driver's seat. Emmett's keeping his lips clamped shut beside him, but I still give him a deathly glare. "And don't even get me started on the backpack. Don't think I didn't see the notepads, pens, and damn laptop in there. It's all completely unnecessary when I can't even read or write."

I'm completely aware that I'm acting like a petulant

child, stomping my foot and spitting my pacifier out because I'm overwhelmed and nervous, but admitting it out loud is never going to happen.

I was fine last night as I enjoyed the evening in the bar with my friend, my men, and Shift. Even Maggie came and sat with us for a while too, and the entire time, I was excited for today, to help Emily carry on with her life. But now... now, I'm regretting it.

Emily shakes her head dismissively at me, aiming a pointed look my way. "Your learning has been coming along amazing and you know it," she states, wagging her finger at me, and I roll my eyes. "And I've also signed us up for the English class for beginners that they offer. So I think everything in there is completely needed."

"Wait, what?" I startle, sitting tall in my seat as I stare at her in confusion. "You don't need that class."

"I know, but you do, and you're doing so much for me, it's only fair I do something for you." She cocks a brow, ready for me to challenge her, but for once, I'm stuck for words.

"This isn't necessary."

"I know."

"You didn't have to," I add, chin pressed to my chest as I peer up at her.

"That's exactly why I'm doing it."

A soft smile touches my lips as my appreciation for her

washes over me. A quick glance out of the corner of my eye shows both Emmett and Shift smiling too. Dammit, sometimes I'm a bitch.

"Thank you," I breathe, reaching across to her, and she squeezes my hand.

"Don't thank me yet, we need to get through your first day," she replies with a wink.

I gulp, turning my attention to the world passing us by as we cross town to the campus where I'm going to be spending a lot more time. I never thought I would see the day that my ass would be anywhere near a college campus. Especially for actual learning and not a job, a target requiring my services.

The fact that she willingly added us to another class for *my* needs warms my once frozen soul. Time and time again, Emily and the Ruthless Brothers have shown me that I have a chance at a future, one that involves family, growth, and stability.

I remain lost in my thoughts as we pass the sign for campus. My nerves get the better of me as I stare at the sheer amount of people here. Small low-rise buildings spread across my view, surrounded by large grassy lawns, sprawling trees, and picnic benches. It's the kind of shit I thought only existed in movies, but apparently, now it's my life.

Shift pulls the SUV into a parking spot at the back of

the lot, and everyone else climbs out before I do. Emmett hovers by my door, but he simply watches me through the glass as I take a few deep breaths, willing myself to get out. The second I pull the handle, he opens the door the rest of the way, offering me his hand as I heave my backpack over my shoulder and climb down.

His arm drapes around my shoulders, pulling me into his side, and we fall into step with Shift and Emily. We garner looks from others walking by, many locking their gazes on the Ruthless Brother emblem on their leather cuts, but no one speaks a word. If anything, it only gives us a wide berth.

Perfect. My social limit has already been reached, and if I can ward people off, then this just might be bearable.

"It's this building over here this morning, as we have a business class first," Emily explains, pointing toward the left, and we follow her lead with Shift right at her side. Why does a business class feel like the most overwhelming? This doesn't feel like it's going to be fun at all. Let's just hope I don't have to fall heavily into reading and writing today. Applying officially to be here as Emily's protector also requires me to pass these damn classes.

All too soon, she stops, and I know this is where Emmett leaves us. The way his fingers flex on my shoulder in comfort tells me he knows it too.

Fuck.

"Ryker is going to try and get away to be here when you finish, Snowflake," he says, turning me to face him, and I nod. "You've got this. You're a damn queen at everything you do and you know it. The fact that it's my sister you're stepping out of your comfort zone for only makes me love you even more."

"Is that possible?" I reply with a grin, and he eliminates the space between us to press his lips to mine. It's over far too soon, but when he leans back, eyes locked on mine, I wet my lips and take a deep breath. "I love you too."

His eyes practically bug out of his head, but I'm already stepping back and racing up the steps with Emily.

"You're something else, Scarlett Reeves," my Viking hollers, making my cheeks heat as we step inside. Emily giggles as she links her arm through mine, guiding me to where we need to go.

"Isn't Shift coming in with us?" I ask, and Emily shakes her head.

"I convinced him that he should wait outside."

"As simple as that?"

"As simple as that," she repeats, her cheeks growing pink as she avoids my gaze. I bite back the smile fighting to spread across my face. I'm so ready for the day she spills the beans on whatever it is the pair of them have going on, but as much as I want the deets, it has to be on her terms.

Following the flow of the other students filling the

hallway, we pass window after window, offering a glimpse inside the classrooms, until we reach the end. When we step through the double doors, my stress levels sky rocket, and the sense of overwhelm weighing heavy on me tingles through my veins.

Emily pushes us to the side out of everyone else's path. "I always sit at the front, so if I move, it may draw attention to you being here. You can join me down there, or get comfortable up here at the back. You're still in the room with me either way."

I exhale sharply, relieved this girl knows me so well. "I'll take the back," I say, and she nods, squeezing my arm tightly as she nudges me to the closest seat to the door.

"Behave, and don't stress about notes and stuff. I've got this," she assures before skipping down the steps and taking a seat right in the front row.

I assess the room as I slowly take my seat, dropping my backpack to my feet. The main exit is where we entered to my right, there's two doors at the bottom, behind the professor's desk, one is labeled as an office, while the other has a fire exit sign. Clear of the getaway points if necessary, I try to drum out the noise coming from the chatter in the room.

My heart rate slows with every passing minute, and when a man steps out of the office, the room quietens. This must be the professor. Emily did tell me his name, but I can't remember it now.

Movement directly to my left pulls my attention as a guy drops into the seat next to me. Floppy blond hair covers half of his face until he rakes it back with his fingers, tucking it behind his ears. His eyes instantly find mine before he runs them over the length of me.

"You're new."

"Am I?"

"Yup, I would know if a hottie like you was running around on campus already," he states, winking at me, and I fight back the eye roll threatening to take over. Perfect, all I need is a creepy guy in class. Hopefully, ignoring him will make him get bored real quick.

My lips draw into a thin line as I turn my attention to the front.

"Hey, don't ignore me. What's your name?" he asks, voice lowering as the professor starts to talk. "I'm Joshua, but you can call me Josh when you're coming on my dick, if you'd like."

My eyes snap to him, surprised at his line, but the grin on his lips tells me he was going for the shock factor. Fucker. Looking at him properly now, I realize he's wearing a blue and white varsity jacket.

Jock.

Of course.

"Has that line ever worked before?"

"Nope, but it got your attention. I can make it up to you if you want?" he offers, unrelenting.

"Thanks, but I have a boyfriend." *Or four*, I think, but he doesn't need to know that.

"That's—"

"Joshua, are you going to continue to irritate the female beside you or are you actually going to attempt to pass this class?" The boom comes from the professor, who is leaning back against the desk in front of the board as he fixes the circular glasses on the bridge of his nose.

Emily glances at me, cringing at the attention she knows I'm hating, but thankfully, Joshua doesn't drag it out. "I'm sorry, Professor, I'll shut up now."

"See to it that you do," he grumbles in response, before immediately redirecting the room back to the board behind him.

Another deep breath, another heavy exhale. I get the feeling today is going to be full of them.

I relax back into my seat, not taking in a word the professor says as the information on the board goes completely over my head. This is definitely not the easy start I was hoping for. My mind is so busy being overwhelmed that it feels like I've only just sat down, but no, the class is ending, and everyone around me rises from their seats.

The class ends, and Emily races up the stairs before I've even got my backpack over my shoulder, pulling me out of the room in a hurry I wasn't expecting.

"What's wrong?" I ask, leaning into her as the hallway fills with people.

"I forgot about Josh Parrish. I'm so sorry," she mumbles, keeping her focus straight ahead until we step outside into the fresh air. I spot Shift instantly waiting at the bottom to the left, and only when we're beside him does she finally stop.

"Don't stress it," I murmur, and Shift tilts his head with intrigue.

"Don't stress what?"

"No—"

"Hey, you snuck off before I could catch your name." An arm wraps around my shoulders, and my body stiffens. Before I can consider my options, I swing my elbow back and hit Joshua in the stomach, making him grunt.

"Fuck. I do like them feisty, baby." Bent, he heaves a breath in, eyes still fixed on me, and my irritation only heightens.

"I'm not feisty, asshole, I'm murderous," I grunt. Shift takes a step toward me.

Joshua's eyes only darken with excitement as he stands back to his full height, running his tongue over his bottom lip. Fucking creep. "Are you this snappy when you're getting fucked?" He wiggles his eyebrows, making my nostrils flare as I thrust my fist straight at his throat. The garbled sound that follows makes me grin, and before he can come back with something else to say, I link my arm through Emily's and hightail it out of there.

Once we're around the corner and he's nowhere in sight, I slow my pace, only to find Shift chuckling as he taps away on his cell phone.

"What's funny?" I grumble, hiking my backpack higher up my shoulder.

He grins, tapping away for a few more seconds before finally lifting his gaze. "The guys aren't going to be happy about that."

"He's no concern. They don't need to worry about irrelevant shit like this when they have bigger stuff to be dealing with," I bite with irritation. I know it's not aimed at him, but fuck, I can't control it.

The guilty look I get in advance makes me pause as he waves his cell at me.

"Oops, too late."

RUTHLESS BROTHERS MC

FIFTEEN

Ryker

My cell phone digs in my palm as I stand at the end of the path, ignoring every motherfucker that interrupts my view. There's a reason I never even considered applying to college, besides the fact that I barely gave any effort to scrape through high school. People. I can't stand them, and there's far too fucking many of them here for my liking.

I can feel eyes on me, or my cut more specifically. They either hate me, want to be me, or want to fuck me. It's a no to all three, but I won't engage in any kind of conversation for them to know that.

I spot the three of them across the walkway as my cell buzzes.

Shift:
Just out of the dining hall now.

His eyes find mine across the space. A smirk teases his lips, and my eyes narrow. Scarlett smiles along with whatever Emily is saying, but she's also scanning the area, always on guard.

She seems at ease at least, but she will forever be on edge no matter where she is. That's the fact of life when you've been raised as she has. I'll shield her from every storm if she lets me, but I know she's independent enough to take on the world by herself and emerge victorious.

I can't imagine the stark contrast this is for her. It's just another one of the things she's willing to do for her family. For *my* family. We owe her everything. I need to work on that, on repaying her in some way. Just not right now though, there are other pressing matters that require my attention.

She spots me from a good distance away, eyebrows pinching in confusion as she picks up her pace. "Hey, you're here early," she says, coming to a stop in front of me.

I shrug. "Shift messaged." Her eyes instantly narrow at him, but all he does is smother the grin threatening to take over his face.

Fucker.

She turns back to me, and I know she knows exactly why I'm here. "I don't know what he said, but—"

Grabbing her arm, I pull her to my side and take a step

away from Shift and Emily. "She'll be back before your next class. How long until then?" Emily's eyes widen as she regards me, considering whether to answer or not, but Shift does it for me.

"Twenty-five minutes."

"Gotcha, send me the location and she'll be there."

There's a clear smirk on Shift's face as I turn away, pulling Scarlett along with me. She doesn't fight my hold as I head toward the building Shift told me about. Fucker knew I wouldn't react well to someone else stepping in on what's mine.

Lessons have to be taught, lines drawn, or I just start taking blood. I don't care either way. I've always been a fair man though, and a single chance can be given.

"Where are we going?" I don't offer her a response or glance in her direction as I remain focused on my destination. She huffs beside me, not putting up a fight like I expected. Turning right up the steps to the last building, she keeps pace, but her curiosity is still there. "This isn't where the next class is." *I know.* "Why am I back at the business class?" she pushes as we near the end of the hall, absent from anyone and everyone.

I spin to face her and lift her feet off the ground before she can process any of it. Her back hits the wall beside the door to her class harder than I would have liked, but I claim her mouth and swallow the whimper.

She kisses me back as fiercely as I claim her, fingers gripping my hair like her life depends on it as her legs tighten around my waist. Aware we don't have as much time as I would like, I tear my mouth from hers, leaving us as breathless as each other.

"Ryker, what's—"

I mute her next question with another bruising kiss, reminding myself along with her exactly who it is she belongs to.

My cock throbs, pressed against her core that it pains me so much to be close, just not close enough.

"Fuck," I grunt, breaking our kiss once again, but this time, I blindly move us into the room. "Where were you sitting?" I grunt, nostrils flaring as I look up at her.

"Ryker…"

"Where. Were. You. Sitting?" It's not a question, it's a demand, and she fucking knows it.

"Here," she whispers, pointing a trembling finger to my left.

I take the few steps required to bring us in front of the seat before lowering her to her feet. This close, she has to tilt her head right back to lock eyes with me, and I thrive on it.

Without uttering a word, I spin her away from me, and her hands instantly hit the desk with a thump. Scarlett peers over her shoulder at me, heat in her eyes as I kick her feet further apart until I have her exactly where I want her.

Running my hands over the globes of her ass, I move in closer as I tease my fingers over her pussy through her tight jeans. She gasps at the touch, just as needy for me as I am for her. I pop open the button of her jeans and lower her zipper. It's only when I pull the material down, along with her panties, to the middle of her thighs, that she questions me.

"What are you doing, Ryker?"

I cock a brow at her. I thought it was obvious, but clearly, she wants me to spell it out. "Do you want me to stop?" I unzip my jeans, and my cock springs free greedily.

She tilts her head at me. "Stop what?"

"Claiming what's mine."

She soaks my words in.

"No," she breathes, or is it a prayer?

"Good." I place one hand at the base of her spine as I line my cock up with the other. I groan at the feel of her needy pussy already wet against the tip of my dick before I slowly sink inside of her.

She moans low and raspy as I fill her, not preparing her with my fingers first, and the feel of her stretching out around my length is like the holy grail. I may have found my new addiction.

Her raw pussy.

"Fuck, Ryker," she gasps, palms flat on the table as she

tilts her pussy toward me. I grin, grabbing hold of her hips as I pull out and slam back in hard and fast. Her mewls echo around us as I take her, harder and faster with every slam of my hips.

Sweat clings to me, need racing through my veins as I make her mine right here. Anyone could walk in, anyone could catch sight of us, and that only turns me on more.

I would fuck my woman in front of the world if it made them all aware she was off the table, that she was mine. But the thought of them seeing her makes me angry, so this will suffice.

"Who do you belong to, Scarlett?"

"No one," she bites out, pushing her hips back into me with urgency, and I slow my pace.

"Who do you belong to, *Rebel*?" I try again, hearing her curse even louder this time.

"Fuck, Ryker," she pleads, and I almost consider that a good enough answer, but I want the acknowledgment on her tongue.

When I stop, she tosses a glare over her shoulder and sighs. "Right now, at this moment, I belong to you, Ryker, and you know it. But I will never belong to anyone ever again."

My cock pulses, loving her truth, and that's all I need to hear as I fuck her harder and faster than before. She slaps her hand on the desk with every cry of pleasure. Reaching around her, my fingers find her center, running over her clit in tight circles as she falls flat against the desk. Her ass is perfectly in the air, leaving just enough room for me to play with her tight nub, and I sense it the second she coils up tight inside, pussy clamping around my cock before she explodes.

"Oh my God, Ryker. Oh my God," she chants, trembling, as I release my load inside of her.

Slowly pulling her back against me, my cock remains nestled in her core as I wrap my arms tightly around her waist and pepper kisses over her neck.

"What the fuck was that, Ryker?" she murmurs deliriously. "Actually, I really don't want to know. It was hot as hell."

I smirk at her judgment as I slip my length from her thighs and tuck myself back into my jeans. She lets me pull her panties up her legs without a word, followed swiftly by her jeans. When she turns to face me, I offer her the response she doesn't likely want.

"That was me making sure little fuckers named Joshua get the message that you're taken," I state, swiping my hair back off my face.

Her eyes narrow. "But how is he—"

Her words cut off as I take a step back and point down to the front of the room. He's turned away from us, roped to a chair facing the board, but from the way her eyes widen, she knows exactly who it is.

I take the steps two at a time as I near the little fucker who appears to still be breathing. "Did you hear that, Joshua?"

He nods meekly as I trudge the remaining distance to him. Scarlett rushes after me, shock clear on her features as she stops beside me.

"Why is his nose busted?" Blood drips down his face. His eyes are also swelling nicely, too. Excellent.

"Because he needed a lesson, and I'm an excellent teacher," I grunt before addressing the little shit, "Now, remember what I said, or next time, I will literally stab you to death. Are we clear?" He nods again, the gag in his mouth making it impossible for him to be heard.

"Ryker," Scarlett murmurs, exasperated with what she's seeing, but I just smile at her too.

"I don't play around, Rebel." I cock my brow at her, challenging her to come back at me, but to my surprise, she shakes her head and moves toward the steps.

"Where are you going?" I holler as she walks away from me, a delicious sway to her hips as she puts more and more distance between us.

"I'm not sticking around to help clean this fucking mess up, so I'm heading to class. Alone." When she reaches the top of the stairs, she whirls around to me, arms folded across her chest as she gives me another pointed glance. "But you bet your sweet ass that I'm making a note of this for the next time Molly pisses me off." She runs a finger across her throat, her hair wild and pupils blown, and then she's gone.

Hot. As. Fuck.

Sighing, I glance at Joshua who refuses to meet my gaze. "Honestly, the best pussy of your life, I swear to God. But she holds my heart, and I'm carving out hers, so there's really no chance for you." Crouching, I whip out my blade and aim it in his direction. "But if you so much as sit in the same fucking row as her again, I will kill you, and I'll enjoy every fucking second of it."

SIXTEEN

Scarlett

Shift pulls the SUV to a stop in front of the compound, while Emily continues to poke her finger at me. "You can't tell me that Ryker showed up that mad and did nothing about the situation, Scarlett. I refuse to believe it."

I move to open my door, but it's locked. Shift beams at me, but only holds his ground for a few more seconds before the click of the locks echo around me. With one foot out of the vehicle, I grab my backpack.

"Honestly, Em, I don't know what you're talking about."

I don't meet her gaze as I rush from my seat and shut the door behind me, but by the time I'm rounding the front of the SUV, she's already there.

Fuck.

She's been pushing me since I met up with them at

our next class. I've tried like hell to ignore her, but there's clearly something written all over my face that gives me away.

"Not even a kiss or a claiming hug to mark you for everyone else?" she asks, cocking a brow at me as I shrug. She shakes her head at me in dismay. "You're a shit liar."

"I am not."

She bursts out laughing. "Scar, you smell like sex, don't give me any of that bullshit."

My jaw hits the floor as Shift chuckles too, keeping his head down as he leads the way toward the clubhouse. I can feel my cheeks heating under her assessment, but I keep my head high and ignore her inquisitive stare.

When it's clear she's not going to get me to kiss and tell, she sighs, linking her arm through mine. "Who is going to whisk you away next? Or do I get to keep you to myself?"

"No one," I grumble, recalling exactly how I left Ryker earlier. I was expecting him to be there at the end of the day, but none of them showed. It seems the prez's little demonstration was enough to relax them.

He fucked me hard, fast, and all-consuming. In the exact spot where I sat when Joshua first approached me, only for the fucker himself to be sitting mere feet away listening. At least he wasn't looking.

I should be mad. I really should. But just thinking

about it makes goosebumps prickle up my arms.

"Well, if that's the case, do you want to watch a movie or something? Pig out on greasy slices and sugary goodness while I go through everything that was mentioned today?"

I cringe, knowing full well she's going to have to touch base on everything. "Yes," I answer, hoping I won't have to put her through this every night after classes.

"Let's at least get you two in here first, shall we?" Shift holds the door open, giving us a pointed stare. I glare at him, while Emily flicks the end of his nose, and he snaps his teeth at her fingertip.

"Are you a shit liar too?" I murmur against her ear so no one else can hear. She frowns at me for a second, but I don't miss the pink trailing up her neck and tainting her cheeks.

"I don't know what you're talking about," she grumbles, avoiding my gaze as Gray hollers my name, bringing me back to the present. Emily quickly releases my arm and pushes me toward the prez's table where Gray sits, eager to get rid of me after my probing.

I relent, hiking my bag further up my shoulder as I cut through the few people standing between us to get to him. Emmett is sitting beside him, the two of them leaning over a folder on the table, but it seems I've distracted their attention.

"Hey," I say, falling into Gray's outstretched arms. He

squeezes me tight, making me smile as exhaustion rips out a heavy exhale from my lips.

"How did everything go today?"

I peer at him, waiting to see the menacing twinkle in his eyes, but there's nothing there. Emmett leans his face against his palm, looking up at me with only warmth.

"It was overwhelming, the classes are insane, but not as crazy as Ryker." I tempt the waters, but they frown at me.

"Is this because of the text Shift sent? He sent another straight after confirming you had it under control, but—"

"Ryker did disappear over lunch unexpectedly," Emmett interjects, cutting Gray off. I huff, shaking my head at the situation. "What did he do?"

"Beat the guy," I start, gaze flicking between both of them, and they laugh.

"I'm going to high-five our prez when I see him," Gray says with a grin, squeezing my side.

"Then gagged him and tied him to a chair in the room where he first hit on me," I add.

"There's a reason he's our leader, Snowflake." Emmett winks at me. Oh he thinks he's one smooth fucker.

"Then fucked me against my desk."

Their eyes widened with surprise. "That fucker better not have been able to see your—"

I wave Emmett off, shaking my head. "No, he had him

turned away. But I didn't fucking know. He just wanted the guy to hear me cry for his dick."

It should be weird as hell talking about fucking someone else to two other guys I'm also getting dirty with, but it's surprisingly... therapeutic. As much as Emily is my best friend, a thing I never thought I would have, this feels too intimate to discuss with her, especially when one of the four guys that are tearing at my heart is her brother.

"Fuck that, my high-five just turned into one with his face because I'm jealous as shit," Gray grumbles, pressing his lips to my cheek with a grin.

My eyes narrow, but they seem too impressed with Ryker's moves to see my side.

Assholes.

Pursing my lips, I look at the folder spread out on the table and my heart stops. "What's this?"

Gray clears his throat, running his free hand over the sheets. "These are some of the ideas Emmett was showing me for if we get a matching tattoo, Sweet Cheeks."

My heart races in my chest. My gut told me that was the reason, and I thought it would make me nervous, but it's excitement pooling in my stomach. "They're all stunning," I reply, glancing over the array of tattoo designs before us.

"Maybe you should let Scarlett choose which one she loves the most for you to get first, then if she ever decides to get it too, you know she likes it," Emmett offers, a soft smile on his lips as he combs over his beard.

"What do you say?" Gray asks, lips brushing against my ear.

I lean out of his hold a little, balancing over the table more to get a better view. There's a pocket watch tattoo, roses, skulls, guns, everything, but my eyes keep being drawn to the one in the far left corner.

"I think this one is perfect." My heart seems to leap faster in my chest as I point it out.

"I think you have excellent taste, Snowflake, because we've been going back to that one every time," Emmett admits.

"Hey, Scarlett, don't make me come over there and cause a scene. You promised me," Emily hollers from the bar where she's chatting with Maggie and Shift. I feel every pair of eyes in the room cast our way. From the Ruthless Bitches in the corner to the prospects scattered around the room.

"You already did," Emmett grumbles, throwing a dirty look his sister's way.

Shit, when have I ever laughed this much?

I'm in just as much danger now as I ever have been, yet there are still moments where it all drifts away and I'm just your everyday girl with fun, laughter, and hope.

It's because of them.

"The boss called," I murmur, tilting my head to face

Gray. I press my lips to his, warmth zapping through my veins at his touch, and he groans against my mouth.

"I may have to call dibs on you soon, Sweet Cheeks."

I nod before leaning over the space toward Emmett, but before I lay claim to his mouth in front of everyone, I move toward his ear. I murmur as quietly as I can so Gray can't hear, waiting for a nod in agreement before he grabs the back of my head and takes my lips.

Fuck.

When he pulls away, I'm dizzy. Every step I take away from them feels like walking on clouds and I love it. As I reach Emily, who now stands at the door leading to the back of the compound, I glance back over my shoulder to see them still watching me.

Damn, my heart is full.

The end credits roll on the third movie of the night as Emily yawns from her spot on the bed. Books are spread out all around us, random sheets of paper, and our laptops. Along with empty bags of chips, candy wrappers, and chocolate bars.

Tonight was way more chill than I expected, and when she sat and started explaining things to me, everything seemed to make more sense. Once she had touched base on everything, our attention shifted to my inadequate reading and writing. Which is such a lie, I feel fucking proud of myself. My growth from the very first time she sat down with me is clear. My handwriting is still a little shaky, but that's more from nerves. I'm never this nervous when I have a gun in my hand. Maybe next session, I hold a pistol in one hand and the pen in the other and see what results I get then.

Reading is completely different, but the progress is coming. I make a mental note to download the Kindle app she told me about, to try and read some books in my spare time too. Not that there's much going spare, but I want to push this. It's important.

I feel normal despite the situation we're in. There should be guilt clawing at my insides for not staying alert and figuring out the enemy's next move, but instead, I feel... safe, protected, at home.

Emily packs the things away around us as I remain in place, thoughts of Kincaid and his men starting to flood my mind as I remember being at their compound gates before freeing myself from their grasp.

I close my eyes, trying to remember what I saw beyond the blood splattering from the men in the SUV with me. I try to recall where I was, what I was actually seeing, smelling, hearing, but it's all too vague. I was drowning in adrenaline. Taking a deep breath, I try to remember what the roads looked like as I escaped and made it home, but just like in my dreams, it's all too fuzzy.

Maybe I need to try them out for real. Head out and survey the surrounding areas.

Emily yawns again, pulling me from my head, and I blink my eyes open to see she's put everything away. "I'm so sorry, I should have helped."

"Don't worry about it, I could tell you were deep in thought." She smiles, stretching out her limbs. I wait for her to ask what I was thinking about, but she doesn't pry.

I don't know what I did to get this girl to like me, but she's like family, the sister I never knew I wanted or needed. Now she's so important to me I would protect her with my life, just as I have done and I will continue to do for the rest of time.

"I'll let you get some sleep." I stand from the bed, stretching my arms above my head and groaning with the perfect feel of tension leaving my bones.

"Aren't you tired too?" she asks as I head for the door, and I nod, turning back.

"Yeah, but I have a plan to put into action first. Then, I can pass out." She smiles at me, again not pushing for further details as I mumble my goodnight and step out into the hallway.

Emmett's door across the hallway is slightly ajar, and anticipation quickly ripples down my spine with excitement and warmth. I rap my knuckles on the wood, and it opens a little, revealing my Viking as he glances in my direction.

"Hey, Snowflake."

"Hey, Viking," I reply, making him smirk as I shut the door behind me. "Have you been expecting me?" I point to everything he has laid out.

"Nope, I just sit like this all the time."

"With Swifty playing in the background? I thought as much." I lean into his side, and he presses a kiss to my temple.

"Are you ready?" he asks, ignoring my jibe at the music playing around the room. I cast my gaze over the equipment he has set up and nod.

"Ink me, Viking."

RUTHLESS BROTHERS MC

SEVENTEEN

Emmett

Scarlett gets comfortable in the seat I've set up for her. Gray had told me mere moments before she stepped in that he had confessed to her what matching tattoos meant to the club, meant to us, and without missing a beat, she leaned across the table and whispered for me to tattoo her first.

She wants this, wants us, and there is no denying it any longer. Once we are done tonight, it will be fresh on her skin and visible to everyone. Only Gray will know what it means at first, but the moment he has it done too, the rest will be history.

"Nervous?"

"Never." She beams; her eyes tired as she rises from her seat, turning on the spot to drop back down, facing the opposite direction. Then, she pulls her hair up into a bun, revealing her delicate neck to me before pointing at it. "I want it here."

With the way she has her hair up so much, it's going to be on display for all to see.

Fuck.

I like that a lot.

My fingers twitch, eager to carve the word *mine* into her, just like when I tattooed her the first time, but this will be just the same.

"I think that would be perfect," I mumble, my throat drying with the thought.

Reaching for the stencil I was working on before she got here, I hold it up to her neck to check the sizing, and it fits perfectly. I know she was happy for me to freehand it last time, but the meaning behind what this will represent felt too risky this time. She deserves the best, and that's what she's going to receive.

We sit in comfortable silence as I prep her skin and transfer the stencil. "Do you want to take a quick look before I get started?" I offer, slipping my hands into black latex gloves, and she shakes her head.

"I trust you."

Those three words hit just as hard as *I love you.* We're all well aware that trust isn't really her thing, but she offers it to us anyway.

Determined to not turn this into a fuck fest before I've

even marked her, I will my cock to soften so I can focus on the task at hand. Shuffling toward the edge of the bed so I'm a little closer, I turn the tattoo gun on. A smile teases the corner of my lips. The buzz of the gun combined with Swifty in the background relaxes me like nothing else.

Scarlett doesn't flinch as I press the ink into her skin, if anything her shoulders relax and she settles in further. We remain quiet for a while before I clear my throat.

"I made an appointment today."

"You did? For what?" she asks, hands flexing on the chair as she restrains herself from turning around.

"For my heart." The organ thunders in my chest, a reminder that it's there and needs my attention.

"You did?" The surprise in her voice is quickly outweighed with awe.

"I did."

"I really wish you were telling me this while I was facing you right now," she admits, a slight chuckle to her words.

"Yeah, but then you could mumble *I told you so* or something and I'm just not ready for that level of sass from you at this time of night," I tease, and I can practically see her eyes rolling in my mind.

I expect a cheeky blast back from her, but silence swirls in the air around us for a few moments before she speaks, soft and quiet. "Did you do this for yourself?"

"I did this for you," I answer honestly, knowing full well that it's not what she wants to hear, but it's what she's getting anyway.

"You know that's not supposed to be the reasoning, right? You're supposed to—"

"I didn't have a reason for it to beat until you."

I could swear she curses under her breath at my words, but it's so quiet I can't be sure. A few minutes pass as I continue to work on the outline of her tattoo, until she clears her throat.

"You have always had a reason for your heart to beat, Emmett. For yourself, for Emily, the memory of your parents…"

"I know what you're saying, Snowflake, but as much as you may look at me and Emily and think we had this whole awesome family vibe going on, we really didn't." Apparently, the hum of the tattoo gun and the Taylor Swift song in the background is turning this into a literal therapy session. I don't want to unload on her, she carries the weight of enough, but I want her to understand me on a level no one else ever has. "My mom died from cancer when I was younger, taking away the caring figure in our lives. The rest of it is filled with the club. I was a part of the Ruthless Brothers before I was even an initiated member. My father only saw these four walls as home, as his life. Most nights, we slept here with a passed-out father leaving two kids unattended." The memory of those dark and confusing times tighten my chest, but the pain isn't for me, it's for Emily, just as it always has been.

"I'm sorry, Emmett. I'm sorry your stability was stripped away."

"Honestly, I got lost in it for a while. The pain, the anger, the frustration that my life was spiraling and I had no control over it. I regret that time so much, but I was just a kid. A hurt and sad kid. Everything changed one night when I saw Emily dancing around on the table top, living her best life to a Taylor Swift song, with two of the Ruthless Bitches who were off their faces. My father was nowhere to be found, my mom buried six feet under, and I realized the only person who could truly take care of her and offer her the stability I craved so much was me." I exhale, speaking the truth taking its toll on me. "I pulled her down from the table, hating that she was upset since everyone was cheering her on, but I offered to read her a bedtime story and her eyes widened. We hadn't had one of those since mom died."

"You are everything to your sister, Emmett."

"She's everything to me too. Which is why I read her a bedtime story every night after. I didn't leave her unattended on the compound and made a point of taking her back to our house, until my father managed to stumble that way too. He loved us, I know he did, but he loved

Mama most, and without her, he couldn't breathe."

I pull the gun from her skin, dipping it into the ink as I catch my breath and give myself a moment.

"I can't even imagine what that would have been like for both of you, but the fact that you stepped up and put her first only strengthened you. You're not reckless or single-minded. You're whole-hearted, family orientated, and a protector. Everything I longed for, and now here you are."

Wetting my lips, I lift off the bed just enough to press a kiss to her cheek. "I'll always be what you need me to be, Snowflake." I catch a glimpse of her lips tilting up as I drop back down again.

"I'll always protect you just as fiercely too." Her words send a shiver down my spine. I've spent so long taking care of everyone else, it feels strange for someone to promise it to me, but I love it.

Drawing the last black line on her flesh, I look at my handiwork with a smile. Do you want this colored in at all or…"

"No, it feels more powerful in black alone." I nod, turning the gun off and laying it on the nightstand beside me.

"You're right. Do you know what the lotus flower represents?" I ask, cleaning the freshly inked area.

"I don't. I was just drawn to it, if that even makes any sense," she admits, and that only makes it that much sweeter that she chose it.

"A black lotus flower represents darkness, death, power, and rebellion. But it can also mean overcoming obstacles, hardship, and whatever life throws at you. I can't think of anything better to represent you, Snowflake."

I secure the wrap over her skin, protecting the area, and she slowly turns to face me.

"Is that for real or are you just giving me some bullshit?" she asks with her eyebrow raised, and I hold up my palm like I'm facing a jury.

"On my life."

She smiles and launches herself into my lap. Her knees drop on either side of my thighs as her arms tighten around my neck. "Thank you."

"For what?"

"For being you."

I band my arms around her waist, taking a moment to absorb every inch of her. The song changes into another, and another, before I finally lean back and meet her gaze.

"So. Do I get to have this tattoo as well?"

She tilts her head to the side as she assesses me. "Do I get to be the one to do it?"

I can't tell if she's being serious or teasing, but I shrug all the same. "We'll see, but this is your thing with Gray first. I want to watch his face when he sees this on your skin without taking that moment away from him."

"Do you see that, Emmett? Such a caring Viking." She strokes her thumb down my cheek, looking at me with such love in her eyes that I might pass out from the intensity of it.

"It's my speciality."

"Wanna go find him now?" she asks, buzzing like it's not almost two in the morning. Some people get a buzz after a tattoo, and I think she may be one of them.

Despite her excitement, I shake my head. "He's on a ride out with Ryker and some of the prospects."

"What do you mean?"

"When you were going through college stuff with Emily, Gray got continuously irritated with Declan, so it was either get him out of here or let him inevitably hurt the fucker. I know we all want the latter, but we—"

"Have to bide our time," she finishes my sentence, and I nod. I can tell it pisses her off; it's driving me insane too. But she wasn't wrong when she declared we should go down this route, it's just sucking major ass right now. "Should I be concerned that no one told me?"

"I didn't really consider that, Snowflake. I'm sorry. You were having a stress-free time, and we wanted to keep it that way. When they left, I came and hid in here to wait for you, and Axel is staked out in the bar area with a fuck-off glare on his face that has me expecting everyone to be in bed already because not many people can handle him."

Scarlett grins, a knowing glint in her eyes. She can handle him perfectly. This is exactly why she was made for us. Ryker, Axel, Gray, and I are all completely different people. Even though our core values may be the same, our passion and love for the club is undeniable. We've all lived different lives that have transformed us into different people, yet she holds us together tighter than we've ever been.

It doesn't make sense, it shouldn't be possible, but here we are.

She yawns, her eyes drooping with tiredness as she peers up at me. "If we're not joining the others on their little mission across town, then do you want to be the big spoon while I pass the fuck out? Apparently going to college is more work than it looks and it's been a long-ass day. I'm exhausted," she admits, nestling her head on my shoulder.

My heart swells as I hold her even tighter. Behind her walls and tough exterior, which is way more than just a facade, is the softest, most lovable fucking woman that will ever exist.

"I wouldn't want to be anywhere else, Snowflake."

EIGHTEEN

Gray

Irritation coils in my gut. I needed a distraction from that motherfucker back at the compound. We've been out here for hours, trying to catch even a glimpse of information on the Devil's Brutes and we've got nothing, which is only serving to piss me off even more.

Dragging a hand down my face, I sigh. The sun will be rising in an hour or so, but our world thrives in the darkness. The rowdy bar we've been at for the past ninety minutes is playing the worst fucking music and is filled with sticky surfaces.

I was close to calling bullshit on the prospects when they kept coming home empty-handed, but seeing it for myself is even more eye-opening. What is our next move supposed to be if there's no one willing to offer up information or murmur about them in the shadows so we can catch a hint of their conversation?

"I think this is a bust," I grunt, glancing at Ryker. I clearly spoke the truth he was avoiding, but it's not likely to change now. We may as well call it time.

"Let's go," he mumbles, rising from the booth, and I follow after him. The prospects catch our movement but don't immediately tail after us. They're showing their worth more than ever. Their ability to listen, take orders, and put the club first is setting a good vibe throughout. They'll likely hang around for another thirty minutes or so, then follow Ryker's next order.

The cool air instantly blasts my face as we step out into the parking lot, a stark contrast from the sweat pit inside. I take a few deep breaths, fixing my cut on my shoulders as we prowl toward our bikes.

Neither of us speaks until we're sitting on our bikes, boots pressed into the gravel beneath our feet. "Where to next?"

"Unless we're in the market for running from club to club asking outright for information, then I guess we need to call it." His jaw tics, irritation at tonight's outcome written all over his face.

"I could eat if you want to stop at the diner on the way home," I offer, and he smirks.

"You're always in the mood to eat."

Facts.

I shrug. "What can I say, I'm a growing boy," I say with a snicker, and he shakes his head at me.

"Let's go then. I'm in the mood for steak and eggs."

Starting up my Harley, I kick up the stand, and roll to the end of the gravel, a few feet or so behind Ryker, before we set off on the quiet roads. I'm never a law abiding citizen on the best of days, but with the tension rippling through my body, the empty roads ahead of us, and my need for food, I floor my Harley.

The wind picks up, whipping around my face and clinging my clothes to me. I can still see the light coming from Ryker's bike until he overtakes me and I find myself in his rearview mirror. We dip and weave past each other again and again until the lights of the town come into view. We stop outside the diner and unclip our helmets.

He's grinning despite the shit circumstances of the evening, but I can feel the smirk on my face too. Speed will do that to you. I crave it, almost as much as I crave my fucking woman.

I internally groan at the thought of her. She's heaven on a bike directing me to hell, and I'm a sucker who will follow her straight into the depths. She went to college today, her first form of public education, and when she sauntered in this evening with Emily, she looked like a breath of fresh air. There was something different about her. I can't quite put my finger on it. She was almost lighter, brighter, and serene. A true glimpse at a normal life for her.

I've been addicted to her piercing eyes, soft skin, and perfect curves since day one, before I even knew her damn name. But now, I find myself drawn to the deeper parts of her, the parts she doesn't let anyone else see. I want to feel her joy, her hope, her happiness, and shoulder the weight of her pain.

"Are you coming, asshole, or are you going to sit there all day?" Ryker hollers, pulling me from my thoughts. I stick my middle finger up at him as I stand, ruffling my hair as I follow him toward the diner. "Where's your head at?" he asks, forever the leader he was born to be.

"Stuck on a hot raven-haired beauty with the softest skin and snarkiest lips I've ever met." The grunt he offers in response tells me my words hit exactly where I wanted them to.

"Fucker," he mutters under his breath as he holds the door open to the diner and we step inside.

The smell of leather and tobacco is thick in the air, drawing my attention to the far right of the room where I see Paisley and a few members of his crew, the Iron Scorpions, sitting around a booth. I blink a few times, glancing out of the window behind me until I spot their bikes parked across the parking lot from ours.

I was clearly too lost in my head to even pay attention, and I instantly berate myself. I need to be alert and aware, now more than ever. There's no space for fuckups.

Ryker doesn't miss a beat, offering Paisley a nod before heading in the other direction to our usual booth.

The second we're seated, a server appears at our side. "Hey, boys, what can I get you this morning?"

"I feel like it's too early to say that yet," I reply with a smirk, glancing up at the redhead I've seen a time or two before. She doesn't have a name tag on, but I'm sure my mom said she was called Fiona or something like that.

"Doll, anything after five is classed as morning." She winks at me, bright blue eyeshadow covering her lids as she taps her pen on her pad.

"Can I please have a coffee and a plate of steak and eggs, Fiona," Ryker says, confirming I got her name right, and I point at him.

"Make that two."

She nods and disappears just as swiftly as she arrived. I think that's what I like most about this place. They get on with their job and ignore us. She's getting extra tips tonight... this morning, whatever the fuck it is.

"Am I missing something so obvious that it's glaring me in the face?" Ryker asks, dragging a hand through his hair.

"What makes you say that?"

"With Banner in charge, we were in the Brutes' pockets, but even as his VP, I never knew anything about it."

"I mean this in the nicest way possible, Brother, but I think that was all a ruse to make him look like he was honoring your father." I grimace at the words on my tongue, but he nods in agreement.

"Same. I get the feeling Billy was the one in on all of the top secret shit. I just got fed bullshit."

My nose tickles with frustration, flaring as I try to calm my bubbling emotions. "Taking him out opened a big can of worms. It was needed, but likely more than we were anticipating," I admit.

Fiona stops by the table, dropping off two hot mugs and some creamer before carrying on her way. Ryker doesn't say anything until he's made up his drink and gulped half of it

"I think Axel was right."

My eyebrows furrow at Ryker's statement. "About what?"

"He was right to take him out. Imagine if I had, just as I had wanted to, then dived straight into handling all of this carnage. It would have been far more fucked up than it already is."

Relief rushes through me. I've kept my mouth shut on the situation the entire time because it's not really for me to interfere. Moves were made around me and I was as clueless as Ryker, but it wasn't my revenge that was taken. Truthfully though, as surprising as Axel and Shift's confession was, once I got over the initial shock, I knew they were right.

"Your silence tells me you already came to that conclusion."

I offer him a tight smile. "We're in the thick of the storm, chaos swirling around us. You taking action and convincing the club that you had their best interests at heart would have been impossible. I'm not sure if we would even still be standing right now," I admit, taking a sip of my own drink.

"Please don't tell him yet. We've had limited conversations since his confession, but I need to talk it out with him properly." I nod, more than happy to keep out of it. "It's hard," he continues, glancing down at his mug. "I loved my dad, I loved my mom, but their decisions were never in my best interests, so feeling that from Axel still feels odd. I know we commit ourselves to the club, to our brotherhood, but what Axel, Emmett, you, and I have is a different level of trust."

"Always," I breathe, feeling just as close to them as I do my own flesh and blood, possibly even more.

"In the past, a move like that would have felt like a betrayal. Ma left when Dad refused to give up the club and put her first. Not me, not *us* as a family, *her.* That's selfish as shit, and I couldn't see past that mindset when it came to the fact someone took Banner's blood from me." His knuckles whiten around the handle of his coffee mug. "If only we all had a Maggie, huh?" he adds with a smile.

"She was born to be a queen, Ryker, she was born for this life. A caregiver, a supporter, a badass woman who doesn't take bullshit. Not everyone is made like that, hell, I'm not sure if she was like that before my old man died, but it's the only way I ever remember her being."

"She's a blessing."

"Agreed," I say, just as our plates are brought over.

Murmuring my thanks, I dive in, appreciating the warmth. We only have my mom now, Ryker's is long gone with no interest in coming back, or so I assume. Axel's mom died at his hands, rightfully so, he never knew his father, and Emmett's parents are both gone too.

This life isn't for the fainthearted, motorcycle club or not; death is always chasing you.

I clear my plate in minutes, Ryker acting a little less like an animal than me. Wiping my mouth with a napkin, I finish the rest of my coffee and brace my arms on the table.

"We need a game plan, a serious one. Ideally, we have several backups too. So we can put an end to this madness and get our feet back on solid ground," I state, determination fighting past the exhaustion threatening to take hold of me.

"Did I fuck us over by not caving to them in the first place?"

"No, never. If we could go back in time to when Banner agreed, I'd shoot his brains out and decline from that point on," I bite, and he nods.

"You're right. We're winging it too much so we don't fuck it all up, but we're leaving ourselves open for attack due to this. We need more allies, because it seems the ones we currently have are more likely to be enemies."

I can agree to that. "What were you thinking? Or who were you considering?"

His eyes cast over my shoulder at the other bikers in here. "They haven't stopped glancing my way the entire time, and my gut's not burning with the need to make an example out of them, so I'm hoping it's in a positive light and they're not picturing my head on a spike."

"Do you want me to go over there and put on a show for them? Lure them to the dark side with my charm, wit, and perky tits?" I offer, and his head falls back with a laugh. The tension that was sinking its claws into him earlier dissolves at my joke. Mission accomplished. It's not like us to get deep and raw, sharing our thoughts and shit, but it's our only form of therapy.

"Can you shake your ass for them too? Just in case they're into heavy trunks," he replies with a smirk, and I give him the finger again.

"Little shit," I grunt, making him snicker again.

"That's President shit to you." My eyes narrow at his

shit joke, but it doesn't erase the smile on his face. "It's as if they heard our conversation because they're on their way over," he says. I have to fight the urge to turn and check for myself, but that would only make us look like gossiping school girls in the corner.

"Ryker, Gray, I wasn't expecting to see you in here," Paisley says in greeting before extending his hand to Ryker. His VP shakes my hand first before we switch, the remainder of the members holding back a little.

"We were out and about and decided to eat before heading home," Ryker vaguely explains.

"I feel that. No one wants to be waking the whores up at this time to cook for us, do we? They'd purposely burn it all to fuck with us," Paisley replies with a chuckle, and I force one of my own.

Each club is run so differently that we don't always see eye-to-eye with operations. If we want food and my mom hasn't already taken care of us, I'll make it myself. The Ruthless Bitches are there under our protection, but I wouldn't trust any of them near the fucking food.

"I'm too scared to find that out for a fact," Ryker murmurs.

Paisley adjusts his stance, pointing over his shoulder as he leans in closer. "If I'm honest, I'm surprised you weren't in here earlier when the Devil's Brutes were here."

I freeze, blood running hot and cold at the news. "They

were here?"

"Oh, like clockwork. They were doing their collection rounds as they always do this time of the week. Strip everyone of their possessions, eat the grub at our sworn neutral ground, and then fuck right back off to the depths of hell they came from," Paisley explains. I can't decide whether he's dropping this information on purpose or completely blasé. "Have you cleared your shit up with them yet?" Ryker scoffs at that.

"If they're still coming in here and fucking with everyone, then no, definitely fucking not."

Paisley stands tall, straightening his cut as he stares at Ryker. "Well, me and my men have had a vote…"

"And…" I push when he forgets to finish his fucking sentence.

"And… we're interested in your thought process. Keep us in the loop." With that, he knocks his fist on the table two times, waiting a brief moment until Ryker returns the motion, and they're out of there in a flash.

"What the fuck just happened?" I scratch my head.

"We just got the details to start piecing together plan A."

NINETEEN

Scarlett

A yawn threatens my lips even though I slept hard last night. My limbs ache from life taking its toll on me, and the back of my neck itches like a bitch for the best possible reason. Slipping into one of Emmett's t-shirts, I tiptoe across the room, peering over my shoulder at him as his chest continues to rise and fall softly.

The door clicks shut behind me. I've laid snuggled in his arms for close to an hour, and if my stomach continues to grumble, he's going to wake up.

Padding barefoot down the hallway, I pull my hair tie out, running my fingers through the length before scooping it back up into a messy bun. I really should attempt to run a brush through it today. The likelihood is slim though, hence the knot on my head.

The smell of bacon tickles my nose as I near the

kitchen, and when I glance around the doorframe, I find Maggie by the stove.

"Morning," I murmur, moving further into the room as she smiles at me.

She's rocking a pair of heeled boots, laced up to mid-thigh, with a pair of skinny jeans, and a ripped Metallica tee. I want to be her when I grow up. She's too fucking cool for all of us.

"Morning. It feels like forever since it's been just the two of us in here," she states, winking at me before glancing back down at the pan she's using.

Stepping up to the coffee machine, I groan in delight when I see it's already full and piping hot. "We really need to make a plan for it more often. It's quiet, the coffee is hot, and I actually like your presence," I reply with a grin, filling a mug with the liquid goodness.

Maggie places a used mug in front of me, nodding at it for me to top her off, and I do just that.

"With college going on as well now, I get the feeling your schedule is going to be looking a little hectic for a while." Her words make me tense, but they're said with an air of approval as opposed to disappointment. Who knew I would find a group of people willing and wanting to support me in everything I do. From a paid assassin to a college student. It seems a pat on the back is waiting just around the corner for me every time.

"There's always time for you, Mags," I promise, fluttering my eyes at her. "Especially if you have any of the good stuff to spare." As I point at the food cooking, she produces a plate from the oven, already topped with scrambled egg and bacon. She places it on the countertop beside me, and I almost fall to my knees with gratitude. "Holy shit, Maggie. I love you."

I cut across the distance to squeeze her arm in appreciation, and she chuckles at my dramatics. "Who knew there was such a soft center under all of your layers," she teases.

Grabbing my mug and plate, I take my usual seat at the dining table, and she quickly follows suit. "I don't know what you're talking about. I don't have layers." I fake a pout before stuffing my face with food, and she chuckles.

"What is it that ogre once said? Like an onion," she muses, and I glare at her.

"If I'm anything, it's a fucking cake. A tasty red velvet heap of deliciousness."

She nods, accepting my description as she reaches for her fork. The pair of us eat away in silence, enjoying the food and liquid gold before us. I woke up this morning, excited and nervous with the prospect of my new tattoo, the worry of impending doom still looming over our heads, and the unknown that comes with attending college. It's a whole other world to me. It's definitely going to take time for me to get comfortable.

"Top off?" Maggie offers as she rises with her mug, and I quickly rush to my feet and take the mug from her.

"No way, you sit your ass down. I'll get the coffees; you made the food," I insist, and she hums, dropping back down into her chair as I fill the mugs up again. Once I've placed them back on the table, I clear our plates despite her protests and rejoin her when everything is cleaned.

"What are your plans for today then?"

"Thankfully, we only have one class today and that's at two p.m., so I have some time. Other than that, I'm hoping to catch up on some new podcasts that have been released and I haven't had a chance to listen to. You?"

"It's almost sweet that you think I leave these four walls," she states, making my eyebrows pinch as I wait for the punchline, but it doesn't come.

"For real, Maggie. We need to change that. Tell me what we can do," I push, and she shakes her head dismissively, waving me off like she regrets even mentioning it. "Don't give me any of that. Tell me what it is you like to do. You should be able to let your hair down every once in a while too, you know." I give her a pointed stare, but she just rolls her eyes at me like I'm being ridiculous.

"Don't worry yourself, Scar—"

"If you don't give me a hint, I'm telling Gray on you, or Shift, or both if necessary." I wag my finger at her in warning, and she chuckles like I'm joking.

"What are you telling me, Sweet Cheeks?"

Gray leans against the doorframe. The back of my neck prickles, but I don't think he has caught sight of it.

"Hey," I breathe, taking him in. He's wearing a pair of shorts and nothing else. There are dark circles under his eyes as if he didn't manage much sleep, and my heart clenches for him. "Did you get much sleep?"

A corner of his mouth tips up as he steps into the room, dropping down into the chair beside me with a heavy sigh. "Don't worry about that, tell me what you were threatening my mom with."

I glance between them as Maggie moves to the coffee machine to grab him a mug too. "You two can be so alike sometimes," I state, pointing between them, and they give me the exact same look, a line forming between their eyebrows as they stare at me.

"No, we're not," they say in unison, only proving my point more, before they roll their eyes at me like I'm being dramatic.

Shaking my head at the craziness of the White family, I settle my eyes on Gray as I point at his mom. "When was the last time your mom left this place and did something for herself?"

"Scar—"

"Nope, you don't get to speak until I say so," I warn,

flicking my gaze to hers as I raise my brow, begging her to challenge me, but she turns back to the coffee machine without a word. I don't think I'll be able to get away with that very often, but right now it looks like I'm getting a free pass.

"What do you mean?" Gray's palm lands on my bare thigh, making my muscles clench, but I focus on the topic of conversation instead of letting my body react to him.

"I mean, I haven't known your mom to be anywhere but here, mainly in the kitchen, since I got here. Do you even leave the compound?" I ask, giving myself whiplash as I glance back at her.

"Of course I do."

"That's not for the purpose of the club? That's not for groceries or other bullshit that's a necessity and for your own enjoyment?" Her cheeks turn pink and the guilty shimmer in her eyes is answer enough. Whirling back around to Gray, I can practically feel the steam shooting out of my ears with rage.

"What is that?"

I flick my gaze back to Gray to find his brows knitting deeper as he slowly raises a finger in my direction.

"What is what?" I ask, irritated that he's changing the subject, but I don't want to passively brush him off either.

"On your neck… is that… is that what I think it is?"

I gulp, my throat going dry as his tongue peeks out

between his full lips.

Shit.

This is not how I wanted it to go. I need to put Maggie first right now, so I keep my face turned to him as he tries to peer around to the back of my neck.

"Don't distract from your mom, Gray. It's important."

His gaze flicks to hers and then back to me. "I will make sure she does whatever it is she wants to do by the end of the week if you turn around and show me your neck."

Fuck.

"Be specific," I mumble. "Maggie, give me something you want to do."

"I don't kn—"

"Now, Mom," Gray interjects, his tone sharp but not harsh.

"I want to go to the diner and see my friends. Friday night would work," she mutters, like she doesn't want to admit it out loud.

Gray nods. "Done. I will personally drive you there if you would like, pick your drunk ass up and bring you home, and even take you out for the day so you can buy something cute to wear or some shit. Deal?"

Maggie pauses for a beat. "Thank you, Gray," she breathes, cutting the distance to her son to plant a kiss on his cheek, but he doesn't take his eyes off me.

"Show. Me. Your. Neck."

I wet my parched lips, my throat as dry as the Sahara desert as I shake my head. "Come and look for yourself." I tilt my head down so my chin touches my chest. I hear the scrape of his chair along the floor, before seeing a blur of his legs as he breezes past me, and I feel his hands on my shoulders.

"When did you get this?"

"Last night."

"Does anyone else have it?"

"Not yet."

I'm pent up with anticipation, trying to read his body language even though he's behind me. His voice is almost croaky, which makes me think he likes it, but I can't be sure.

The hand that wraps around my throat a second later has me on pins as he lifts me to my feet and spins me on the spot. Our eyes zero in on each other immediately, and I find his wider than I've ever seen them before.

"I fucking love you, Scarlett," he whispers before crushing his lips to mine.

My hands fly to his bare chest, his fingers digging into my hips at my waist as he shows me with his mouth just how much he means those words.

Holy shit.

He tears his lips from mine all too quickly, but before I can protest, his hands are at the back of my thighs, and my stomach hits his shoulder a moment later. He's carrying me from the room before I can contemplate which way is up, but he turns to the right instead of going left to the rooms, placing me on the prez's booth table in one swift move.

His eyes are wild. I widen my thighs, and he steps between them, claiming my lips once again as he cups the back of my neck, feeling the dried ink on my skin.

"Why aren't we in your room right now?" I mumble between panting and kissing him, clawing my nails into his flesh as I crave every ounce of him.

"Too far," he grunts. "I just needed to be away from my mother. I wasn't thinking," he adds, words stilted as he continues to press his lips all over my face and down my neck, making my back arch with pleasure.

I rasp a chuckle from my lips, my skin heating from his touch as I ready myself to fuck it all to hell and take his dick here and now, when the door swings open. The noise doesn't stop us, the irritation just flickering beneath my skin at the sound, but the words that travel through the air next halt us.

"Please, Kincaid. You promised me."

I blink up at Gray through the sex-induced fog, but he's glancing toward the booth by the double doors that lead in from the outside.

I'd know that voice anywhere. It's like nails on a

chalkboard and I've been desperate to erase it for some time now.

"No... but you said... I'm putting everything on the line here for you. You promised me if I gave you intel on everyone here, their locations, their inner workings at the club, *everything*, that you would protect me and I could be with Declan. He loves me, I know he does. Otherwise, he wouldn't work with me to help you." The pleading is cringy as fuck, an icy bucket of water over our heated moment from seconds ago.

"He was already working for me, you dumb bitch. Now, are you going to—"

Whatever Kincaid was about to say is cut off as Gray rushes with lightning speed to where she's sitting, hiding in a booth around the corner. I hurry to catch up, just as he snatches the cell phone from her grasp with a snarl.

Molly squeals, face paling as she realizes she's been caught red-handed. What kind of dumb bitch actually takes a call from the enemy in the fucking main room of the compound?

I take another step toward them, shaking my head in disgust at her as Gray lifts the phone to his ear despite it being on speaker phone.

"Well done, Kincaid. You just added another dead body to the ever growing pile at your expense."

TWENTY

Scarlett

A tremor runs through Molly as Gray launches the cell phone across the room and it shatters into tiny pieces. His shoulders rise and fall, his anger a tangible thing, tainting the air. But he's not calming down, he's only getting angrier.

Cutting the distance between us, I gently place my hand on his shoulder and he startles at the touch until he realizes it's me. "Get the others, Gray."

He shakes his head. "Scarlett…"

"I need you to get a handle on yourself. I can keep an eye on this dumb bitch until you get back."

Gray huffs, sneering at the Ruthless Bitch that has truly fucked us over. "I don't trust that she'll still be breathing by the time I get back, Sweet Cheeks."

Despite the seriousness of the situation, I drop my

hand to my chest and gasp. "*Me*? What would little old *me* do?" He smirks, his shoulders relaxing just an inch, but it's the reaction I wanted. "Fine, I won't do anything serious at least, maybe just a little maiming," I offer. He glances between the pair of us one last time before nodding.

"Oh my God, you can't leave me with her, Gray. Please, I can explain *everything*," Molly interjects, clambering to her feet as her wild eyes search his. She reaches out to touch his arm, just as I had done, but he deflects her touch and sidesteps her in one swift move.

"You don't want me to stay, Molly, I can promise you that." He sneers, and I clench my thighs together. It shouldn't be so hot for him to look like that, but he's usually the calm one, the funny guy. Seeing him like this is like watching an entirely different person.

"Get the others, Gray. I've got her." I'm eager to encourage him along as he takes a step back, but before he moves, he cocks a brow at me.

"How are you so calm right now, Scar?"

I offer him a soft smile. "This is what I'm trained for. It's what I know. On the inside, I'm raging, my heart is thundering, but I can take this all in stride," I answer honestly. He offers me one final nod, not really knowing what to say to me in response, before he storms toward the door at the back to find his brothers.

The second he's out of earshot, I turn around to the

bitch who interrupted what was going to be an exceptional *fucking* time, only to find her hands planted on her hips and a snarl on her lips.

"You can't do shit to me," she hisses, rolling her shoulders back and looking down her nose at me. "Kincaid will protect me. *Declan* will protect me."

I can't stop the roar of laughter that falls from my lips, a little snort adding to the mix as I stare at her serious-as-fuck face and punch her in it. "Oh my God, you actually believe that... don't you?" My laughter angers her by the way her face turns red. Perfect. "How do you think that's going to happen exactly? Neither of them is here right now, not when you need them most. Kincaid won't do shit to save you, he's happy to watch people die for his cause. You're not going to be any different."

"Well, Declan—"

"Declan what?" I interrupt, stepping closer to her as I raise my eyebrows. "What is he going to do? He's not going to suddenly claim you as his old lady and save you from the wrath of the Ruthless Brothers. He's far from a knight in shining armor, Molly. Aren't you aware? Or were you too hungry for his dick to see with anything but rose-tinted glasses?"

She shakes her head like I'm the delusional one. "I've told them what you're capable of. What you've done since you got here."

"You don't know what I'm capable of." I sneer, eyes flashing wider with the adrenaline coursing through my veins and tempting me to put an end to her now.

"I watched you kill his men with my own eyes. He didn't believe me at first, neither did Declan. Not until Graham murmured some things about your past that made him second-guess himself. But I promised on my life that you took down Kincaid's men, and I wasn't lying."

It's my turn to shake my head. "That was easy. I was using guns, but I much prefer a more hands-on approach since my speciality is torture," I bite, watching as she gulps, taking a small step away from me.

The door to the right opens from the Ruthless Bitches' end of the compound and before they can take a full step into the room, I'm yelling at the top of my lungs. "Get the fuck out. Now!" I don't get a response or a bite back in any form. All we get is the soft sound of the door closing again. Turning my attention back to Molly, I pout.

"You know, I'm really sad I'm actually going to be killing you for a legit reason now, and not because you looked at or touched my men one too many times." I tap my finger on my lips as I assess her.

"You're sick," she grunts, folding her arms over her chest to create a barrier between us.

"You haven't seen anything yet."

She huffs. "You're a dumb bitch who... ah—"

I slam my fist into her face, and her nose crunches under my touch. It's like a beacon for me every time she pisses me off, and now is no different. If she crumbles at this, imagine what's going to follow.

"Sorry, what did you say I was? I didn't hear you," I goad, a smug grin on my face.

"Fuck you," she spits, blood hitting the floor. "You know, Ryker won't let you kill me." A smile spreads across her face, blood staining her teeth as I grin right back.

"Didn't you hear… our agreement changed, and you're ripe for the picking. That was before you fucked the club over too, so you're done."

"Bullshit. You're just a whore like the rest of us, he—"

I punched her again, harder this time. She falls to the floor with a cry, mumbling curses under her breath, and I relish in the sound. "You're just never going to learn, are you? I'm going to enjoy cutting that tongue from your mouth." The idea shoots a tingle through my veins.

"You wouldn't," she whimpers, looking up at me through her hair falling over her face.

Challenge accepted. When I grip her throat, she yelps, trying to push away from me, but she doesn't get anywhere. Yanking her toward me, I press my fingers deep into her flesh as I pry her lips open with my free hand.

"Sweet Cheeks, you said *no serious injuries*." Gray's voice from behind me makes me pause, and I turn to find him standing there with Ryker, Emmett, and Axel. Each of them are bleary-eyed and confused as fuck, but the anger that vibrates from them is palpable.

"But listening to her whine is just awful. Really, I'm doing us a favor." I smile from ear to ear, hoping they'll see my way of thinking.

"You're not supposed to look so delicious with a feral glint in your eyes, Reaper," Axel grunts, and my heart skips a fucking beat in my chest.

"You're one to talk," I manage to rasp back, my pulse ringing in my ears, and he grins.

"How long?" Ryker asks, stepping closer to look at the deceiver in my grasp.

"Screw you," Molly bites, and I'm almost pleased she's taking the same tone with him as she was with me, but it also pisses me off that she thinks she can talk to my man like that. "I never would have helped him if you had just chosen me. But no, you chose *her* instead."

"*Her* has a name, you stupid bitch," I grunt, shoving her away from me as I stand tall.

Ryker moves to my side, standing in solidarity with me. Even though we're not touching, I can feel his body heat at my side. "You were *never* a consideration, Molly, no matter how fucking twisted your mind is. That's what it all was, in your head."

"Please," she sobs, crawling toward him on her hands

and knees. How the mighty has fallen.

"That's it, Molly. Get on your knees and beg him for forgiveness," I snap, crouching again to meet her eyes. "Beg him to forgive you for betraying the club, beg him to save your life. Go on, let me hear you." I feel as deranged as I'm sure I sound, but I've hated this fucking whore since I got here, and now there's an actual reason to fuck her up. It's exciting!

She peers up at Ryker, hope filling her eyes like there's a chance of him saving her. It's irrelevant how much she has pissed me off or fucked over the club. There's no coming back from that.

"Is it worth getting any information out of her?" Emmett asks, and I glance over my shoulder to see him. He scrubs a hand down his face, distracting me from the situation at hand.

"I mean, it would be more than fun to interrogate her." I gleam, excitement bubbling inside of me. "But the reality is Kincaid was likely only using her as his eyes and ears. The fact that she knows anything is slim to none."

"Do you know anything?" Ryker asks her. She wants to say yes so there's a reason to keep her alive, but if she's still breathing, she's going to be in pain. It's as simple as that.

"I-I… Ryker, p-please."

She's truly a fallen woman. Rising slowly to my feet,

we all know what's coming next, even Molly. That's why she's resorted to pleading once more.

"She doesn't know shit. She didn't even know Declan already worked for Kincaid, she thought he was doing it for her," Gray states, recalling her conversation on the cell phone.

Her eyes widen, her bottom lip trembling as tears start to track down her face. "You're right," Ryker murmurs, taking a step back. "Do you want the honors, Rebel?"

"I can't go down there," I admit, pointing to the door leading to the cellar, and Ryker nods.

"I can clean up from wherever you need, Reaper. Just say the word." I glance at Axel, his words settling over me like a warm blanket.

"How do you want to ride your way into Hell, Molly?" I offer a soft smile.

"I-I don't," she mumbles, responding to me for the first time without snark on her tongue. Wow, there really is a first time for everything.

"I remember Matt's old lady at the Ice Reapers, Jeni, I think she was called. She told me about this time they attached a traitor to bikes with a rope, and all drove off in different directions, tearing that motherfucker limb from limb." Molly whitens at my little story.

"I mean, I'll clean it up, but it doesn't get any messier than that, Scar," Axel says with a teasing grin on his lips.

"Fine, less mess." I tap my chin, thinking, drawing out the anticipation for the little bitch before me. "I like the idea of a sword fight, but I don't think my opponent is up to scratch."

Ryker chuckles beside me, surprisingly more relaxed than I expected him to be. I'm aiming for way too dramatic in my mind, and she really doesn't deserve that level of energy from me. But I also want it to be epic.

"Has anyone got a weapon to hand? I don't feel like getting my hands dirty." I look at the four men surrounding me to find two guns, a blade, and a pair of brass knuckles being offered out to me. "Wow, a selection, you really do love me," I preen, taking a moment to decide before settling on the blade in Emmett's hand.

Lunging at Molly, I wrap my hand around her hair tight, relishing the sound of her hissing before slicing the sharp edge through her locks, and they tumble to the floor. "No," she cries, like she's not going to die any minute now anyway.

"That's for the comments you made about Emily," I grunt, turning back to my men to pull the brass knuckles from Axel's hold. Slipping my fingers inside the rings, I waste no time launching my fist at her face again, her scream ripping from her stomach as blood splatters everywhere.

The metal clangs on the floor as I release them from

my hold. "That was for the bullshit about Axel," I bite, seething, then I grab both of the guns from Ryker and Gray. "And this is for not telling the epic tale of how I slaughtered Kincaid's men properly. I wielded two guns in nothing but a tee and slaughtered his men one by one. Rest in pieces, bitch."

Bang.

Bang.

TWENTY ONE

Scarlett

Axel arranges the cleanup of the dead Ruthless Bitch, while Gray takes my hand in his and leads me toward the bathroom. Emmett turns the shower on, and Ryker sticks his head in with a fresh fluffy towel as Gray undresses me.

There's a quiet ambience around us, but instead of feeling further away from them, it feels like a warm blanket holding us all close. The hot water from the shower hits my skin, and I tilt my face up to let it wash away the blood that hit me moments earlier. Blindly reaching for the body wash, I come up empty-handed, only to feel calloused fingers run over my bare skin from behind.

Glancing over my shoulder, I expect to see Gray, but it's Emmett. He's stripped down to his boxers as he lathers the body wash over my skin. The move is hypnotic as he cleans me from head to toe. When he's done with my body, he pulls my hair from the mess on my head and proceeds to wash my locks. I'm pliant to his silent commands, tilting my head, lifting my arm, and everything else he needs from me until he cuts the water off and holds out a towel for me.

A soft smile spreads across my face. "Thank you," I say, breaking the silence. Tightening the towel around my body, Gray escorts me to his room with his hand at the base of my spine. "I'm not made of glass, you know," I grumble, even though I'm loving the treatment.

"You're made of the strongest stuff known to man, Scar, there's no doubt about that. But that doesn't mean we can't treat you like you're precious, because you are."

Damn these men! Always making me putty. Ryker is poised at the foot of Gray's bed with a small pile of clothes in his hands. His face lights up when his gaze settles on mine, reminding me there's simply a man behind the role of the *president* I saw moments ago.

"Do you want a minute to get dressed alone?" he asks. The door clicks shut behind me as Emmett moves into the room too.

"I'm good," I rasp, feeling all three of them watch me as I dry myself off and slip into a pair of boxers, one of their t-shirts, and a ridiculously big pair of shorts.

"Do you want to rest, get the fuck out of here, or relax?" Gray asks, and I frown.

"You know I've killed people before, right? I've killed people *here* before. Like, lots of them. I don't need this soft treatment every time I take someone's life," I state, my lips rubbing together nervously. This really does feel weird as hell.

"You deserve it though," Emmett replies, sweeping a hand through his hair. "You've clearly shown you're willing to get blood on your hands for us, the club, and everybody else you care about. That's likely because it's all you've ever known, but the aftermath of that doesn't have to be the same as it always was."

His words tighten my chest as I attempt to take a steady breath.

"Is that okay with you?" Ryker asks, cocking a brow at me, and I nod. "Good... Can I ask you a question?"

"Sure."

"It's not an easy one."

"They never are," I murmur, intrigued and slightly nervous with where he's going with this.

"Why did you stay?" My eyebrows pinch, and he rushes to explain, "Why did you stay with the Reapers after your father's death? Why didn't you just burn it all to the ground and run?"

He wasn't joking, this is deep as fuck.

Flicking my damp hair over my shoulder, my skin heats under their watchful gazes. I know the truth, feel it in my bones, but it's weak as hell and I don't really want to admit it out loud. I've never spoken it out loud, but one look at these men, and I know they won't judge me for it. I've laid the rest of myself bare to Axel, telling him parts of my past that hurt my soul like fuck. They deserve this from me.

"Because it was all I knew. It may not have been safe or somewhere to call home, but the fear of the unknown outside of those walls hung heavily on my shoulders. I had my bags packed and ready to go the second I turned eighteen, determined to leave, but even when the opportunity finally arose and you guys appeared, I still chose to come with you instead of fending for myself."

"All you've ever done is fend for yourself, Snowflake. Don't forget that."

As always, they have a way of making me feel worthy even when I doubt it so much my heart hurts. Everything happens for a reason; this is the path I was supposed to take, and if it leads me to my Ruthless Brothers, then I would walk this road time and time again.

I'm certain of it.

A knock comes from the door, before it opens just a little to reveal Axel on the other side. "Hey, Reaper," he says with a smirk, wiping the pain and uncertainty from my skin. "Shift is out here declaring that he's better than you at Apex and the last time you destroyed him was a total fluke. Care to prove him wrong, or do you want me to beat the fuck out of him for talking shit?"

I chuckle at his playfulness. A rare occasion I definitely want to make the most of.

With my mind made up, I wag my finger at him. "You tell that motherfucker to get the game set up because I'm going to slaughter him again for good measure."

The door clicks shut behind him, but I still hear him holler to Shift at the top of his lungs. My body relaxes as I turn to face Ryker. "Don't we need a game plan to combat the fact that Molly talked?" He's the leader here, but I need to be sure we're not taking our eye off the ball.

Grinning, he rises from the bed, tossing his arm around my shoulders as he pulls me to the door. "I've upped security, and for now, that's all we need. Our priority is you."

"Fuck, Scar," Shift grumbles, dropping his controller into his lap with a huff as everyone around us laughs.

"Oh, poor baby," Gray says with a fake cry, only making it funnier as I smirk at his brother.

"I believe this challenge was set by you. I only rose to the occasion." I shrug, like it's as simple as that, but we've been at this for hours and I've taken him down again and again. It's far more enjoyable than I was anticipating, and it definitely was exactly what we needed. Just like Ryker said it would be.

Emmett's arms band around my waist, pulling me further into his lap, and I rest my head on his shoulder. Gray is to my right, Shift beside him, and Emily on the arm. Leaving Ryker and Axel to sprawl across the other sofa, happy to watch the carnage before them.

Lips press against my pulse, making me shiver, and I peer at Emmett with half-mast eyes. He doesn't look at me though, tucking his nose into the crook of my neck as he inhales. His warmth is short-lived as he trails featherlight kisses over the back of my neck, where his ink lies, and I smile.

"Screw you all, assholes. I play better when it's not split screen," Shift insists, rising from the sofa with a sigh.

"I would still beat you," I state, and he glares at me.

"No, we would play on the same team, Scar. And then your awesomeness would make me look just as fucking cool." A round of laughter envelops the room again.

This is how I've always wanted things to be—calm, relaxed, and seeping in a kind of love that can't be explained. This must be what family feels like. I would jump in front of a bullet for Emily and Shift just as quickly as I would for Ryker, Axel, Gray, and Emmett. I just wish Duffer was here to feel it too.

My throat clogs up at the thought of him, my eyes closing of their own accord as I try to calm my breathing that quickly hitches at the sadness that creeps down my spine.

"Where did you just go, Snowflake?" Emmett whispers, running his free hand through the hair that's sprung free from my hair tie. "And don't say nowhere. I literally felt a change," he adds, calling me out before I can even utter the two magic words: *I'm fine.*

Blinking my eyes open, I smile at him, though I know it doesn't meet my eyes. "I just wish Duffer was here to feel all of this," I admit, deciding the truth may have some healing qualities to it.

He has to be remembered, even if that's from me saying his name out loud every day.

"He would be diving on the controller to try and match you," Emily muses, drawing my gaze her way to find a soft smile on her face and a distant look in her eyes.

"I would have probably let him win."

"No, you wouldn't." Shift scoffs, shaking his head at me.

"You're probably right," I say with a chuckle, and Emily reaches across Gray to squeeze my fingers.

"If anything, he would have insisted he was going easy on you."

"That sounds like the Dylan we all knew," Ryker chirps

in, before taking a drink of his beer and my heart warms.

Dylan.

He was more than just Duffer to them.

This is exactly what he deserves, the love he should have always received.

A silent bubble casts over the room, everyone's heads dipping in thought for a moment as we remember Dylan and those we've lost.

Gray clears his throat, the first to pull his chin from his chest. "So, when do I get my matching tattoo?" He distracts from the sadness in the room, as he always does, and Emmett shuffles beneath me, keeping me pinned to him while he looks at his friend.

"Whenever you want. I promised Scarlett that I would do yours next, so whenever you're ready."

"I want it now," Gray blurts, wagging his eyebrows at me, not even pausing for a beat to consider it.

"What matching tattoo?" Ryker asks, intrigue coloring his features.

Emmett spins me on his lap, turning my back to Axel and Ryker to reveal the black lotus freshly marked into my skin.

"Fuck," someone curses, and my skin prickles with heat. I think it's Axel, but I can't be sure. It was raspy as hell, that's for sure.

"Let me go and get my things, Snowflake," Emmett

murmurs, lifting me to my feet as he stands. No sooner do my toes touch the floor am I straight back up in the air again as Gray pulls me into his lap.

"Shall I order some pizzas?" Shift asks, and Emily stands with him.

"I'll help. Otherwise, you'll just order six meat feasts," she insists, and Shift laughs.

"That's because pineapple doesn't belong on pizza, Em."

"What? Yes, it does!"

They continue to bicker as they step out of the door. I don't miss the inquisitive look on Gray's face as they leave. He's catching on to the feelings and emotions that swarm around them too.

Ryker clears his throat, leaning forward to brace his arms on his knees. I tilt my head in his direction to find an almost nervous look on his face. He assesses me for an extra moment, before exhaling harshly. "I want it as well."

"Want what?" Emmett asks, stepping back into the room with a cart filled with all of his supplies.

"Matching." I gulp, in a state of shock I didn't know was possible. "Is that okay?" he asks, gaze still locked on mine, and I nod, taking a second to find out how to use my damn tongue again.

"Always," I croak.

"Okay, Brothers, form an orderly line," Emmett orders

with a grin, pointing to the coffee table for Gray to take a seat first.

Ryker strips out of his cut and tee, bearing his abs to me as he winks, and I nestle further into the seat as Emmett goes through the motions. The hum of the tattoo gun is like a symphony for my damn heart as the stenciled outline becomes permanent with every stroke of the needle.

I'm not sure I blink the entire time, it feels like only seconds have passed when Emmett declares him done. Gray bounces on his feet, eyes peering into my soul as he steps toward me.

"How does it look, Sweet Cheeks?"

He turns, revealing the exact same tattoo as mine. "It looks good on you."

"Your mark always looks good on me."

Fuck.

That's hot.

"My turn," Ryker announces as Gray presses his lips to mine, before taking the seat beside me.

I'm completely engrossed in the process all over again like I've never seen it before. It's exhilarating watching someone mark themselves with a tattoo exactly the same as yours to show the world that they are yours and you are theirs.

I'm sure Emmett does it even faster this time, because I barely manage to calm my breathing before Ryker's kneeling down in front of me, back turned to show me the symbol on his skin. Shuffling forward in my seat, I press my lips to the skin just to the left, sealing my approval. Capturing my hand in his, he brings my knuckles to his lips, silently returning the sentiment. As he rises to his feet, movement to my left catches my attention and I startle when Axel strips out of his tee and lowers himself to the coffee table.

Holy. Fucking. Shit.

Emmett doesn't say a word, looking from the back of Axel's head to my face and back again. I want to ask him if he's sure, tell him that he doesn't have to do this, but I can see the steely determination in his gaze.

The urge to leap across the room is real, the desire to smother him with my limbs and show him how much this means to me is barely controllable, but I manage to hold it at bay as the hum of the gun starts up again.

His eyes remain fixed on mine the entire time he's seated, my heart galloping in my chest, completely uncontainable. I've never felt more alive.

The second the sound of the gun stops and Emmett nods that he's done, I drop to my knees on the floor in front of the sofa where I'm sitting. I hold myself still, eyes fixed on the grumpy man that has captured my heart along with the other three Ruthless Brothers in this room.

Silently, he falls to his knees from the coffee table, a

meter or two away from me. My pulse rings in my ears, unsure what's going to happen next as the room watches us, and then he floors me with a simple crook of his finger, calling me closer.

Running my tongue over my bottom lip, I drop to my hands, and he slowly eliminates the space between us. When I can't get any closer without touching him, he tucks his hand under my chin and slowly lifts me up to my knees again.

When we're eye to eye, he drops his hand and leans in close until we're nose to nose. His lips touch mine for the briefest second, maybe millisecond, it's over so quickly I'm almost sure it didn't happen. But the heat where he touched and the pounding of my heart confirms it.

His hands wrap around my wrists, pulling my attention from his face, but as he slowly lifts them, I find myself looking deep into his eyes again as he places my palms against his cheeks. His beard is rough under my touch, his skin soft. His body shakes with every breath he takes, making it clear that this isn't easy for him, and tears prick the corners of my eyes despite my best efforts to remain calm.

Thank you, I mouth, and he offers the smallest smile in response.

He rises to his feet in the next moment, pulling me along with him, and when he's certain I'm not going to faint with bewilderment, he releases his hold on me.

"Are you going to do the honors, Scarlett?" Emmett asks, distracting me. My eyebrows pinch in confusion, until he waggles the tattoo gun in his hand.

I balk, sure he's playing a prank on me, but when I shake my head, he nods his eagerly.

"You can't be serious, Emmett. I have no idea what I'm doing, and it won't look anything like it's supposed to," I insist, but he shrugs like that's irrelevant. "Maybe you're hungry. You're not thinking clearly. Where's your sister with that damn pizza?" I ask, glancing toward the door, but she doesn't magically appear.

"Pizza? We all know they weren't ordering pizza any time soon." My eyes widen, but when I see the amusement in his gaze, I know he's not mad. "Any other man in the world and I would be digging his grave right now, but if there's anyone I trust with her, it's him."

"How long have you known?" I ask.

"He's always been protective of her, more than necessary, and it only increased when she came home from the mall that day. She, however, has had his name written inside little hearts since she could write," he muses.

"Why don't you tell them you know and that you're not mad?"

He grins. "Because it's fun making him think otherwise." The others chuckle, and I shake my head disapprovingly, but if that's the extent of his feelings on the situation, then I approve. "Nevermind distracting me though. It's not going to change my mind."

"It's not?"

He tears off his cut and tee, before dropping down into the same spot his brothers have taken.

"Ink me, Snowflake."

TWENTY TWO

Scarlett

The truck rumbles as the four of us squish into the front. Axel insisted on driving me to college today, Emily and Shift in tow. After our moment last night, the ink still fresh on his neck, I was eager to agree. But his thigh has been pressed against mine for the better part of the drive, and I think I may self-combust.

From. A. Fucking. Thigh. Touch.

I should be embarrassed, but I'm too aroused for that. And when he gives my knee the occasional squeeze, I barely keep my lips shut and the groan at the back of my throat. I'm sure he's doing it on purpose, knowing full well he can do whatever he wants to me, all the while respecting his boundaries until he says otherwise.

Emily is to my right, with Shift pushed up against the truck door. They're not looking at each other, faking indifference, but I can see he's drawing small circles on the side of her leg where he thinks no one will be able to notice.

Amused, I rest my head back, anxious to be back at school again after skipping on day two. It wasn't planned, but when a girl's gotta die, a girl's gotta die. Clearly, college classes were the furthest thing from my mind. That being said, despite everything that happened yesterday, life has to continue as normal. Which means I get to experience campus life while the guys back at the compound handle breaking the news that the evil witch is dead.

I would have enjoyed witnessing the fake crocodile tears streaming down the Ruthless Bitches' faces, but alas, duty calls. As the familiar sign looms ahead, I sigh. It feels like it's been an eternity since I was last here, and a flash in my mind reminds me what happened when I was here the last time.

Ryker.

Fuck.

I can't think of that with Axel's close proximity. I can't handle it.

The truck rolls to a stop at the drop-off point, and Shift murmurs his thanks before climbing out. Emily shuffles after him, leaving just the two of us, and I don't want to leave.

"Don't have too much fun in there, will you?"

"I would never," I say with a smirk, still not moving, and he leans toward me to press his lips against my forehead, warming my soul. "I thought we agreed that I was going to be the death of you, not the other way around," I groan, loving the sound of his chuckle echoing around us.

"I don't think my dick has ever been as hard as it is now."

"You can't say shit like that to me. It's torture."

"Tell me about it," he grunts, making a deliberate show of adjusting himself through his jeans.

Dead. I'm fucking dead. D.E.A.D.

"Come on, lover boy, let our girl go," Emily hollers, and my eyes narrow even though I don't turn in her direction. The amusement on Axel's face quickly reconfirms that the glare is now for him.

Shuffling along the bench, I'm just about to step down from the cab, when Axel speaks. "I'll be seeing you soon, Reaper. *Real* soon."

My blood heats as I turn to face him, the desire storming in his eyes catches me off guard as I try to find a worthy response. He knows he's thrown me off balance, but he doesn't get to win this twisted game unraveling between us.

"I love you, Axel."

I jump down as quickly as possible, slamming the door shut behind me before I rush to catch up with the others.

Axel's slack jaw, wide eyes, and pink-tinged cheeks will forever be imprinted in my mind.

Chancing a glance over my shoulder, I smile when I find the truck unmoved. *Take that, asshat.* I doubt myself for a second, worried he'll think it was a joke under the circumstances. I just have to hope that he knows I would never play with those words unnecessarily, especially not with him.

"Who knew Axel would go soft for someone, huh?" Emily asks, nudging me as Shift leans forward from the other side of her to meet my gaze.

"If it was going to be anyone, it was written in the stars that it would be Scar."

I bite back my grin at his words. My heart feels full, my soul alive, and my body energized.

Lost in my own mind, I follow after Emily. It's only when we're half way up the steps to business class that I realize Shift is still walking with us. Despite the crowds moving around us, I stop to stare at him.

"What are you doing?"

The way he rubs at the back of his neck, the guilty look in his eyes, tells me he knows exactly what I'm talking about. Emily stands between us, eyebrows pinched as she glances from one to the other.

"Do you really think Ryker is going to let me wait outside again?" There's humor to his tone, but I know for a fact that he's definitely not joking. That's exactly something my hot fucking president would do.

"That's ridiculous," I grumble, still complaining even though I know my fight is going to be weak.

He shrugs. "Ryker's the boss."

I narrow my eyes, ignoring the people having to move around us. "And I'm your friend."

"Exactly. I'm going to say your safety is paramount here, Scarlett."

I shake my head at him. "Safety from what? Some guy's poor attempt at hitting on me. He got the message already."

Shift shrugs again, making it clear that his actions aren't going to change, but it doesn't calm the annoyance inside of me.

"We need to move or we're going to be late," Emily interrupts, and I sigh, reluctantly nodding for her to lead the way.

The three of us move in silence as we follow the crowd, before stepping into our classroom. My table from the other day is free, and the spot beside it is empty. One glance around the room and I spot Joshua in the middle row, as far to the left as possible, with his head down and shoulders hunched.

I turn to Shift, only to find him clocking Joshua's location too. I give him a pointed stare, but he still remains by the door, leaving Emily to head down to her seat. Huffing, I drop into my spot, annoyed that I'm here to protect Emily, only for Shift to be here to protect me.

When I say I love these Ruthless Brothers, I definitely don't mean all of the time. Only when it suits me and they're not being a total pain in my ass.

Motherfuckers.

Just like last time, the class goes by in a whirlwind, and I feel like I have a healthy dose of whiplash. I tried harder, even pulled my notepad and pen out to try and take notes, but I know Emily is going to have her hands full explaining the lesson to me again. At least it's Friday, so we can do it some time over the weekend.

Everyone rises from their seats when it's time. Joshua rushes down the steps and heads through the fire exit without a glance back. I spin to look at Shift, but he's too busy watching Emily make her way up the stairs with the other people from her row.

Once the three of us are together, I make sure I'm walking on the right side of Emily as Shift covers her left. But I still manage to jab him in the arm with my finger.

"Hey, what the fuck, Scar?"

"Please, you know there was no reason for you to be there at all. You can report that back to your prez with a sweet middle finger aimed in his direction too," I grumble, still irritated.

"Noted."

Emily smiles at the pair of us, but doesn't say a word. The silence gives me a second to stop being so dramatic and get over it. It's a simple reminder that there were three of us the last time something happened, and one of us paid the price. I don't have this on my own, and as much as my pride doesn't want him to be hovering over our every move, it's the whole point of us being here.

"Where are we heading next, Em?" I ask, being too lazy to pull the details out, but she doesn't complain.

"We actually have our first English class."

Shit.

I really, *really* need to pay attention then. Nodding, I try to psych myself up.

"Do you want to grab a coffee on the way? It starts in thirty minutes," she offers.

"Definitely. Please tell me we're going to the bagel place, because you *know* I've been craving that spicy goodness." I cross my fingers, repeating the word *please* like a mantra in my mind until she nods.

"It's the only place to go."

"These are on me, an apology for being all up in your faces despite the original plan," Shift offers, fluttering his eyelashes at us. Emily giggles, and as much as I try to give him my worst stare, it falls flat.

"Apology accepted," I state, making him grin, but I wag

a finger at him too. "But if it's going to happen everyday. We're going to need a daily apology too."

"Fuck," he groans, mumbling something about upping the allowance Ryker gave him to take care of us.

The crowd thins out as we head toward the cafe. All the while, I try to think positive thoughts about the next class. If there's anywhere I have to apply myself, it's in English. She's in that class because of me, *for* me, and I refuse to let her regret it.

Emily and Shift chat about some new television show I haven't heard of, and I take the opportunity to pull my cell phone out.

Scarlett:

Is there any other reason I should be aware of for Shift needing to be IN classes today?

I'm just about to put it away, not expecting an immediate reply, when my cell vibrates.

Ryker:

Other than making sure no man walks within ten feet of you? Nope.

Scarlett:

You're an asshole.

Ryker:

But I'm your asshole.

Scarlett:

Cute, but this isn't over.

Ryker:

I didn't think it would be. But if you behave and be a good girl, I'll be sure to make it worth your while.

I don't offer him a response. Someone's been talking about my kinks. It was definitely Emmett. He called me a good girl, and then Gray did, and now Ryker. I don't think Axel knows how to call me anything other than Reaper.

The cafe appears in the distance, distracting me from the heat I can feel at my neck. I'm definitely flushed, but if Emily or Shift notice, they don't mention it. Stepping inside, I'm relieved to see only a few people ahead of us in the line. When it's our turn, Shift orders a cinnamon bagel with a black coffee, Emily a blueberry one with a latte, while I go for my usual cheddar jalapeño special with cream cheese, and a vanilla latte.

As we exit the store, I'm smiling ear to ear with my goodies in hand, taking a big bite of the cheesy goodness when I stop dead in my tracks, bagel frozen at my lips.

"What's up?" Shift asks, strategically standing in front

of Emily in defense mode instantly.

"Cop," I murmur, nodding toward the police car parked up across the street with the deputy and another guy talking by the hood.

"Fuck," Shift grumbles. *My thoughts exactly.*

As if sensing our stares, his head lifts in our direction, his eyes narrowing as he assesses me, like he's trying to remember how he recognizes my face. Instant panic courses through my veins, just as it does every time the police are in the vicinity. I can't chew the food in my mouth, my body is like ice as I watch his every move.

He can't remember me from the home invasion, I had a balaclava on, but I ran into him at the diner first, with Ryker, and the conversation definitely wasn't friendly. The deputy's eyes narrow as they lock onto Shift's cut. He's quickly piecing two and two together before he lifts a cell phone to his ear.

"Why do I have a bad feeling?" Emily asks, pulling my attention away from the fucker, and Shift does the same.

"He saw me at the diner with Ryker a few weeks ago and it was… less than pleasant," I offer, not wanting to get too deep into it here. His appearance literally confirms that you can't trust who may or may not be around.

"I'm calling it in, Scar," Shift states, and I nod.

The deputy's in the driver seat now, eyes locked on me as the cell still remains at his ear.

Fuck.

My gut twists, a telltale sign that nothing good is coming.

RUTHLESS BROTHERS MC

TWENTY THREE

Gray

"**M**olly is gone."

The room drips in silence, making it even more clear that the mouthiest Ruthless Bitch is no longer with us.

"What do you mean?" Ruthie asks, a tremble to her bottom lip contorting her face as she blinks up at Ryker.

"She's dead," Axel grunts, blunter than Ryker's approach, and the girls gasp.

Standing in front of the booth where the girls gather around, I can't quite decide who is genuinely shocked and who couldn't give a shit less. The reality of this life most of the time is that it's a dog eat dog world because all we've ever known is the need to survive. This is no different. As long as it doesn't have a directional arrow pointing at them as a repercussion, then they'll get over it.

"Do we know why?" Candy asks, face stoic as she glances over the four of us.

"Because she was helping the enemy," Emmett states, folding his arms over his chest as a few of the girls' eyes widen in shock.

"The Brutes?"

"She was a direct line for Kincaid himself," I grumble, swiping a hand down my face as the memory flashes in my mind. Of all the times that woman has interrupted me, yesterday was the worst. But if there was any reason to put some trophy worthy sex on hold, it's for a betrayal like that.

"Did anybody know?" Axel asks, casting a deathly stare over each of them, and they shake their heads profusely. "If anyone approaches you about pulling the same bullshit as she did, just remember this moment. We're only family if you remain loyal." Once he's had a nod of confirmation from each of them, he waves his hand. "Good, now fuck off."

I don't wait around to see more, heading straight for Church with my brothers following behind me. I'm not expecting anyone to be inside, but when I find Declan and Graham taking up the bottom end of the table, waiting patiently, I keep my surprise muted as I find my seat.

"Graham, Declan," Ryker murmurs, clicking the door shut behind him. If he's as surprised as I am, he's doing well at keeping it hidden. "To what do we owe the pleasure?"

Emmett sits beside me, Axel across the table, and Ryker in the president's seat. Graham relaxes back in his chair and points to his son. My fists tighten in my lap, knuckles burning with the need to plow them into his fucking face.

"Is it true? Is Molly dead?" Declan asks, swiping his thumb over his lips.

"Yes." The vein at his temple pulses at the answer as he tries to bite back his anger. "Is there a problem with that?" Ryker asks, face impassive as he stares him down.

There's nothing harder than acting casual when you know you have a traitor in your grasp. Loyalty seems hard to come by these days.

After what feels like an eternity, Declan shrugs. "Nope, it's just a shame because she had such a good pussy."

No, you just lost your little ally in here, motherfucker.

"Was there anything else?" I ask, eager to get on with my day and the promises I made and the need to uphold.

"I'm just trying to understand more about it. You say she was working with the enemy, with Kincaid," he states, pointing at the door. "We overheard your conversation with the Bitches, but I'm just trying to figure out how you found out about her secret."

I hold back a scoff, but my nostrils flare despite my best efforts. This man's more worried that he'll get caught. Pity he doesn't realize he already is.

"She was heard on a phone call with him," Axel grunts, not even bothering to look at Declan.

"By who? I hope it was a reliable source because—"

"It was me... and Scarlett. Two witnesses. But this is Ruthless Brothers business, and we handle things how we see fit." I hate that I muttered her name in his vicinity, and the nudge I get from Emmett tells me he's pissed too. It doesn't make a difference though; he's never going to be anywhere with her alone ever again.

She's ours. The ink on the back of my neck confirms it.

Graham sighs. "Thank you for explaining, I know it's out of courtesy," he offers, a tired smile on his face and I nod. "You say the word and I'll rally the extra men down here quicker than you can say done, okay?"

"Thank you, Graham," Ryker murmurs, jutting his chin at him, and the two men rise. Declan drags his feet like he's considering saying something, but he eventually shuts the door behind him without saying a word.

The second they're gone, the tension seeps from the room and we let out a relieved sigh.

"His time is coming," I grunt, and Axel jabs a finger across the table at me.

"Your time is coming if you utter her name in front of him again," he bites, and I roll my eyes. I'm not oblivious to the fact that I said her name to state my claim, to confirm she was with me.

"Whatever," I grumble, rising to my feet. "Are we done? I have some plans to uphold."

"What plans?" Emmett asks, and I smile.

"I have a date with my mama."

"Ma, I was not prepared for all of this."

It should be impossible to shop for this long. No one requires this many bags surely, but if anyone deserves it, it's her. Next time, I'm bringing Shift along though, because this is definitely a two-man job.

"Honey, you're never prepared for anything girly. But you're doing a good job. Just one more shop," she soothes, patting my cheek before pointing at the next one.

Fuck.

"You're definitely making the most of this, aren't you?"

"Yup."

A smile ghosts my lips as I side step the crowd walking toward us and follow her into the store. The second she starts trying to buy underwear, I'm fucking out. I have my limits.

One more shop turns into six, and I'm sure I've covered every inch of the mall a hundred times over. It should be impossible, but here we are.

"Want to grab some lunch?" she asks, handing me

another bag.

"Sure. Where do you want to go?"

"There's supposed to be a cute little taco place here if you want to try it?" Her eyes light up with hope, and I can't say no, I'm a complete sucker for her.

"At this point, I'm willing to eat anything. I'm exhausted." She beams at me, practically skipping along to the food court. I unload all of the bags from my arms and drop them at her feet before placing our orders.

Two. Of everything.

When I walk back toward her with a tray of food piled high, she grins, rubbing her hands together with excitement. Yep. Definitely my mom.

"I love you, Gray," she squeals, barely letting me set the tray down before she reaches for the first taco she can get her hands on.

The noise of the people drifts away as we sit and eat in comfortable silence. Seeing her like this fills me with love and appreciation for her. She needs this more often and I've let her down.

"I'm sorry we haven't been doing this for you more often, Mom, but we'll change that, okay?" I say, wiping my mouth with a napkin.

She smiles softly in acknowledgment. "We live a crazy lifestyle, Gray. It's not the norm for us to be able to take our foot off the gas and just appreciate life for a minute, but I'm glad we're doing it now."

"Well, I appreciate *you*, we all do. Everything you do for the club, for my brothers, for me and Shift. I'm eternally grateful. We shouldn't just expect it though, not when you don't get anything in return."

Her eyes gleam and crinkle as she smiles. "Scarlett is a good influence on you."

"She's a good influence on all of us."

"Agreed." She glances off, lost in thought, and I give her a moment. "Everything you're saying to me, you need to say to her too, Gray. She would single-handedly give her soul over to you guys and protect that club with her life, but she needs gratitude and appreciation in return as well."

"You're right, I'm going to make sure of it." My heart feels full at the mere thought of her. I want to give her everything, and never because it's in response but because she deserves it first.

"You love her a lot, don't you?" my mother muses, a wistful smile on her face and I nod. "The way you look at her, it's just how your father used to look at me. He would have liked her."

"He would have liked her sassy mouth and no-bullshit attitude," I mutter in agreement, and she grins.

"He would've loved to see you happy too."

My heart warms, but I don't reply, saying anything else

would spoil the moment. Reaching between us, I lift her hand and press a kiss to her knuckles. She squeezes my hand tighter, eyes shimmering as she takes in the warmth between us.

"Let's head home, honey, I've got a lot of things to organize before I go out later," she says.

I grab all of her things and head to the SUV I brought. It's a good job we came in the damn thing with everything she bought. It's as if she saw the size of the trunk and thought 'challenge accepted.'

Driving us home, I let her take control of the radio, and she plays some country music, singing along as she watches out of the window. I glance at her out of the corner of my eye a time or two and my heart constricts. Even as her child, I will never know how hard her life has been, what she went through before I was big enough to understand, but I'm here for her now. To protect her, to appreciate her, and to make her smile just like she is at this moment.

All too quickly, we're pulling into the compound, and I spot Axel outside, smoking. "Brother, help a guy out," I holler as I jump down from the SUV, pointing at the trunk as my mom chuckles.

"I'll get the coffee machine going," she says with a grin, heading inside.

"What's up?" Axel asks, rounding the vehicle with me, and I point to all the bags as the trunk opens. I may have carried them all while I was there, but there's no way in hell I'm doing it now if there's someone here to help me.

No thanks.

"What the fuck did she buy, man? Is there anything even left *at* the mall?" he asks, tossing the butt of his cigarette away as he leans in to grab some of the bags.

"Don't even get me started. That woman is a weapon when it comes to shopping. As if she needed any more talents than she already rocks," I grumble, grabbing the other half and heading inside. "Are they back from the campus yet?" I ask, and Axel nods.

"Yeah, she went for a nap. I think she might actually be in your room."

My dick twitches at the thought of her in my bed, and my steps quicken. When I enter the bar area, my mom points at the booth in the corner, insisting that we drop everything there.

Swiping a hand down my face, I glance at the time. "Axel, could you do me a favor?"

"I'd rather I didn't."

I roll my eyes at him like usual, but he stays where he is, waiting to see what I want. "Could you take my mom to the diner tonight? She's having food with some of her friends, but I was hoping to catch Scarlett for a bit. We were having a… moment yesterday before Molly interrupted, and I was hoping to skip back to that."

He cocks a brow at me, making it clear that my discreet phrasing is pointless.

"You mean you want to fuck her."

"I want to love her," I correct, giving him a pointed stare, and it's his turn to roll his eyes this time.

"Fine, but you fucking owe me."

"When do I not?" I beam and dash toward the back of the compound before he can change his mind.

I try to quietly step into my room, but my excitement has the better of me, and I slam the door shut behind me a little louder than necessary. She doesn't stir from her spot on the bed though. She has one of the pillows length ways, snuggling it tight as her damp black hair fans out around her.

She's a true vision of beauty, and she's all ours.

One of my white t-shirts is draped over her, but she must have shuffled in her sleep because it's ridden up to her waist and it's clear she's not wearing any panties. This is exactly how I expect to be greeted going forward. I refuse anything else.

Shaking out of my cut, I drape it over my chair, before removing everything else but my boxers. I climb onto the bed beside her, but as I lay my head on the pillow, she flutters her lashes.

"Hey," she breathes, a tired smile dragging across her face, and I lift my hand to cup her cheek.

"I'm sorry, I wasn't trying to wake you."

"You weren't?"

"Technically no, but I'm not sad that it happened," I admit, making her hum in amusement.

"Did you tell Ryker about my praise kink or was it Emmett?" she asks, eyes still not quite open, and I frown at her in confusion. When I don't respond right away, she peers up at me and must sense that I need her to be more specific because I have no idea what she's talking about. "Did you tell him that I like being called a good girl?"

"Definitely." Her jaw falls slack and her eyes widen. "What? Every single one of us should know what it's like when you're that turned on. It's an experience. Besides, sharing is caring, and it's worthwhile on your end and we both know it." She pats her palm against my chest, glaring at me, but I shrug.

I kiss the corner of her mouth. "You know you love it when I tell you you're a *good girl*, or what you'll get if you act like a *good girl*. Don't tell me I'm wrong because I'll call bullshit so fast you'll—"

Her lips crush against mine, stopping my threat, but I don't mind. Not when she's going to shut me up with these resources. She demands control, gripping my hair like her life depends on it, and I let her have it. Molding my lips to hers, I pull her flush against my body, the skin on skin contact heating my veins.

Pushing her to her back, I grin when her thighs fall open, inviting me in. She reaches for the waistband of my boxers, and before I can move to slip them off, she's pulling at the material. A tearing sound echoes around us as I gape at my torn boxers now clinging to just one thigh.

"I see the addiction to that." Desire swirls in her eyes as my cock springs free.

"I need you. Now," I bite, every inch of my body thrumming with need to fill her with my dick.

"Then take me."

I should be worshiping her, lapping at every inch of her skin as she groans beneath me, but feral needs take over and I'm left a servant to our desires.

Lining my cock with her entrance, I sink inside of her and I groan, low and hoarse, as her pussy clenches around my length. Molten lava wraps around me, heightening the pleasure flickering through my blood as she gapes up at me.

She moves to touch her clit, but I bat her hand away, replacing it with my own as I sink all of the way inside her. I give us both a moment to adjust, but with every breath I take, my heart rate only increases instead of calming.

"Please, Gray," she begs, palms running over my body.

I pull out, loving the way her core pleads for me to stay, so when I slip back inside her, I'm welcomed immediately. My tentative moves quickly pick up, my hips taking off on their own accord as I slam into her harder and faster with every thrust.

She clings to me just as I cling to her. Eyes locked on one another as our gasps intertwine between us. Her nipples are pebbled beneath my t-shirt she's wearing, and I bow my head to nip at them, making her core tighten around me.

God, she's heaven.

We've fucked crazier, been dirtier, yet this feels the most intense. We're wearing each other's marks, and this is nothing less than a claiming.

"Shit, Gray, I'm going to… Oh fuck," she groans, her words slurring as her body tenses beneath mine.

"That's it. Keep your eyes on me like a good girl," I purr, and she tumbles over the edge, eyes barely open, but they remain locked on mine.

At the squeeze of her pussy as she climaxes around my cock, milking me for all I have and drowning me in her essence, I can't resist the urge to follow her over the cliffs of ecstasy. Wave after wave crashes through my veins. I find purchase in the crook of her neck as I catch my breath.

"I hope you don't have any plans tonight, Sweet Cheeks."

"Why?"

"Because I'm far from done with you."

TWENTY FOUR

Scarlett

Friday evening was spent locked in Gray's arms, dirtying up his sheets. The ache between my thighs is still present two days later. Saturday was spent recapping the college work from Friday and practicing my reading and writing.

Thoughts of the deputy still lingered in the back of my mind, but nothing had stemmed from it. He hadn't reared his ugly head with another drop-in at the club, so I was counting that as a win… for now at least. Ryker promised they would keep an eye on the situation, and Axel had Shift tap into the security cameras we set up when we were there.

Nothing out of the ordinary. Nothing to be concerned about.

So why does it feel like the calm before the storm?

This uncertain zone where I am waiting for the other shoe to drop. Not just with regards to the deputy, but the Devil's Brutes too. We're sitting and waiting again, as if we're offering them the upper hand, which they definitely don't deserve.

The irritation and agitation of it has me sitting up in bed. Axel's smell surrounds me.

He was adamant he wanted me to rest up in his bed last night, but he didn't join me. He slept on a cot beside me, but the fact that we were in the same room while he slept felt like progress. That's when we're at our most vulnerable, and he offered me a snippet of that. I'm willing to cling to anything he has to give at this point, and he doesn't take that fact lightly.

"I was wondering when you would actually move," he states groggily, and I peer over the bed to see him rubbing at his eyes. A thin sheet is draped over his thighs, revealing his bare chest and tight black boxer shorts. He looks like sin, probably tastes like it too. "Get your head out of the gutter," he adds, making me blink up at him with a smirk.

"You shouldn't put it there to begin with," I retort, squinting my eyes in defiance, but he just hums in amusement at me. "How did you know I was awake anyway?" I ask, watching the muscles in his back move as he sits up, and I have to clench my thighs if I want any chance of being able to breathe.

"Your breathing changed about twenty minutes ago, then you started getting huffy in the last five," he explains, scooping his hair into a bun before he starts to get dressed. My tongue peeks out, wetting my parched lips as I enjoy the show. "So... what's driving your mind crazy?"

"The Brutes, the deputy, Declan, anyone and everyone on our radar. I can't stand sitting around. I feel helpless, and I really fucking hate it."

"We are playing a blind game so I get where you're coming from. I feel it too. As much as we have the extra men here now, we're not entirely sure where it is that we're heading. Gray and Ryker got a snippet of information about them frequenting the diner like clockwork, but we want to see that with our eyes first before we make a move. Besides, it's neutral territory, we would have to devise a plan to hit them in transit."

I exhale heavily, but it doesn't alleviate the tension in my shoulders. Axel takes a seat beside me, lacing his fingers with mine in a sweet gesture that makes my body tingle.

"It's a bit of a long shot, but do you feel like taking a drive with me?" I meet his gaze, lost to his stormy eyes as they peer into my soul.

"Whatever you need, Reaper."

My favorite—*our*—favorite murder case podcast plays through the sound system in the truck. It feels weird being the one behind the wheel, but when I asked, Axel just waved the keys at me and took the shotgun seat without a word.

His faith in me is unprecedented, especially when he has no idea what we're doing. I don't want to say it out loud and jinx it, or get his hopes up if I'm a total letdown.

"I want you on the back of Hattie eventually," he says, startling me since we've been sitting in peace and quiet for the past twenty-five minutes.

"What?" I ask, cutting my gaze to him for a second before turning back to the road.

"Hattie, my bike. I want you on the back of her eventually."

My breath catches, my mind going a mile a minute as I rub my lips together. "With you driving?" I ask, testing the waters, and he nods.

"*Obviously*, I might lo—I might care for you a lot, but nobody drives my baby," he retorts, and my heart flutters.

"I only want to ride her if you're driving, Axel, I just didn't want to get my hopes up." I keep my eyes fixed on the road, but sense him turning in my direction. If I do, he'll be able to read my eyes instantly, see the love blooming there for him.

After I blurted it at him in the parking lot and hightailed

it out of there, he didn't mention it at all. But he almost uttered those words just now and I think I might pass out from all the emotion coursing through my veins.

I try to change the subject so I can focus on the task at hand. "Why did you name her Hattie?"

Silence greets me as I slow the truck, still rolling as I consider which way to turn, and choose the left turn, before we get to it. As we head down the road, I'm almost sure that he's not going to answer. But as always, he's full of surprises.

"She was the girl who lived next door to me when I was young." My lips press together as he speaks, not wanting to interrupt him or push for more than he's ready for. "We were about eight, I think. Did nothing but play catch or tag on the grassy field by the trailers, but every day when she showed up and smiled at me, I forgot all about my terrors at home. She was a sliver of light and hope in a dark and twisted world, and I clung to her more than she would ever have known."

I chance a glance at him briefly, before returning my attention to the road. Maybe I should have let him drive, I can't focus. "Would?"

"Yeah," he rasps. "We didn't live in a safe neighborhood, not many trailer parks are located in the nice parts of town, but that one was the worst of the worst I stayed in." He takes a moment, running his hand over his beard as he gets lost in his thoughts. "I also didn't realize how dark her home life was too, until one day she didn't show. Or the next day, or the one after that. Then there were cops, taped off areas and horror consuming the park. Listening in on conversations that weren't meant for me, I learned that she was dead. Her momma's boyfriend had been hurting her, and when her real pop found out, he went in guns blazing. Only thing was, the bullet ricocheted and went straight through Hattie's chest."

Holy shit.

"That's awful, Axel. I'm so sorry," I say, knowing it doesn't cover the pain, but I needed to acknowledge him in the only way that I could.

"It's life, Scar. We live, we breathe, we die. It's never our choice. Not the being born part or the dying part. We just live our life as it's intended. Sometimes, we find hope and sunbeams at the end of a storm, other times we meet our maker far too soon. Just like Dylan did. He'll be your Hattie forever, Reaper, and I'm sorry you have to feel that."

At the mention of him, my heart clenches, but for the first time, my initial reaction isn't filled with pain so drenching it licks over my skin like gasoline. This time, it's determination and strength that pumps through my veins.

"I hate that I'm breathing and he isn't," I admit, managing to keep my voice calm as I take the next right turn. "I hate that I'm in college and he's just fucking dead,

Ax, but most of all, I hate that he doesn't get to see this side of me. Me, somewhat resembling a whole person. Not entirely broken anymore, or trained like a dog to sit, roll over, and kneel on demand."

"He saw it, Scar. I'm certain of it. The confidence that you have wielded since the moment you stepped foot onto our territory is nothing shy of awe-inspiring. You were never broken, you were always you, but now, you just shine brighter."

Words fail me as I try to scramble to put something together but fall flat. I wasn't seeking his words, his reassurances, but he offered them anyway and it was exactly what I needed. Especially coming from the man that hated me for what felt like forever.

"Thank you," I manage to murmur, raspy as shit, but before he can respond to me, I slam on the brakes and drive us over to the side, my heart pounding like crazy.

"What the fuck, Reaper? I didn't think you were leading me to my impending doom just yet," he grunts, and I turn to him with wide eyes. "What the fuck am I missing? There are no other vehicles out here and you're driving like a crazy woman, slamming on the brakes like you're saving us from disaster."

I shake my head, disbelief flickering through me as I try to find the words, and settle on three. "I found it."

"Found what?" he asks, glancing outside of the truck.

"You have to help me out here, otherwise I—"

"Do you see the fencing further down the road?" I interject, pointing in the direction, and he nods.

"What of it?"

"I'm ninety-nine percent sure that's where I killed the two men in the SUV." I let my words sink in, watching his face scrunch up in confusion before realization dawns on him.

"Drive closer. I need that extra one percent, Reaper," he says, and I quickly put the truck in drive and roll closer. We cover a few more meters but when we notice a couple of bikes and men standing at the open gate, I pull over.

"Is that…"

"Declan? Yeah, I think it is."

We edge forward, squinting in our seats as we confirm it's the filthy fucker himself.

"It's time we called them out," I state, anger and relief warring inside of me. We've finally got their compound location, but there are still traitors in our nest.

"We have to bide our time," Axel replies, leaning back in his seat with a huff. He pinches at the bridge of his nose, frustration getting the better of him too.

"I'm sick of fucking biding our time, Axel. It's not getting us anywhere. This is important, and we can use this."

"We don't know how many men are on the other side

of that fence, and acting irrationally with the Ice Reapers is what fucked everything up for us and triggered all of this to begin with," he grunts, not liking the answer on his tongue anymore than I like hearing it.

Knowing we're not going to be making a move today, and not wanting to get caught as soon as we actually have something to our advantage, I turn the truck around and start heading to the compound, confident I know where I'm going now. "What triggered all of this was me killing Banner," I say.

"That was going to happen whether it was you who did it or someone else. It was a job, I listed it, and I wasn't backing down on it."

"But—"

"It doesn't matter, there's no room for mistakes this time. Not when they've had you in their grasp. Over my dead body," he bites, and I sigh with annoyance, slamming my fist into the wheel as the pent-up anger inside of me refuses to go. Huffing at myself, my nostrils flaring, Axel's hand clamps down on my thigh. "Keep up with that noise and I'll put you in your place, Reaper."

I barely recognize his voice, it's so deep and thick, but it doesn't ease the rising tension inside of me. "You fucking wouldn't," I grunt, hands tightening on the steering wheel as I press down on the accelerator more.

He doesn't correct me as we ride back to the compound.

The podcast still plays in the background, but none of it is sinking in as I remain lost in my head. The strain I'm feeling doesn't subside when the compound comes into view, nor when I park the truck, a little harsher on the brakes than I intended, but I don't apologize.

I'm fully aware it's not his fault, but I feel trapped.

Hopping down from the cab, I slam the door shut behind me and storm toward the building, relieved as hell that the bar area is magically empty when I step inside.

"Where are you going, Scarlett?" Axel asks, like it's not fucking obvious.

Whirling around to face him, I swing my arms out and drop them back down to my side with a slap. "To bring those fuckers to the table. We need to figure this out. Now," I bite, and as he stalks toward me, I shake my head at him.

"I warned you in the truck, Reaper."

My eyebrows knit together, ready to call bullshit on him, when his shoulder connects with my stomach and I'm hoisted into the air.

"What the fuck, Ax? Put me down right now," I yell, wiggling in his hold but it doesn't really get me anywhere. His palm comes down on my ass cheek without warning. He kicks open the door leading to our rooms at the back. He doesn't apologize or soothe the sore spot as he continues walking.

"It's time your bratty ass got a reminder," he says,

opening his bedroom door and waltzing inside like I weigh nothing, before slamming the door shut behind us.

He lowers me to my feet so slowly, and I might explode from impatience. Once I'm firmly on the ground, I fold my arms over my chest and glare at him.

"A reminder of what?" I ask, giving him a pointed stare, but if it affects him it doesn't show. A salacious grin spreads over his face, and his eyes darken.

"Of what I can do to you."

TWENTY FIVE

Axel

Scarlett stands toe-to-toe with me, eyes wide and jaw slack. She has every opportunity to reach out and touch me right now. I can sense the desire in the tension of her shoulders and the flex of her hands, but she doesn't.

For me.

She's constantly evaluating me and my needs, and always so accurate in understanding my wants, as I do hers. The feel of someone putting you first is indescribable. Even now, when I'm looming over her and calling her a brat, she still does it.

Clearing her throat, she looks up at me. "What is it you want to do to me?"

I tuck her hair behind her ear. "Everything. But right now, I'm going to tie you up until my words sink in."

"Because I want to act now?" she clarifies, eyebrows

pinching together, and I nod.

"You're acting rashly and you need to remember the bigger picture. For that to happen, you need to disassociate from it all and look at it again later with a clearer head," I explain, and she huffs at me, just like she did in the truck.

"And you think tying me up is going to clear my head?" She cocks a brow like I've lost my mind, but I know what I'm doing. Especially when it comes to her.

"I'm betting on it, yeah." Her tongue sweeps across her bottom lip, her pupils dilating a little as my words settle over her. "Strip for me, Reaper."

"You're insane."

"You don't want this?" I ask, knowing full well if she says no, it's a bold-faced lie.

"Of course I fucking do," she grumbles, then shakes her jacket off, before whipping her t-shirt over her head. The defiance in her eyes is real, the smug look alluring as she watches me stare at her tits, neatly encased in a red lace bra.

She's going for the shock factor. Again. Just like she did on campus the other day. She's a weapon of mass destruction and I'm ready for her to detonate.

Her gaze remains on mine while she kicks her boots off, then she leans forward slightly, tucking her hands beneath the waistband of her jeans. She reveals the matching lace panties so fucking slowly that I almost tear the denim from her thighs, but the little show she's putting on is too fucking good to disrupt.

Scarlett *Reaper* Reeves is the most enticing woman I will ever witness for as long as I live.

She plants her hands on her hips, and I shake my head. "This hot little two-piece can go too," I grunt, refraining from adjusting myself in my pants.

Her classic eye roll makes me bite back a grin as she reaches behind her back to unclasp her bra. Her sweet tits bounce as she drops the fabric at her side, but as she moves to her panties, I lift my hand.

"Wait."

To my surprise, she stops with her palms flat against her stomach. I rub my lips together, excitement and nerves warring inside of me as I reach for the scrap of material and tear the lace with my hands.

"What the fuck?" Scarlett blurts, and it only makes my grin widen.

"I've wanted to know how it feels to do that for the longest time."

"And?"

Reluctantly lifting my gaze from her pretty pink pussy, I meet her eyes. "You're going to need to do another shopping trip, because that's how you undress every single time from now on."

"Fuck," she rasps, not moving to cover or hide herself

from me. If anything, she stands taller, pride clinging to her.

Standing before her, I remove my cut and black tee, along with my boots and socks, until I'm standing in just my boxer shorts and jeans.

"No man should look hot standing with jeans on, but there's something about your bare feet and chest on display, mixed with the cords in your arms that make me wet as fuck." Smirking at her, I tie my hair in the bun, and she groans. "Will you stop, I'm going to need a damn towel."

I twirl my finger, hinting for her to turn around, and she does. Making sure to keep enough distance between us, I slowly braid her hair, securing it with a hair tie before leaning forward to press a kiss against her shoulder.

"Are you ready?"

"Desperate," she breathes.

As much as I want to rush through all of this, I don't. Slowly gathering the rope I need while she remains with her feet planted at the foot of the bed. "If this gets too much for you at any time, just say the word, Scarlett, and I'll stop," I say, dropping the ropes beside her on the bed in an array of colors.

"I know."

"Any preference?" I ask, referring to the rope, and her hand instantly reaches out to touch the deep purple.

I take it from the bed and drop to my knees behind her.

Her soft skin beckons me closer, but I focus on the rope instead. Starting at her thighs, I weave and wrap until it's tangled around her upper legs, ass, and waist.

As I reach for another string of rope, pink this time, she rubs her thighs together, and the gasp that bursts from her lips is undeniable. I've strategically placed the purple rope to offer the perfect friction at her core when she adds just the right amount of pressure. Just like she is now.

Looping the pink around the purple rope where it ends at her waist, I change the patterning up to intertwine the soft material around her breast. It nestles perfectly under her tits, before framing them like the stunning prize they are. I end the pink twine at her throat, brushing my fingers over her pulse. I can feel how much she's enjoying it.

The blue rope calls to me as I move to complete the final part of my design, but first, I lift her arms in the air. I link the blue to the pink and start to band her arms together until I finish with a decorative fusion knot at her wrists.

"You can drop your arms for a second if you need to," I offer, and she does, looking at the intricate detail in awe. Getting rid of the rest of the rope, I turn to face her from my closet, and take her in.

She's a complete vision.

"This is stunning, Axel," she murmurs as I prowl back toward her. She peers over her shoulder at me, pupils blown as she looks at me with awe and... love.

"Yes, you are." She smiles, a toe-curling, heart-melting grin that makes my gut clench. "Arms back up, Reaper," I command when I come to a stop beside her, and she moves, doing as I ask without question.

Grabbing her waist, I lift her onto the bed, thrumming with need at the feel of her skin encased in my ropes. I climb up beside her, reaching up to the ceiling as I lower the new addition to my room.

"Since when has there been a fucking hook in here?" Scarlett blurts, looking up at the ceiling with wide eyes.

"Since yesterday."

I hook the rope at her wrists over the lowered hook. I pull against it, testing to make sure the tension travels from one rope to another as it should. When I'm satisfied that she's safe, I jump down off the bed. Her feet are still pressed into the sheets, and her arms are stretched out above her head like she's a goddamn wet dream.

"Now, what are you going to do to me?" she asks, looking down at me with hooded eyes and I sweep my tongue over my lips.

I stroke my finger over her cheek, and she leans into the touch, before I slowly ghost down her throat and over her collarbone. She gulps, which makes my dick strain against my jeans. Running my hand over the trails of the rope around her chest, I tease at her taut nipples, but continue down until I reach the apex of her thighs.

"Now, I'm going to taste you," I croak, eyes zeroed in on her glistening clit and folds. Before she can even consider a response, I lean forward and swipe my tongue from her core to her clit.

Fuck.

"Oh my god, Axel," she groans, legs trembling.

One taste isn't enough. I don't think it ever will be. Just like every other inch of her, she's addicting, and I've just found her nectar. Grabbing the backs of her thighs, I lift her in the air with ease, the hook making it effortless, until each leg is draped over my shoulders and her pussy is in my face.

"Ax—"

My name is cut from her lips as she groans, which probably has something to do with my tongue deep in her cunt. I lick, nip, taste, and tease like a man starved. I have been. For too many years, I've feared anything intimate with a woman, but this is different... this is *everything*.

I'm sure I'm leaving bruises on the globes of her ass cheeks. I'm feasting on her so much, the sound of my name is now a chant on her lips for anyone within a one-mile radius to hear.

"I'm so close, Axel. Oh my God," she cries out, and I rake my teeth over her clit, a little harder this time, and she shudders above me. Flicking my tongue down to her entrance, I groan as she climaxes over me. My chin is dripping with her juices, and it's the best sensation I've ever fucking felt.

When I'm sure she has nothing left to give, I slowly lower her to the bed again. She can barely hold her weight up, so I quickly untie the rope from the hook and lower her to the bed.

"Holy shit, Axel," she mutters, eyes barely open as she lies down on my sheets.

Taking a step back from the bed, my heart thundering in my chest, I know I need more, but more than that, I'm certain it's what I want. Unzipping my jeans, I drag my boxer shorts down my legs with the denim and discard them without care. My cock begs for attention, desperate to feel her, and I wrap my hand around my thick length, trying to calm myself.

Her arms were resting on her stomach, but as I take a step toward her, she lifts them over her head.

Fuck.

This is why it could only ever have been her.

Rounding the bed, I lift the hook that's tucked between my headboard, and latch the rope to it.

"Axel, you don't have to do this," she whispers as I move to the bottom of the bed again.

"If I don't feel you in the next thirty seconds, Scarlett, I think I might die," I whisper, my pulse ringing in my ears as I place one knee on the bed.

I don't have to ask her to hold this position; I don't have to clarify that she can't try to free her arms right now, she already knows it. It's written all over her face, along with the love, need, and fire flashing in her eyes.

When I'm set perfectly between her thighs, I slowly run my hands from her knees to her core, feeling goosebumps prickle over her skin. Which feels like heaven combined with the rope wrapped around her too.

Grabbing my cock, I exhale slowly, lining myself up with her entrance and the heat already pooling in my stomach is unbearable.

With my eyes locked on hers, my hands tightly gripping her waist, and the tip of my cock at her core, I remove the remaining distance between us and slam my length inside her.

My brain shuts down, my body blazes at the feel of her as her moans echo around the room. Perspiration clings to every inch of me as I hold position for a second, trying to catch my breath, but need takes over and pleasure ripples through my veins. Tightening my hold on her waist, I pull out and slam straight back into her tight pussy.

With my jaw slack, tendrils of hair falling around my face, and a pink flush rising over my chest, I look like a crazed man, but I can't stop. I need her. Every inch.

All I can hear above the ringing of my pulse is my name on her lips as she begs for more. Eager to please, I pull out, much to her protest, and flip her over with one swift move. Her braid trails down her back, the rope decorating her beautifully as I pull her up to her knees and thrust back inside of her.

"Shit, Axel. Please," she screams, every syllable hitting me square in the dick. Slapping my hand down on her ass cheek, the rope course beneath my touch, she shivers beneath me, before her pussy tightens around my cock in a deathly grip.

She explodes, taking everything from me as my moves become jagged and messy, spiraling me over the edge of ecstasy with her.

I feel like I'm coming forever, spilling into her thrust after thrust until I'm spent and sprawled over her back. A tangle of limbs, I press a kiss to her shoulder.

"How are you feeling?"

"Like heaven," she breathes, eyes closed, and my chest clenches.

"Heaven is when I take care of you now, Reaper," I murmur, peppering two more kisses to her cheek before I lean up.

"What does that mean?"

"It means you get a bath filled with bubbles, a massage, and whatever else your icy fucking heart desires."

"I knew there was a reason I was meant to love you, Axel."

"Ditto, Reaper, ditto."

TWENTY SIX

Scarlett

The bed and sheets are soft, fluffy clouds. All snuggly and dream-like, but it's real. Oh-so-fucking real. When I stand though, my legs turn to jelly and it's a little harder to walk to the door than I expected.

"Throw these on, Scar, then at least if we run into anyone, I don't have to slaughter them for laying eyes on you," Axel states, showering me with even more of that crazy-ass love I'm addicted to.

I take the t-shirt and boxer shorts from his hands and quickly dress, but when I move toward the door once more, he sweeps me off in bridal-style and carries me the rest of the way. His heart pounds against my cheek, and his musky scent wraps around me, while I try like hell to keep my hands to myself.

He unlocks the door with me in his arms like it's not an

inconvenience, but he comes to a halt halfway across the threshold. A frown darkens his features and panic worms its way into my chest. When I glance up to see what the issue is, I find Ryker, Gray, and Emmett leaning against the opposite wall.

Their arms are folded, eyebrows raised, and mouths open.

My cheeks instantly heat as realization washes over me. "Uh, I think we had an audience," I murmur, making Gray chuckle as he pushes off the wall.

"An audience? NASA called, they heard you from the space station." He's grinning with bewilderment, but I just shrug as Axel slowly lowers me to the ground.

"I'm not going to apologize. I hope whatever extraterrestrial life form that's out there heard how good Axel's dick is."

Ryker swipes a hand over his mouth, failing to hide his grin, while Emmett shakes his head in disbelief.

"Oh shit, I'm sorry. I'm not saying it to make you feel embarrassed," Gray quickly rushes out, waving his hand. "I was just confused when I heard the sweet sounds of you climaxing, but saw the three of us sitting together. Which meant only one thing, and I had to be here to see it so I could believe it."

Axel's hands ghost over my waist, making me shiver. "We don't have to make a big deal out of this," I state, feeling protective of Axel, but as usual, Gray doesn't get the hint.

"Behave, of course this is a big fucking deal because—"

Axel steps from behind me and presses his palm into Gray's face, knocking him back a step or two without actually hitting him. A chuckle ripples from my gut, and a bark of laughter echoes around us.

"You're getting on my nerves, and I need a smoke. Are you coming, Reaper?" He stalks toward the back exit without looking over his shoulder, and I'm almost bouncing on the balls of my feet and clapping my hands like a damn seal in excitement over him.

I need to get a grip. If I wasn't crazy about Ryker, Gray, and Emmett already, I'd think there was something seriously wrong with me. But because of them, I can decipher the feelings and emotions ricocheting around in my head.

Fuck, I love these guys.

Winking at the others, I skip after him. "Obviously," I finally reply, and when he reaches the door, he turns to glance over his shoulder.

"Since you're all here, you can come too." He nods to follow him, but Ryker waves him off.

"I'm good."

"It's *not* a request. We know shit," he replies before stepping outside and leaving everyone behind. The fucker knows we'll follow him. It's a good thing he's hot.

"Fine," Emmett grumbles, sweeping me up off the floor and carrying me just as Axel had been. I snuggle into his chest, fully aware that I smell like Axel right now, but he doesn't complain. The cool air outside brushes over my skin, sending a chill down my spine. I warm a little when he takes us into the garage, but I don't make any attempt to leave Emmett's arms.

"Are you going to tell them or am I?" Axel asks, lighting up a cigarette and leaning against a large tool box, and I smirk at him. That's a silly question. That's exactly what I wanted to do the second we found it. A smirk grows across his face as he wags his finger at me. "Remember before when I said you needed a clearer head and all that shit. How does it feel right now?"

My eyes narrow. I forgot about that, and that's entirely his fault, just as he intended. Pursing my lips, I intensify my glare but it falls flat. "You're pushing it, Mister," I grumble.

"Can somebody clue us in?" Ryker says, swiping a clear spot on the table set up against the far wall to take a seat.

"Yeah," Gray adds, coming to stand directly between where Emmett holds me and Axel stands. "Like, are you guys good? Am I ever going to be required for another Gray sandwich because that shit literally made my life?

And—"

"Not that, you fucking idiot," Ryker grunts, smacking the back of Gray's head and catching him off guard. I hadn't even noticed that Mr. President moved from the damn table, so I can't imagine how startled Gray feels.

"What they want to tell us, he means," Emmett explains.

"Fine, I guess that's important too," Gray relents, moving to stand beside Axel with his arms folded over his chest.

Emmett reluctantly puts me down, and I fold my arms in an attempt to replace the warmth I just left behind.

"We found the compound."

"What?" Ryker's eyes widen in surprise.

"Well, technically Reaper did," Axel adds, taking a drag of his cigarette as Gray gapes at me in surprise.

"How?" Emmett asks, hand on my shoulder as he turns me to look at him.

"From memory."

"Memory?" Emmett's brows furrow.

"This crazy-ass woman took me on a wild drive. I didn't know what was going on. I could have sworn she was lost a time or two, but she was retracing her steps from when she was taken. Even found Declan at the gates too, confirming what we already knew."

Ryker paces in front of us, aware of how serious this information is, as we all give him a moment to process.

"Fucker. How do we get on the inside?" he murmurs more to himself than anyone else, but Axel still replies.

"I don't know, and that's the part we have to figure out. But at least we know *where* we're fucking heading."

Ryker spins to face me. He takes two long strides, eliminating the distance between us before I'm in his arms, feet off the ground as he spins me on the spot.

"Fuck, you're amazing, Rebel." I preen in his hold, basking in the compliment.

"Thanks, it's my specialty, but what's the plan? Whatever it is, you better count me the fuck in."

"Always. You're our Ruthless Rebel. That means something," he murmurs against my ear, and I shiver. Nothing has ever felt quite like this.

I'm home.

"For now, we need to act normal and make sure this stays between us. I can't risk Declan getting a whiff of this." I nod in agreement, hating that it feels like we're pausing again, but this time it makes sense. It would be foolish to go in blind. "Can you do it again for me, Rebel? I want to survey the borders," he asks, and I know with certainty that this time, things could finally be swaying in our direction.

"Of course, but first, Axel promised me a bubble bath, a massage, and anything else I wanted. That has to come first."

"Worshiping our woman?" Emmett adds. "Fuck yeah, it does."

"Not you, fuckers, she's mine for the rest of the day. Anyone who tries to question me can meet my fucking left hook because I've waited long enough," Axel grunts.

My heart is full, the prospect of hope on the horizon for the club is like a breath of fresh air.

It's just like Emily said. *Families who slay together, stay together.* And we're getting closer and closer to proving her right.

With my Ruthless Men beside me, nothing is going to stand in our way.

TWENTY SEVEN

Scarlett

Patrolling the Devil's Brutes' compound last night was exactly as disappointing and exhilarating as I expected it to be. I got us there much quicker this time, remembering the route much better, but every step we took around the perimeter had me itching to climb over the fence and cause a riot.

Ryker refused. As did the others.

Fuckers.

I get it, I do, but they're not the ones now on the way to Jasperville University to spend the day taking classes that don't even compare to getting revenge. Nope, that's me.

Shift is driving today, Emily and I tucked in the back with a two-bike escort behind us.

A yawn parts my lips as I swipe a hand down my face, covering my tonsils from Emily's view, but she smirks at me, confirming I failed.

"Someone needs to get more sleep," she snickers, wagging her eyebrows at me, and I grin. She doesn't know about our late night drive. She's assuming I was up late getting up to much more fun things, but alas, that's not the case. Not that I can tell her that though.

I hate to lie, so I shrug. "It's not my fault your brother's co—"

"Ew! Ew! Ew! Shut up," she screeches, covering her ears with her hands as she squeezes her eyes shut.

Shift chuckles up front, which only makes Emily stamp her feet. "Don't laugh, Shaun. It's not funny."

My eyes widen at the name on her lips, but it's Shift's response to it that has me even more intrigued. His eyes darken, teeth nipping into his bottom lip as he glances in the rearview mirror at her.

Deciding winding her up is more fun than talking about me, I tap her on the shoulder. "Who's Shaun?"

Emily freezes, gaping at Shift. When I flicker my gaze to Shift, he keeps his eyes pinned on the road. Silence blankets us.

"Wait… Is Shift's real name Shaun? I didn't know that." I think she's vibrating, her eyes are on the verge of falling out of her damn face as she tries to scramble a response. "Three names for one man. Who knew the infamous Kronkz could be such a cool kid. We talked about deep shit, man, and I'm only just now realizing I never even knew your name." I lift a hand to my chest in mock horror, aiming a pointed look his way for when he eventually looks at me in the rearview mirror.

He sighs, shaking his head.

"Fuck," he grunts, slapping his hand against the steering wheel. "She knows, Em."

My eyebrows furrow as I look at Emily, who's now so pale I think she's about to pass out.

"Knows what?"

"Don't push, Scar. She's going to hyperventilate any fucking second, and if she gets upset, I'm going to be a pissy little bitch. Even to you."

My smile grows. "That's the kind of response I want to hear from your lips. I don't give a fuck who you're talking to. Do you hear me?" I cock a brow at him.

He wraps his arm behind his seat as he pulls into the campus parking lot, squeezing her knee in silent support and she quickly brushes him off.

"Em, it's okay. If you two hadn't been looking at each other with hearts in your eyes, you might have been able to keep it a secret, but it's not. It's fucking adorable if anything," I offer, squeezing her cheeks playfully.

"Oh, shit. We're not ready for people to know, Scarlett. Not. Ready."

What she means is she's not ready for Emmett to know,

but I don't clarify. They're her emotions, not mine.

The SUV comes to a stop, and before I can utter a word of reassurance at her, my door swings open and I'm lifted from my seat. Gray holds me in his arms until we're on the sidewalk, where he proceeds to lower me to my feet oh-so-fucking slowly. Making sure every inch of me brushes against every inch of him.

"Hurry the fuck up, asshole," Emmett grumbles, glancing at me from over Gray's shoulder, but my view of him is quickly cut off as Gray presses his lips to mine. Wrapping my arms around his neck, I take my time, kissing his lips until they're locked in my memory.

"Have a good day, Sweet Cheeks," he murmurs when he reluctantly takes a step back, and Emmett occupies his spot.

"It's a good thing you're a fucking queen, Snowflake. I have zero patience, but waiting for you is still a gift," he says, making me swoon. He molds his mouth to mine in the next moment.

All too soon, he backs away too, leaving me needy and wanting before a full day of classes.

Motherfuckers.

I'm still standing in the same spot as the revs of their engines echo around us and they take off. "Who did you say is the one with hearts in their eyes?" Shift muses, tapping his fingers on his arm as he assesses me. I stick my middle finger up at him, giving him a fuck you smile, and Emily chuckles, linking her arm through mine.

"Can we talk about this later?" she asks quietly, leaving me confused, but when she nods at Shift, I understand.

"Whenever and wherever you want," I reassure, and she relaxes beside me.

She leads the way to class, and I panic when I realize I didn't grab my backpack when we were leaving the SUV, but I spot it on Shift's shoulder with Emily's perched on the other.

"I'm not ready for this class today," I admit, and Emily shakes her head.

"You're going to be fine."

"The only time I've ever had a needle and cotton in my hands is to stitch up a wound. Creating beautiful clothing isn't the same as that. Like at all." Uncertainty flusters me, but I trust in her as we make our way to the building.

Making our way through the crowd, I keep glancing around at everyone, hating the vulnerability from the masses, just as I do every time we're here. A flash of black catches my attention in the distance to the far left. Familiar dark and twisted eyes, combined with swept back hair and a leather cut flicker in my peripheral vision, making me pause.

Kincaid.

People continue to pass around me as I stand taller, but

when I focus on the spot I was sure I saw him in, I come up blank. Not a hint of leather in sight.

"What's up? Is everything okay?" Shift asks, sensing the unsettling inside of me.

I nod, but it still takes me another moment to glance at him. "I could have sworn I just saw Kincaid," I mutter, making Shift's eyes widen.

"Where?"

"Over there." I point where the movement caught my attention, but clearly I was imagining it because there's definitely no one there except students walking by.

"I'll have some prospects sent over to scan the area." Shift pulls his cell phone out and starts tapping away.

"Is that necessary?" I ask. "I could have just been seeing things with all the pent-up worry going on in my head," I admit, not wanting to cause a stir for no reason.

"To protect the two of you, everything and anything is necessary."

It was all in my fucking head as expected. I guess it's better to be on high alert as opposed to being too relaxed, but I hate that I caused an issue and had the prospects trailing campus for no reason.

No one else other than those in Ruthless Brothers'

leather has been seen wearing a cut. Emily's right; I need to get some damn sleep.

Thankfully, the design class was all about research and we could work in pairs, so I let Emily lead the way, helping with what I could so she didn't feel like she was carrying dead weight. We had a two-hour break for lunch, which was spent at my favorite bagel spot, and now, we have the fun of business class to enjoy this afternoon. Once I get through this, we have one more class and then we can head home and pass the fuck out.

I wasn't prepared for how busy this would feel. It's keeping me on my toes in an entirely different way than the rest of my life, but it's worth it to see Emily be so engrossed in it all. Shit, even I may have enjoyed myself this morning. Not that I'm going to admit that just yet. Not before I get through this god-awful class at least.

"Ryker's agreed to me waiting outside of the classroom doors," Shift states as we take the steps up to the business building.

"Every day you get to take a step further back, huh?" I reply with a grin. "It feels like a fun game for us to enjoy and to make your life hell."

Emily giggles between us. She's barely been able to look at Shift all day since this morning's revelations, but I guess it's going to take her a minute. He doesn't push her, not once, but I do spot him tapping away on his cell phone a few times, and Emily's cheeks turn pink as she gets a text message.

It's cute as hell and totally what he deserves. I'm more excited for her to finally talk to me about it so I can give him the warning talk. It has me all kinds of excited.

"Don't push or I'll just come and sit inside anyways," he grumbles as we reach the doors to the classroom.

I roll my eyes at him as I step inside, not missing the way their fingers brush before Emily follows after me. She takes her usual seat at the front, and I get comfortable at the back. My lips purse when I notice the person sitting directly in front of me.

Joshua.

Great.

Someone forgot or is living life a little too close to the edge right now. If Shift sees him there, then he'll probably sit himself between us to make sure Ryker is happy with the level of protection he's offering. I don't need any further drama though, we're already sinking in it. So I shuffle down in my seat, pulling my things from my bags as the professor appears and begins the class.

I'm getting quicker with the keyboard, my fingers don't ache from using muscles I never even knew I had like they do when I'm writing, and it's easier to piece the letters together. I'm still not ready to start whipping out a hundred words a minute, unless the word is *a*, but I'm taking whatever progress I can get.

When I'm sure a migraine is coming on from looking at the screen so much, the professor thankfully calls the class to an end, and I rush to pack all of my stuff away. The next class is to do with make-up, which is going to be intriguing at least. It has me nervous because I can't do anything like Emily can, but it beats having to overcome words and shit, so we're taking it as a win.

Hitching my bag on my shoulder, I move to the stairs to get ready for Emily, when Joshua turns and blocks my view.

"Hey."

"Fuck off," I grunt, shoving at his arm to move him to the side, but he doesn't budge.

"I was wondering—"

"Honestly, take a hint and get the fuck out of my way," I bite, in no mood to deal with his bullshit right now, but he just smirks at me like I'm funny. He's about to see what funny definitely doesn't look like in a second, with a goddamn audience if necessary.

"It's amusing how raspy your voice gets when you're angry. It reminds me of your groans when you're fucked like a whore." His top lip lifts in a snarl, and I scoff at the audacity coming from him.

"Listen, shithead, do us both a favor and save us a hell of a lot of time by getting out of my vicinity. It's not the man fucking this whore you should be worried about. It's the whore herself."

People continue to move around us, and I count to three in my head. When he's still standing where he is, I shove at his chest, making him stumble back a step and it gives me enough room to maneuver around him.

Irritation claws at my insides at his presence, but I'm too focused on Emily to let it drown me. Especially when I don't have eyes on her. Frowning, I glance along the front row again, before head counting every single person walking up the stairs, but I don't see her bouncy blonde hair anywhere.

What the fuck?

Taking another step down the stairs, my heart starts to pound, my body going rigid as I come up blank again. I try to take a deep breath, but it falls short as I spin on the spot and march toward the doors, expecting to see her standing side-by-side with Shift, but my gut twists when I find him leaning against the wall. Alone.

"Shift, is she with you?" I holler, his eyes quickly lifting to mine as he stands tall.

"What? No. Why?"

My body tingles as I spin on the spot to face the room again. My backpack falls at my feet. I can't find her.

I can't *fucking* find her. Why the hell can't I find her?

I don't manage a single step into the room before

Joshua is thrusting a piece of paper against my chest. "You're going to want this, whore."

Clutching at it with one hand, I glare at him, and when he goes to take a step away from me, I slam my free fist into his throat. "Grab him, Shift," I yell, and he follows my order. My attention switches to the cream colored envelope against my chest.

Fear coats my skin as I tremble, tearing into it as quickly as I can, while wanting to delay the inevitable I know is coming. My eyes scan over the text, words written too small for me to decipher as quickly as I need to and my throat clogs with anger at myself for being a failure.

It takes me a split second to know I can't break this down word for word. I can barely see past the end of my own nose. So I glance at the bottom of the note to see who the sender is, and chills run down my spine as my heart breaks in two.

Kincaid.

TWENTY EIGHT

Scarlett

Bile burns the back of my throat as I scope out the building, coming up empty-handed, just as I did in the last building. Where the fuck is she? I feel exhausted and useless all at once.

How did Kincaid manage to make her completely disappear into thin air? She was there one moment and gone the next. I can barely breathe if I let myself wallow in the panic of it. Instead, I channel all of my focus into fucking finding her.

Shift called the club, bringing every brother to campus to search for her, and I haven't seen any texts come through to confirm someone has. She shouldn't be missing in the first place. I'll forever beat myself up for this. I can't even bring myself to lean on any of my men at the moment.

Gray was the first to try and hold me, with Ryker being

second. Even Axel insisted on checking on me, but my heart fucking broke when it was Emmett's turn. I don't deserve anything from any of them. I let them down, I let myself down, but most of all, I let Emily down.

Fuck.

Frustrated, I step out into the courtyard. We've split up, desperate to cover as much ground as possible, but the disappointment flashing in Shift's eyes as he rushes out of the building beside me tells me he's had no luck either.

I fucking hate this place. It's too wide of a scope to have a lock down of any kind. My gut tells me she's gone, but a tiny slither of hope has me holding out. Every second we're looking in the wrong place is another moment she's left in danger.

Now in hindsight, all I can think about is how she offered me the gift of reading and writing, and I didn't even have the common decency to offer her something I know; how to protect herself.

I want to scream, cry, and exhale the feelings and emotions clogging up my throat, but I can't. That would show weakness, just like Kincaid wants. He fucking knows he's hit a soft spot for me, and he's going to twist that knife deeper and deeper until he's satisfied there's nothing of me remaining. It feels like Duffer all over again, only this time, it's not so quick. I knew he was dead the moment he hit the ground, but I have no idea of Emily's circumstances and that is both a blessing and a curse.

Huffing, I dig my hand into my pocket, retrieving the crumpled letter. I straighten it out, and though my eyes drag over the words on the page, I barely read them. Instead, I repeat them from memory, forever seared into my damn soul.

I thought I already killed this bitch.
When Molly was adamant I hadn't, I called bullshit.
*Then the always watching eyes I have saw her. But more importantly, they saw how **YOU** are with her.*
It seems the Ruthless Brothers MC doesn't want to take my threats seriously, but I know you will. You know what I'm capable of, Scarlett.
I'm going to enjoy watching you drop to your knees for me after all this time. Even more than that, I'm going to enjoy making you mine for them to see.
Get ready, little Scarlett, time's up.
Kincaid.

He knows he can use me to get the Ruthless Brothers to bow to him and his rules, and he knows he can get to me through Emily. If he so much as hurts a single hair on her head I will break his fucking neck. Well, I'm going to do that either way, but extra painful if necessary.

"Scar," Shift rasps, coming toward me, and I stuff the

letter away. He doesn't need to see it again, he already knows. The heartbreak brimming in his eyes is palpable, twisting my heart even tighter. He's lost, so fucking lost, and I can't fix it.

"We're going to find her, Shift," I murmur, and he nods, solemn, not trusting my promise as a sea of Ruthless Brothers move toward us from every direction. Not one of them has a blue-eyed, blonde-haired, button-nose girl with them. I didn't think it was possible to sink any further, but here we are.

I catch sight of my Viking joining us from the right, but I can't bring myself to turn and look at him. It's too painful.

"No luck?" Ryker asks, confirming just how bleak everything is looking, and everyone shakes their head.

"Fuck," Emmett bites, deep and gravelly, making my body stiffen at his pain. My eyes close, trying to take a second to gather my emotions, but it's pointless. We're in this mess because of me and everyone here knows it.

"I say we question the fucker tucked away in Shift's trunk," Gray states, referring to Joshua and his current location, and I nod, ready to move out toward the parking lot, but a hand on my shoulder halts me.

From the dark brown boots and denim jeans, I know it's Emmett without even lifting my head, which keeps me locked in place with my eyes fixed on the ground.

"Look at me, Scarlett." I shake my head slightly, shoulders slumped as he sighs. "Everybody, get ready to head out except for you four prospects. I want you patrolling every inch of this campus on repeat. If you've passed the same spot four times, do it a fifth. Understood?"

"Yes, VP."

I start to sidestep him, but his grip on my shoulder tightens.

When the sound of retreating footsteps tapers off in the distance, his other hand lifts to my shoulder as well, adjusting my stance so I'm standing toe-to-toe with him. "Look at me, Snowflake," he repeats, using my nickname this time, but even though it clenches my chest, it doesn't ease any of the turmoil I'm drowning in so I remain where I am. "Scarlett," he grunts, pushing my chin up to look at him, but my eyes drift closed at the same time. "I can't help you, if you don't help me."

I scoff. "You help me? I don't think so. I deserve to feel like this," I say, making him shake my shoulder forcefully.

"Bullshit. I can sense that you think this is all your fault, but you need to hear it from me. It. Is. Not." His grip on my chin grows tighter, and my eyes open instinctively. "There you are," he breathes, not relaxing his hold as he looks at me.

Looking into his swirling blue eyes, every piece of emotion I'm feeling rushes to the surface and I feel myself crumbling. "I'm so sorry."

"I'll let you get those three words off your chest, Snowflake, but I don't want to fucking hear them again. This isn't your fault."

"How are you this calm?" I rasp, nostrils flaring as tears threaten the back of my eyelids.

"Because I know you won't rest until we find her, and between us, we're going to rain down hell on this fucking town. She's coming home to us. There's no alternative." His words stoke my fire, and I exhale, latching on to them with everything I have. "Just to clarify though, it's not your fault Kincaid has some point to prove, it's not your fault he's a raging asshole, and it's definitely not your fault that he took her to hurt you, which in turn, will hurt us. You're allowed to have a weakness, Scar, someone you care for, someone worth fighting for."

His eyes drill into mine, and even as I nod, I can't stop the anguish seeping into my response.

"I took my eye off her, Emmett. The whole reason I'm here is for her and I couldn't even last a week."

"It wasn't by choice and you know it. You had some motherfucker in your face causing issues, just as he was likely paid to do. But just like with everything else, you're going to help get the answers we need out of him, aren't you?" It's a statement, not a question of my strength or ability. "I believe in you, Snowflake, I believe in us, and I believe it isn't her time. But I need your head in the game."

"I should be pep-talking you, not the other way around." I swipe my hand down my face and he releases his hold to offer me his hand instead. I take it without question, and he pulls me to where the bikes and SUVs are lined up.

There aren't really any students around at this time. They're either in classes, eating, or done for the day. Audience or not we were searching every corner of this damn place.

"What do we do now?" I ask as he holds out a helmet for me, and I tug it over my head, desperate to get on the bike instead of riding in the SUV.

"We take this motherfucker home and beat the shit out of him until we find the truth," he says. His jaw is so tight it could cut steel, and the determination in his eyes tells me it *has* to be that simple for us to achieve it.

"Make him bleed, Emmett."

Another grunt echoes around the garage. All the doors are shut and locked, but for extra measure, Axel is standing guard at the garage door and Gray is by the main door. No fucker is getting in or out until we have answers.

I was relieved when they opted to boycott their usual torture location, not wanting to spook Declan or give him the opportunity to rat us out to Kincaid.

The stress on Axel's face makes my heart ache. Emily may not be *his* sister, but she's a part of his family, our most delicate flower, and she's in the hands of the devil. Gray's expression is grim, irritation at how long this is taking is getting the better of him.

Ryker remains behind Joshua, looming over him as Emmett lands blow after blow on the motherfucker, but no matter how much blood splatters around us, Joshua continues to play dumb. I'm reaching my limit with him, but it seems he's more than some dumb jock.

"Where's my sister?" Emmett grunts, but Joshua just offers a bloody smile.

"I don't know shit, man." His head lulls to the side, and he manages a nonchalant shrug like this is all normal to him.

I'm ready to step in and get my hands dirty, but as I take one step toward the center of the room, Shift stops me. He takes my planned path instead, squeezing Emmett's shoulder. My Viking looks up at him with a narrowed stare, but whatever he sees in Shift's face is enough to make him take a step back and offer the floor to him.

Shift shakes off his cut, eyes narrowing at Joshua in his seat. His arms are tied with rope behind the back of the chair, and his ankles are strapped to the legs with cable ties. My oldest friend cracks his neck from side to side as he assesses the asshole holding out on us.

"I'm going to ask you a few questions, and every time you don't give me the response I want, I'm going to torture you. Agreed?"

"I don't know what—" His bullshit is cut off with a hiss when Shift lurches toward his face. I don't realize there's a blade in his hand until I see the track marks left on Joshua's cheek as blood seeps down to his neck.

"The answer I was looking for was agreed or yes. Either would have sufficed. Do I need to repeat myself?"

"No," Joshua grumbles, and Shift throws his hand out toward him again, but this time, he pats him on his other cheek with the side of the blade.

"Good boy." Shift crouches. "Let's start from the beginning, yeah? Did you know Kincaid before he approached you with this job?" Joshua shakes his head. "I can't fucking hear you," Shift bites, aiming the blade so the tip rests on his thigh.

"No."

He twirls the blade, but doesn't add any more force. "When did he approach you?"

"I don't kn—Ah, fuck, man!" His bullshit response morphs into cries of pain as Shift slams the blade into his thigh.

"I said, no crap. If you're not going to give me the answers I want, you're just going to feel the wrath of my torture. I really can't make it any easier for you to understand than that." The cords in Shift's arm flex, the tension visible on him from head to toe. "Is it worth me asking you again or should I just give you a matching wound on the other side?"

"Fuck, no. It was this morning. He approached me this morning."

"And what did he say?"

"I-I can't think with that thing sticking out of my leg," he grunts in response, making Shift tear it from him. The guttural grunts echo around the room, and I shake my head at his foolishness. He may be talking a big game right now, but I'm pretty sure he would have preferred that to stay where it was.

"What did he say?"

"He offered me five thousand dollars to distract Scarlett and give her the letter."

I huff. "I'm sure that five grand doesn't sound quite so worthwhile now, does it?"

Joshua glares at me, but doesn't speak. That doesn't stop Ryker from yanking at his head to tilt his face back so he can snarl at him. "What did I fucking tell you about looking in her direction? Don't make me start stabbing you for that too."

That shouldn't be hot, it really shouldn't, but it is. I'm saving this thought for later though, now is about pain, not pleasure.

Ryker releases his head, and his chin rests on his chest for a second until he catches sight of Shift twirling the blood-stained knife in front of him. "Last question and I'll let you leave." I didn't think it was possible for Shift's voice to turn so dark, drenched in anger and ready to cause war. "Where did he take her, Joshua?"

"I'm not sure..." Shift lifts the blade, and Joshua yelps. "Wait, wait, wait, please, fuck... I'm not sure, but he mentioned something about you not knowing where he's hiding so it doesn't matter once they're behind the compound lines, you'll never even know."

That's all we need. It's frustrating as hell that we just didn't storm it to begin with, but we just need to get over there now.

"What are we doing with this fucker?" Axel asks from the door. The echo of a gunshot rings out around us, and I glance to my right to see Emmett standing side by side with Shift, a gun in his hand and Joshua limp in his seat.

We'll have to clean that mess up later, because now, we have to put a plan in motion. We may have no idea of what awaits us inside, but he's certainly wrong about one thing. We know exactly where he's hiding. He just doesn't know we're coming.

TWENTY NINE

Scarlett

I wait by the SUVs as the bikes line up in the front yard. Axel does a skim of the interior before waving Ryker, Gray, and Emmett inside so they could gather the weapons we need.

Standing shoulder to shoulder with Shift, I'm at a loss for words, but I feel the need to soothe the rage building inside of him. I've never seen this side of him before. It's usually me causing mayhem and him behind a screen, but I shouldn't be surprised that he can handle himself like this too.

"Are you okay?" I ask, hating how it sounds on my tongue. Of course he's not, but I don't know what else to ask to gauge where his head is at.

"I will be when I see her, touch her, smell her." My heart swells with each of his words.

"You're going to get all of that, Shift. I promise," nudging him with my shoulder.

"That's *if* Emmett doesn't fucking kill me first."

My eyebrows furrow in confusion, but then I remember that I know all of the things this fool doesn't. "What do you think he's going to kill you for?" I need to clarify what he means before I start ranting at him.

His eyes whip to mine with a pointed stare. "You know what we spoke of this morning, Scar."

I smile at him despite the pain we're drenched in. "He already knows. But he's sadistic as hell and wanted you both to squirm over it for a bit," I admit, spoiling Emmett's fun, but it's no longer about that.

"Since when?"

"Since forever. But definitely now after you just destroyed that motherfucker in there. You went harder than even I did, and she's my fucking sister." Shift stills beside me, eyes widening as he turns to see Emmett coming through the double doors with his arms laden with guns.

My friend gulps beside me, clearly intimidated by all of the weapons Emmett's carrying, but my phenomenal Viking reassures him, just as he did with me. "We're going to bring her home, take care of her, and make sure we can help her in whatever way she needs. We don't know what that looks like just yet, but the fact is that she *is* coming home. Straight to me, straight to Scar, and straight to you." Emmett holds out a few guns in my direction and I take them so they can slap hands together, sealing a pact between them. "I trust her with you and with you alone."

"Even after what I did in there?" Shift murmurs, nodding toward the garage, and Emmett grunts.

"*Especially* because of what you did in there."

My eyes dart to Axel, Ryker, and Gray as they filter out of the compound, giving these two a moment. Maggie appears in the doorway after them, eyes wide and skin pale. She knows. Before I can even take a step, she's cutting the distance between us until her arms are wrapped around my neck.

"Bring her home." She presses a kiss to my cheek, squeezing my shoulders before hightailing it back inside. Well, that was a whirlwind.

Wordlessly, we load the vehicles up with weapons, but a niggling thought keeps playing at the back of my mind. Ryker shuts the trunk on the SUV and turns to face everyone, but before he can speak, I step forward.

"It's not going to work if we just storm in there." It's hilarious that I'm saying this now after all of the conversations I've had with Axel, but it's true.

"What do you mean?" Gray asks, coming to stand beside me.

"We need the upper hand."

"We can't get the upper hand without being inside first.

It's no longer an option. The only alternative would be to call on Graham and Declan, but the men we brought here as backup can no longer be trusted to have our back, so it looks like this." Ryker waves his arms around at the five of us.

Shaking my head, I know I'm going to be hit by wall after wall with them, but I push on. Pulling the tattered letter from my pocket, I press my finger beside the bottom of the words and turn it for each of them to see.

"It specifically says, 'I'm going to enjoy watching you drop to your knees for me after all this time. Even more than that, I'm going to enjoy making you mine for them to see.' Which means we need to follow the path he's leading us down."

"How does that look to you?" Emmett asks, folding his arms over his chest as if he's bracing for the impact of my words.

"It's the food chain, he's hitting our weak spots, going through Emily to get to me to inevitably get to you. Offer him the next thing on the chain... me."

"Fuck. No," Ryker bites, tension instantly rippling from him.

"Listen to me first, Ryker, before you start making decisions. It's *your* turn to see the bigger picture, like you always tell me. I can walk in there, all wired up so you can assess what we're dealing with and then hit them hard."

He's already shaking his head before I finish, Gray and Emmett following suit, and my chest tightens with the words I know I'm going to say next that will piss them off even more. "I'm not asking for permission. I'm asking Shift if he has the recording equipment to wire me up or not before I do it."

"Rebel…" Ryker starts, but I wave my hand at him.

"I might be your Ruthless Rebel, but you're not my prez. I don't have to take your orders." He knows this, the darkening of his eyes confirms it. We've had this conversation before, but until the shit really hits the fan, things never sink in.

"Scarlett, I'm not letting you. I can't, the danger, shit, Sweet Cheeks, I love you," Gray interjects, siding with Ryker.

Before I can utter those magical three words back as I continue to break his heart, Axel moves between us, standing in front of me protectively.

"We promised her that we wouldn't try to control her actions, like you're doing now. We promised her a home, a family, and we all fucking know how crazy this woman is."

"She's putting herself in danger," Emmett grunts, but there's no strength to his words. He's already conceding.

"Maybe," Axel grunts, glancing over his shoulder with a sad smile touching the corners of his mouth. "But she's also doing what she does best. Surviving."

I roll my Harley to a stop by the gates leading into the Devil's Brutes' compound. It's now or never, and for the first time, I'm walking toward danger with a tinge of nerves rocking my body. I take my helmet off and ruffle my hair, before I swing my leg over the machine and stretch out my limbs. I can already feel the eyes of the Brutes at the guard booth by the gates, but I take my time.

They need to think I'm girly, obsessed with looking cute for Kincaid. Not that I'm here to fucking slaughter him. I'm mic'd up with audio and visual for the guys, but it was too risky putting an earpiece in, so they can hear me, but I can't catch a word back. I'm going in blind and deaf, but the disadvantage doesn't matter.

Running my hands over my fitted combat pants, I lift them to straighten my leather jacket as I move to their little booth. "Hey," I say with a smile, flicking my hair over my shoulder. They run their eyes over me from head to toe, and I giggle under their attention. It's probably a good thing I can't hear my guys right now. They wouldn't be impressed.

"What are you doing around here, little lady?" the older guy asks, a thin beard reaching down to his chest as he peers at me.

"Kincaid."

"Impossible. He never invites pussy over, no matter how good it is," he replies, a leery grin on his face as he scratches his cheek.

"He does for mine," I promise, nodding toward the phone hooked up on the wall. "Why don't you give him a call and tell him Scarlett's here. He'll want me."

The pair of them eye me like I'm crazy, but the younger guy with a cigarette hanging out of his mouth relents. "When he declines the offer, I'll take you for a spin, yeah?" he says, wagging his eyebrows, but I don't respond, knowing full well he just earned a bullet through his skull from one of my guys later.

His eyes remain locked on me as he hits the call button and brings the phone to his ear. It rings a few times before a muffled sound comes through the phone. I wish I was close enough to hear what was being said. "Prez, there's a lady here claiming you invited her… I'm not lying, I swear," he says with a chuckle, dragging on his cigarette. "I told her that too, offered her a good time, but she's insisting that if I tell you her name is Scarlett, you'll—" His face pales, the voice coming through the phone booming now, but I still can't piece it together. "Yes, boss. Sorry, boss," he mumbles, before dropping the phone and rushing to press the button that controls the gates.

Taking a step back, I smile at them, but he's whispering into the older guy's ear, both avoiding my gaze purposely. I take that as my cue to head inside. I don't rush my pace as I make my way up the driveway. I slow down close to where I'm sure I was the last time I was on this side of the gates. A crimson fleck on the ground makes me wonder if it's from when I crushed that cunt's skull with the SUV door, but I'll never be sure.

The building comes into view. It looks a little bigger than the Ruthless Brothers', and the layout is a little different too. It's still a single-story, but it goes out wide to both the left and right of the main doors sitting front and center of the property where Kincaid stands.

There's a wicked grin on his face as I approach, and when I'm a few yards out, he knocks on the door behind him and two men step out. Dressed in black jeans, black tees, and their black leather cuts, they look like something off the television, but unfortunately, this is my reality.

"Search her, boys," Kincaid orders, and I come to a stop where I am.

I bite back the smile on my lips. I told the guys he would do this, and they didn't believe me, but with Shift's reassurance that I knew what I was doing, they listened to me. I know they trust me and my judgment, but I think putting me in danger goes against their nature. It's not a quick fix, and I'm sure I would be the same if it was the other way around.

One of them pats their hands over my arms, along my shoulders, down my back and around my waist, while the other starts at my feet, tucking their hands into my combat boots before working their way up my legs, and coming to my hips. I'm expecting one of them to go for the apex of my thighs, but unsurprisingly, Kincaid stops them.

"That's enough, don't touch her anywhere else." He crooks his finger for me to follow him. "Take a break, boys, this is personal."

Fixing my smile, I saunter in after him. The doors lead into a hallway. I make sure to move my whole body as I'm looking around so the guys can catch a glimpse too. Church is to the left, a club area to the right, and another corridor at the end of the walkway leading off in both directions.

He steps into the large open space of the club, a bar at the very back with a door beside it, while the rest of the space is filled with tables and chairs. Two women are talking together at one of the setups near the liquor, and he whistles, gaining their attention. "Out, now," he grunts, and they rush to their feet, barreling past us without a word, but the fear on their faces was clear.

I'm not shocked. He's a completely different kind of leader than Ryker. He's much more like my father, gaining control by wielding fear instead of trust. That's why they're not in the same league. Ryker stands for everything that's essential to the club as a whole, this man only cares for himself. Even when I was a child, it was the same.

"I'm not going to lie, Scarlett, I'm shocked to see you. Especially alone," he states, coming to a stop by the bar, and I keep a few feet between us. "How did you get away from them?"

"From who?"

"Don't play dumb, Scarlett," he grunts, reaching for an empty glass and a bottle of tequila. He pours himself a shot and downs it, but when I still haven't responded, he specifies, "How did you get away from the Ruthless Brothers?"

I shrug. "It wasn't hard. They don't track my every movement, so I got on my bike and came out here."

"And how did you know where to look for me?" He braces his elbows on the table, assessing me as I shrug again.

"Does it matter? I didn't tell them where to find you."

"How, Scarlett?" He bites, slamming his glass down.

"When I escaped your men at the gates."

His eyes rake over me from head to toe. "How is it you escaped them exactly?"

We're getting off track here, and I really don't have the energy to waste on this. "I feel like we should get to the point of why I'm here now. Where is she?" I ask, and he shrugs, feigning innocence, but the glint in his eyes tells me he knows exactly what I'm talking about.

"Who?"

"The girl you took when you had your little letter dropped off for me earlier," I reply, pulling the cream paper from my pocket and waving it between us.

His smile spreads as he shakes his head. "You're telling me all I had to do was kidnap someone you care about? I could have done this years ago and eliminated all of this time between us?"

"I had no one I cared about years ago," I admit, as he circles his finger around the rim of the glass.

"You could have had me. You could have always had me, Scarlett, but you let your daddy take you from the room that night," he states, shaking his head in disappointment. He edges closer to me, reaching out to touch my chin with his finger, the move surprisingly gentle. "Imagine what our lives could have been like if you had let me take you away to safety back then."

"I don't think you were offering me safety, Kincaid. I was a child, and you were offering me things I shouldn't have even known existed." I make sure to keep my tone neutral, but inside, my heart feels like it's going to burst at the seams.

"Hmm, I would have offered you anything you wanted if I'd had your pussy that night."

"Are you forgetting how old I was?" I retort, but he's

completely unfazed. For such a beautiful man, his soul is twisted beyond repair.

He shrugs. "You would have been mine."

"I can be yours now if you let her go."

Kincaid rocks back on his heels, pursing his lips. "But you're not a virgin now, are you, little Scarlett?"

"No," I admit, shaking my head lightly. "I lost that to a one-night stand that's back to haunt me," I explain, faking a shiver.

"Back to haunt you? Tell me more." He drops his hand from my face, tucking them into his pockets as he tilts his head.

"It's nothing, just some guy from another club. I didn't realize he was connected to the Ruthless Brothers and now it's not so safe there for me anymore." His eyebrows furrow, slowly piecing together who I mean, but I explain further to push the final nail into the coffin because I know it's going to piss him off. "His name is Declan? His dad is called Graham or something, he—"

"I know who he is. I didn't realize he took something that was mine," he murmurs, sweeping his tongue over his bottom lip as he looks at me. "I must admit; after the stories Molly fed me about you, I was sure you were a little tornado of rage, but here you are, as pliant as I remember."

Huffing, I roll my eyes. "Molly? Please, that girl was jealous of me the second I stepped through the doors at the Ruthless Brothers. I was fresh meat, new pussy, but she kept spinning webs of lies to try to keep the men away from me. If anything, she did me a favor. I was looking for safety and security, not a bunch of STDs," I retort, lying through my teeth. "I haven't seen her the past few days though, so things were starting to get a bit rougher for me. Which is why everything with my friend was a surprise, but... I'm hoping you can be my savior."

Holy shit, I'm really laying it on thick. I'm even doubting myself right now, god fucking knows what the guys are thinking.

"You are something else, Scarlett Reeves."

"Is that a good thing or a bad thing?" I ask, fluttering my lashes as I stuff the letter back in my pocket.

"That's yet to be decided," he grunts, folding his arms over his chest.

"How about you let my friend go," I repeat, not wanting to utter her name to him. He doesn't deserve it. "And I'll give you what you want... What is it you asked for? Me on my knees..."

I slowly move to drop down to one knee, but he reaches out and stops me with his hand on my arm. "Not here," he breathes. Pulling me back up to my full height, he slips his hand to mine, lifting my knuckles to his lips as he kisses them, and I have to hold the bile burning up my throat. "Doing this for you doesn't erase what the Ruthless

Brothers owe me."

"Obviously, that's their debt to settle. I just want to protect myself and my friend. You can offer that, Kincaid."

He groans and shakes his head. "My name sounds so good on your lips."

I smirk, pressing my teeth into my tongue so hard I'm sure I taste copper. "Take me to her and I'll say it all you want."

He grips my hand tighter and turns for the door beside the bar. It's not until he pushes it open that I realize where it leads, and my heart plummets in my chest.

The basement.

Fuck, fuck, fuck, fuck, fuck.

My feet stumble, my entire body going numb, but I push through the pain. She's worth it.

Exhaling harshly, I try to refrain from trembling, but the way Kincaid looks back over his shoulder tells me he feels it. We reach the bottom step and I feel light-headed, especially when I blink around the room and don't see the telltale traits of Emily's face anywhere. It's just a basement, with a table set up in the middle, and it slowly fucking dawns on me, that this is exactly where I was when I first met Kincaid… where he…

"Where is she?" I ask through clenched teeth, and he smirks at me.

"She's not here."

"I'm gathering that, where the fuck is she?" I grunt, struggling to keep my composure with my surroundings overwhelming me.

"In the one place you'll never look." He releases my hand and moves around the table, eyes still fixed on me the entire time.

Confusion clouds my vision as a red mist casts over me. I repeat Joshua's words in my head.

Once. Twice. Three times, and then it clicks.

He mentioned something about you not knowing where he's hiding so it doesn't matter once they're behind the compound lines.

Kincaid wasn't referring to himself when he said that to Joshua, and he wasn't talking about his own compound.

Fuck.

"You fucker, I know where she is," I state, not really talking to him now. I'm praying the signal goes through to the guys while I'm down here because it's them that I need to hear this if they haven't managed to work it out for themselves.

"You don't know shit," he says with a chuckle, taking off his cut and laying it out flat on the table.

"She's with Declan at the Ruthless Brothers' compound."

THIRTY

Scarlett

"**W**hy would you be assuming she's with Declan?" His head tilts to the side, eyes boring into me as he braces his palms on the large worktop between us. There's a handgun and a dirty blade before him, and I can't decide whether he's going to reach for them or not. As long as he's not catching on to the fact that I'm talking to someone else and not him, I can handle the consequences. Cocking a brow at him, I match him with a pointed stare of my own, but before I can answer him, he continues, "I'm guessing it's for the exact same reason I know you're talking a whole lot of bullshit about the Ruthless Brothers."

As he utters the last word, the door at the top of the stairs slams shut, and the gut-wrenching sound of a lock slamming into place vibrates through me. I try with all my strength to remain as composed as possible, but my eyes drift closed with the fear that trickles down my spine.

There's a fucking reason I don't go into basements anymore, and my worst fear is playing out before me.

"I don't know what you mean," I murmur, sticking with playing dumb as I flutter my eyelids open.

"Don't play games with me, Scarlett," he snarls, slamming his fist against the table. "I saw you with two of them this morning on campus. I'm not stupid."

Shit. So I had seen him. Fucking creeper.

Sighing, I tuck my hair behind my ear. "You saw exactly what I wanted everyone around me to see and them to feel. There's nothing more to it than that."

"Bull. Shit."

I shrug, which only seems to irritate him further. "You can believe what you want. I know the truth."

Slowly, he moves around the table between us, dragging his fingers over it as he keeps his gaze fixed on me. "I think I'm starting to believe Molly more and more, little Scarlett."

"Hmm, that's never good for anyone." I shake my head in amusement, holding my ground as he leans back against the table a few steps away from me.

"How would you come to the assumption that your friend is with Declan?" Apparently, he's not going to let that comment go, and I need to address it if I want to play it off.

"Because I know he's working for you." I roll my eyes as an extra measure, downplaying the entire thing as his gaze narrows.

"How?"

"Because I have a functioning brain, that's how," I grumble, folding my arms over my chest. I'm definitely channeling my inner Molly right now. She gave me a few good pointers on how to be a dumb bitch.

Kincaid smirks, but it's still a touch too close to manic and crazed for my liking. "I like it when you get sassy. It's going to make punishing you so much more fun."

Yup. Definitely manic and crazed.

Smiling at him like I'm acutely aware of his threat is harder than I care to admit. "Fine, I know he's working for you because he was obvious as hell when you sent your men to the compound. The last time at least. I watched how he responded to the situation. If anything, you should be proud you have a loyal servant in him. With Ryker and the guys preoccupied with the Devil's Brutes' arrival, he sidled up to the table, hand poised on his weapon ready to take anyone and everyone out." I take a step toward him this time, making it clear I'm docile and not a threat to him. "And before you ask, I notice these things because you don't grow up with a father like mine and not learn to watch for this kind of stuff. Especially with the Ice Reapers, everyone always had a hidden agenda."

He steeples his fingers on his lips, glancing down at me like he's trying to make me feel smaller under his intense gaze. "And you haven't told them?"

My eyebrows pinch. "Why would I be the one to tell them? I'm not a Ruthless Brother, I'm just a whore."

"Not to them, you're not, that's what Molly said at least. Even Declan agrees that they're blinded by you."

Bingo. Way to confirm he's one of your fucking weasels.

"I think the question that remains is, do I blind you? Or could you see me as an asset too? If that's what it takes for you to free my friend, I'll do it."

He takes a step toward me, then another, and another, until there's barely any space between us. "You're a mystery to me, Scarlett," he says, and I still can't fully gauge his mindset.

"How about you make the call and release her, give me evidence that you've done so, and I won't be so mysterious by the time we're done," I offer, relaxing every tense muscle in my body to make him think he has a calming effect over me. I know he's able to read body language just as well as I can, his background may not be as twisted as mine, or possibly it is, but I know it's as merciless. The need to survive is as strong for him as it is for me.

He drops his hands to his sides, smiling slightly as he eliminates the remaining space between us, and I almost think I have him until he engulfs my throat with his giant hand. My eyes widen, but not from the surprise of his move. It's from the burning need inside of me to get his fucking paws off me, but he's never going to believe I'm pliant if I fight him right now.

"We're locked down here, Scarlett. I can take you whether I do what you ask or not," he bites, rattling me in his hold.

"Are you trying to relive our youth?" I rasp, smirking at him like his hold doesn't faze me. "I didn't realize your kink was non-consensual sex. It's not something I've been involved with before." I've heard of it being consensually done, but that's definitely not what he's hinting at. The gleam in his eyes tells me he wants it to hurt, on his terms, and against my will.

He's cruel, heartless, and vile.

Without responding, he spins and pushes me backward so the table edge slams into the base of my spine, and I grunt, but at least he's dropped his hold on me for a second.

I brace my hands behind me on the table top, eyeing his moves as he slowly stalks toward me. "Molly said you were powerful with a weapon, destructive, and the reason half of my men are dead."

Shaking my head, I stare directly into his eyes. "Did you fuck her by any chance? Because if you did, then she thinks you're hers, just like she did with the Ruthless

Brothers. Some of the shit she's said about me has caused me nothing but issues." Sighing, I wet my lips. "Honestly, Kincaid, I'm just a girl trying to survive by whatever means necessary. This life isn't normal, not like it is for the rest of the world. In this little sliver of life, it's all about making it to the next day. I'm not trying to get in anyone's way, but I'm trying to protect myself too."

I want to puke at the bullshit spewing from my mouth, especially because I can't tell whether he's falling for it or not.

He braces his hands on either side of the table at my waist, leaning in close so the tips of our noses are almost touching. "Why do you keep talking about her like she's not dead?"

"Wait, what?" I balk, searching his eyes and lifting my hand to my chest like his words hurt me. "She's not dead."

"It seems those boys don't keep you quite as close as you think, do they?"

"What do you mean? They didn't kill her. They wouldn't. Shit, even when I threatened it in fits of anger, they still intervened."

He shakes his head, trailing his hands down my sides until he slips his fingers through the belt loops on my pants. Seamlessly, he lifts me up onto the table, just like that, forcing his way between my thighs.

"I can't decide whether you're lying or not..."

"That's irrelevant to me. I already told you, I know the truth and I have no reason at all to lie to you."

"You also want to survive, Scarlett. You just told me that yourself." He leans in closer, bringing his lips to my ear. "You're a snake just like your father was, and you coming here does nothing to help your friend. All it does is render you defenseless to me." He grabs my crotch, claiming it as his, at the same time I feel the leather handle of the blade behind me.

"I've never been helpless, Kincaid. Not ever." I sink my teeth into his ear, biting hard as I drive the blade blindly into his stomach. His skin tears at my mouth as he grunts, pushing to get away from me. He staggers back, blood gushing down his neck from the wound, or loss of flesh at the bottom of his ear... leaving the small piece between my lips.

I spit it out in disgust, threatening to puke everywhere, but manage to keep a hold of the blade in my hand as he gapes at me. His mouth slams shut, settling into a thin line as his nostrils flare and anger ripples from him.

"You stupid fucking bitch, you're going to regret that," he hisses, before lunging at me. I swipe the dagger at him as I try to jump down to my feet. I catch his chest with the tip, but he still manages to slam his fist into the side of my head.

I lose my footing as my boots hit the ground, and I

can't keep my balance as I topple sideways to the floor, clutching the blade like my life depends on it. My cheek burns from the contact of his fist, and he doesn't give me a second to recover, kicking me in the stomach and knocking the air from my lungs.

Motherfucker.

Swinging my legs and arms, I try to catch him with whatever I can, but he doesn't make it easy. I hate fighting scrappy like this; there's no precision, no finesse, just survival.

"Bitch, keep still," he grunts, grabbing at my hair, but I slam the knife into his arm the second he lifts my head off the ground, and a guttural groan burns from his lips. His grip slackens as liquid drops onto my face, and I realize immediately that it's blood.

Clutching the knife in my hand, I manage to kick him to the side and rise to my knees, but before I can try to get to my feet, a boot smashes me in the face. Black spots form behind the back of my eyelids, the world spinning around me as the pounding of my heart rings in my ears. I sloppily swipe a hand down my face, crimson staining my palms as I smear Kincaid's blood across my skin. It does nothing to clear my foggy vision, only making the situation ten times harder from my position on the floor.

I knew taking him down would be hard, but fuck, have I overestimated myself?

"Look what you've done," he yells, waving his bleeding arm everywhere as blood seeps into his clothes from the wound, along with the mess from his ear. Yet he's still on top right now, looking down at me with fury as I struggle to even breathe, never mind fighting back.

He reaches for the collar of my t-shirt, lifting my back off the ground as he growls in my face, and I'm slowly sinking into a dark pit of despair. My body can't catch up to my brain, even though neither are working at full speed, but I'm helpless in his hands.

A slam sounds around us, overwhelming my already frazzled senses, and he snarls, "Shut the fucking door behind you, boys, we don't need everyone watching the fun we're about to have."

My tongue is like lead in my mouth. I will my arms to lift and fight back, for my legs to kick out at him, but thinking it and doing it are two very different things.

Footsteps echo down the stairs as Kincaid's snarl turns into a sinister smile, pleased with the backup he's got, but when he glances over his shoulder, the look on his face quickly drops. My world spins once more as he lifts me, and with my next breath, my back is plastered to his chest, our bodies aligned from head to toe.

Blinking, I instantly understand the reason why I've suddenly become a human shield.

Two to be more specific.

"Are you with me, Rebel?" I nod subtly at Ryker, hating how much of a failure I look at this moment. So much so that I barely meet his gaze, or Axel's, as he stands beside him. They've both got a gun aimed in our direction, and Kincaid chuckles.

"Lower your fucking guns or she dies."

"How about you let go of her and I don't torture you as much as I planned. I'll make it quick and relatively painless," Ryker counter offers, but that only seems to piss Kincaid off as he rattles me in his grasp. I'm still not completely functional, so there is nothing I can do but accept it.

"Drop your weapons or I kill her," he bites back, reaching for my limp arm and lifting it in the air so the dagger in my hand is aimed at myself. His fingers wrap around mine before I can try to drop it, but panic doesn't set in, if anything, I can see clearer than ever.

Lifting my blurry eyes to Ryker, I exhale. "Take the shot."

His gaze flickers between Kincaid and me, but when the president of the Devil's Brutes tightens his hold on me, Ryker slowly lowers his gun to the floor.

Fuck.

My eyes slam shut, frustration getting the better of me. I hate that I'm being used as a weapon against them, a barrier in the way of bringing this fucker down. I can chase the fuckers hurting *my* weakness, but actively being someone else's weakness feels like the end.

Taking another deep breath, I force my eyes open, blinking a few times so I can focus a little better, but this time, I settle my stare on Axel who is already staring intently at me.

"Take the fucking shot, Ax," I repeat, firmer this time, and the world slows.

His hand flexes around the gun, his tongue flicking out as he considers his options. Kincaid's chest rumbles with a chuckle against my back, the sound piercing to my ears as he clenches my fist tighter. The tip of the blade presses into my neck, nicking the skin. Ryker inches forward, considering whether to get his gun back or not, but none of that matters.

A cold glaze drops over Axel's features, his decision made as he aims the gun up by an inch. The laughter stops, the hold on me softens at the same time a boom rings out, and a bullet flies in my direction.

Kincaid ducks, leaving me to stand on my own wobbly feet as I accept my fate, falling backwards as the world goes black.

RUTHLESS BROTHERS MC

THIRTY ONE

Emmett

Wind whips by us as we speed down road after road. My foot is pressed down so hard on the accelerator pedal, I'm surprised it hasn't broken through the floor of the SUV. Fear creeps down my spine as I put more and more distance between me and the woman I love, but hopefully cutting the distance between me and my sister.

My heart is torn, split between the two people it beats for. Anger zaps through my veins, and I slam my fist into the steering wheel. "I'm never going to forgive myself for driving away from her."

"Emmett, you and I both know she would never forgive herself or us if we didn't," Shift states from his seat beside me. I know it's true, but it doesn't ease the tension rising inside of me.

I grunt in response, no words summarizing my thoughts

as I pray for the SUV to go faster. The quicker I get back to the compound, the quicker I can hopefully be free to race back to Scarlett.

My mind replays everything we watched and heard on the setup Shift had put together. When she pieced together where Emily must be, my heart soared, but then I realized the distance between the two. My soul plummeted when Ryker gave the order I couldn't dare speak.

Shift and I were to leave, while the three of them stayed to get her out.

After watching her put on a show for him, luring him in with a web of bullshit to release Emily, I could barely breathe. I was sure the end was coming, ready to cause a damn riot in their compound, but when he opened the doors to the basement, my blood ran cold. The sound of her breathing became more labored with every step she took down there. We were already packing and ready to hit them hard when she said Declan's name.

Fuck.

It's causing me more pain that Shift left the camera feed with the others, leaving us blind. It's a blessing and a curse all at once. I need to know what's happening, but fear would pull me off the road and away from my current assignment. That would only make the distance between us mean nothing at all, and I need to trust the other guys.

Swerving between cars on a busy afternoon wasn't how

I was planning on spending my time, but when I finally see the compound up ahead, none of it matters. I hear Shift murmuring on his cell beside me, and the gate opens in time for me to not brake, before we come skidding to a stop at the compound doors.

I don't switch the engine off, I don't shut the door behind me, and I don't look at anyone or anything until I'm through the main door and have eyes on Declan. He's sitting in a booth with his father and some of their men. As I charge toward him, the thud of my boots hitting the ground is masked by the bass from the music. I see a flash of Maggie in my peripheral vision, but brush her off for Shift to handle as I grab the back of Declan's cut and yank him from his seat.

"Where the fuck is she?" I growl, pushing him toward the table behind him as he bends backward, arms up in surrender between us.

"What the fuck, Emmett?"

"Where. The. Fuck. Is. She?"

"What are you talking about?"

Rage slams through me at his bullshit attempt at playing dumb. "I will carve out your organs one at a fucking time, before severing your dick and making you choke on it if you don't tell me where the fuck she is in the next ten seconds."

"Boys, what the fuck is happening right now?" Graham

grunts as the music cuts out and the room goes silent.

I tighten my hold on Declan as I glare at his father. "Fuck off, Graham. Your son's been working with Kincaid the entire time you've been here."

"What?" His shocked grunt isn't a surprise, it was obvious he had no clue.

"Yeah. Just like Molly was, but we wanted to see how things played out. Unfortunately, your time's up," I snap, pulling Declan back up as I snarl in his face. "Now, where the fuck is she?"

"I still don't know—"

Screw this motherfucker.

Rearing my fist back, I smash him in the face. The crunch that sounds out and the blood that instantly pours from his mouth and nose is nowhere near as satisfying as I had hoped.

"What the fuck?" he splutters, pissing me off more as Graham slowly rises to his feet at my right.

"This is your final chance, Declan," Shift warns, knocking the safety off his gun and aiming it in the asshole's direction. "Tell us where Emily is or I will put a bullet between your eyes. I really don't give a shit."

"You can't touch me." He sneers, spitting blood onto my cut. I lift my hand back once more, but this time, a hand closes around mine. Turning my head to stare Graham down, I'm ready to give him a fucking warning by association, but he stops me with a shake of his head.

Resignation drops his features, disappointment carving frown lines into his forehead as he turns to look at his son.

"Tell them, son, or I'll watch it happen."

"You aren't listening to me… none of you can touch me," he repeats, swiping the back of his hand across his face.

"That's exactly what Molly said before we killed her. See where I'm going with this," I grind out, really hating that it's taking this long to get answers.

He shakes his head. "I'm under the protection of local law enforcement."

"That means absolutely nothing to—"

My cell phone rings in my pocket, cutting me off. I can't leave it in case it's something to do with Scarlett, so I toss Declan toward Shift as I reach into my pocket for it. My eyebrows knit in confusion as the incoming call flashes with an unknown number.

Nothing good ever comes from an unknown number.

Steeling my spine, I press the green button and lift the device to my ear "Hello?"

"Emmett, it's been a while… again." Ice slices through my veins at Hartman's voice in my ear and my gaze narrows on the traitor now in Shift's grasp. "I have your sister here. Unfortunately, I've had to arrest her for intentionally inflicting physical harm to me, knowingly placing me in imminent danger, and deliberately laying hands on me to provoke me."

"Bullshit," I bite, a film of red coating my vision.

"It's true. I have witnesses of her hitting me with intent to cause harm."

"Intention to fucking escape you, there's a difference."

"Hmm, that's to be seen really, but for now, she'll do well in my custody. It may tame her a little." He's practically singing, the smug tone to his voice is infuriating.

Shift nudges my shoulder while still restraining Declan, and when he nods at the cell, I know he wants to know what's going on. Putting the cell on speakerphone, I lift it higher in the air. "When I get down to the station, I'm going to murder you."

"Are you threatening an officer?" This cunt really knows how to get under my skin.

"It's not a threat, it's a promise of vengeance."

He chuckles, excited with the uproar he's causing. "Good luck with that… I'm not even at the fucking station."

The muscles in my neck bunch, my anger reflecting back at me in Shift's eyes.

"Then you haven't actually booked her? You're just detaining her because you know this is a bunch of bullshit." Silence extends between us, pain ricocheting through me before he clears his throat.

"Semantics. Payback's a bitch."

The call ends, driving me insane as I turn my focus to Declan.

"Where is he?"

He chuckles, head lulling back as he hums. "Don't know. Don't care."

"Shame," Shift bites, lifting his gun to Declan's temple and pulling the trigger without missing a beat. His body slumps to the floor as Shift swipes at an invisible piece of lint on his jacket.

Every inch of my body tingles with the eyes watching us, but the most important ones are Graham's, who stands with his palms pressed against the table before him, looking down at his dead son with a solemn look on his face.

"I will not retaliate for this, but my men are no longer at your disposal," he says, and I shrug.

"Then get your shit packed and get the fuck out of here. I have bigger issues to deal with than wondering where you are." He nods once, staring down at Declan as he draws the sign of the cross at his chest, before turning to leave.

"How the fuck do we figure out where he is?" Shift asks, jaw set tight with frustration as my nostrils flare with anger.

"Check the security cameras," I grunt, recalling Axel taking Scarlett with him to set them up at the deputy's home. Shift is already moving, not bothering to respond to me as he goes in search of the only lead we have.

THIRTY TWO

Scarlett

It feels like I'm floating in water, drifting out to sea without any support or any worries to go with it. It's a thought that confuses me, because I've never actually been to the ocean. Not open water like that, the closest I've been is to the waterfall… I think?

"Come on, Scarlett. You have to wake up." The voice sounds familiar, but it's like they're miles away, like whispers on the wind. A hand strokes down my face, and I try my best to lean into the touch.

My fingers trail from someone's eyebrow, down to their chin which is covered in a beard. It takes me a moment, but I manage to blink my eyes open to see one of the hottest guys I've ever laid eyes on.

His face softens as he looks deep into my eyes, and I get the sense that he's familiar. I feel comfortable in his presence, which is reassuring, but the brain fog is taking its toll on me. Frowning, I clutch his t-shirt with one hand and cup his cheek with the other. "Am I dead? Is this heaven?"

I breathe, and a chuckle echoes in my ears like the sweetest music.

"You wish, Reaper."

My eyes slam shut, the word Reaper on his tongue jolting me from my bleariness. "Axel?"

"You got it. Can you remember your name?"

I peer up at him, eyebrows furrowed. "Scarlett. Why are you asking me that?"

"Do you know where you are?" I slowly lift my head to glance around the room, not entirely sure where I am until I lay eyes on the dead body beside me.

Kincaid.

"We're at the Devil's Brutes' compound," I mumble, my memory coming back to me in small pieces.

"And who is your favorite Ruthless Brother?" he asks, and I turn to glare at him.

"Don't be an asshole, Axel," I grumble, and a chuckle sounds from behind me.

"Yeah, Axel, don't be an asshole," Ryker mocks, brushing his hair back off his face as he smiles at me.

"So, I'm not dead or in heaven then?"

"You think that's where you're heading?" Axel asks, cocking a brow at me, and I pout, stroking my hand obsessively down his face while my hand at his t-shirt yanks him closer.

"Obviously not, but where else would I have the luxury of being able to touch you?" I sound delirious, feel it too, when I pause, slowly ticking over what it is I'm actually doing. I pull my hand away from him like he's on fire. "Oh my God, I'm so fucking sorry," I rush, my chest constricting with panic.

"Shut up, you idiot. I'm just glad you're okay. Like I almost lost you for a second time, your touch lets me know you're real. That being said, I'd rather we didn't go for a third, okay?"

"Uh-huh," I mumble in agreement as he grabs my hand from my chest and puts it back on his face. "Did the bullet hit me?"

"Please, does it feel like the bullet hit you? I'm a good fucking shot, Scar," he retorts, and Ryker scoffs.

Tilting my head to the side, my grin spreads. "You are?"

His eyes narrow, but he presses a kiss to the center of my palm before releasing my hand and rising to his feet. He offers to help me stand and I take it. The room tilts and sways as I try to get my balance and the back of my head hurts like a bitch.

"What happened if it wasn't the bullet?" I ask, glancing around the room, but my gaze quickly locks on Kincaid, and I can't tear it away.

"You didn't have your balance when he released his hold on you and you smacked your head on the table," Ryker explains, coming to stand in front of me with a soft smile on his face. "I'm sorry I couldn't make the shot, Rebel. With you between us, I was too scared."

I can tell he hates to admit that, and despite the fact that I hate being their weakness, it makes my heart melt that he put me first.

"Thank you... both of you. What the hell do we do now? His men must be coming if..."

"There's no fucker coming. The compound is empty, bar the couple of dead guys we killed. I don't know if there will be others heading back here, but I think now is a good time to leave." Footsteps echo down the stairs, and I glance up to see Gray trudging toward us with blood splattered over his face and clothes.

"Gray," I murmur, relieved to see him as a wicked smile spreads across his face.

"Hey, Sweet Cheeks, we've got a lot of chatting to do, but for now, we need to get the fuck out of here. I'm excellent at burning MCs down, but preferably while we're not in it," he remarks with a wink before pulling me into his chest.

"I love you," I murmur softly, saying it to all of them, though my head is buried in Gray's t-shirt.

"We love you too," they mutter, and my heart soars. Where's my fourth?

"Where's Emmett? Wait, why the hell are you guys all here when I told you where to look for Emily?" I push out of Gray's hold, glaring at the three of them.

"I was waiting for this," Ryker states, throwing his arm around my shoulder as he guides me back toward the stairs. "You didn't think we were all going to race back to the compound and leave you here alone when we literally fucking saw you go down into a basement, did you?"

"Well…"

"Sometimes, you're crazier than I think," Axel says, wagging a finger at me before leading the way.

"Shift and Emmett raced back to the compound. We haven't heard from them since," Gray explains, and worry rattles me. I hate the feeling more than anything else in the world. Worry, anxiousness, fear, they all roll through me, now more than ever since there are people to be concerned for.

Stepping into the club area, I notice four dead Brutes. I move around them, slower than usual, it seems the knock to the head took more out of me than I want to admit. Axel travels through to the main doors which are already open, and surveys the area one last time, while Gray holds up behind us as an extra precaution.

More dead Brutes scatter the ground out here, but Axel

doesn't pay them any mind as he moves to our SUV which is parked hazardously in the middle of the driveway. Axel climbs into the driver's seat, and Ryker tucks me into the back before sliding in beside me. I panic for a second when I realize Gray isn't with us and Axel's starting the engine.

"What about…" I trail off as Gray runs like hell from the compound as Axel leans across the center console to swing the passenger door open. He leaps into the seat, slamming the door shut behind him.

"Let's go," he yells, manic excitement glinting across his face as Axel does just that. We're barely at the gates when a boom rattles the ground, vibrating the vehicle, and I glance over my shoulder to see billowing smoke and flames cascading over the compound. Gray claps his hands excitedly, and Axel grins.

"And they say I'm the crazy one," he grunts, speeding out of there without another backward glance.

"We're all fucking Ruthless, it's a requirement," Gray replies, settling into his seat as Ryker drapes his arm around my shoulders and pulls me into his side.

Tension starts to seep from my bones, exhaustion threatening to take over, but I refuse to sleep. "We need to call Emmett," I murmur, and Gray waves his cell phone at me.

"Already on it." Emmett's name flashes across the

screen before he answers it and immediately puts it on speakerphone.

"Brother."

"He doesn't have her." My heart seizes up at the anguish in Emmett's voice.

"What?" Axel bites, hands gripping the steering wheel so tightly I think it's going to snap off.

"Hartman does. He's claiming he arrested her, but they're not at lock up, or so he says," Emmett explains, without really explaining anything.

"How and why the fuck does he have her?" Ryker hisses from beside me, and Axel seems to hit the accelerator even harder.

"All part of Declan's plan apparently."

"And where is that motherfucker now?" I bite, furious that I didn't just let them kill him when they wanted to.

"Dead... Shift did it."

I can't tell if he sounds pleased or irritated by that fact. Like he expected it to be his right, but Shift took it anyway.

"Have Shift pull up the security feed we set up," Axel orders, and Emmett sighs through the line.

"Already on it, but nothing is coming up at his house. They're not there."

"Shit."

We need a plan, an action, something... we can't be at a dead end.

"Pass me the fucking cell phone," Maggie snaps, in frustration.

My eyebrows pinch as I sit up straight and glance at Ryker who looks just as confused as me.

"Maggie?"

A huff comes through the line like she's taking a deep breath but it's doing nothing to calm her stress. "I spoke to Delia at the diner."

Gray sits tall in his seat. "What? Why?"

"She's my friend, Gray, the one I went to see on Friday, you idiot," she grumbles, but that doesn't seem to pacify him.

"Wait what?"

"Not now, Gray."

"When did you speak with her?" He pushes, still not giving up on the fact his mom has a friend.

"Just now," she says with a sigh.

"Why?"

"If you would shut up for a fucking minute, you would know because I'm trying to explain," she grouches, making me grin despite the circumstances.

A snarl comes through the line, but it's not from her. "Can you get to the point? The woman I love is in danger and you guys are driving me insane."

Shift.

Fuck.

That shuts Gray up as I lean forward in my seat, desperate to be closer to the cell phone like it will make a difference.

"The Sheriff has gone out of town and left Hartman in charge, but the other officers and staff can't stand him. So he refuses to go back to lock up where they will call him out on his bullshit." That confirms that he's not lying about being there, so there's no use checking it out, but it still doesn't give us a direction to go in.

"If he's not there and not at his house, then I don't know where to fucking look," I murmur, head in my hands as I try to stop the throbbing in my skull.

"Of course he's not…he's at the fucking diner, claiming neutral ground," Maggie hisses, making my spine stiffen, and I sit up straight, eyes wide as I gape at Ryker.

"That motherfucker. We're going to have to draw him out. But how?" Axel says, my brain ticking into overdrive to come up with a solution.

"Who said anything about drawing him out?" Maggie retorts, almost pleased with herself, but there's an agreement in place. There always has been.

"We would be starting a war with everyone if we waded in on neutral ground and caused a riot," Ryker states.

"That may be the case for anyone else, but when a corrupt cop is holding the child of Delia's late husband's best friend hostage, then she feels like a debt is owed."

My mind swirls as I try to piece together what she means. I guess Eric, Emmett, and Emily's father must have been close with Delia's husband.

Holy shit.

This town really is too small to handle all of the drama.

"What does that mean for us, Ma?" Shift asks, his voice carrying through the cell phone as the hairs on the back of my neck stand on end with adrenaline.

"It means that motherfucker isn't ready for the ruthless riot coming his way."

THIRTY THREE

Scarlett

There's no time to clean up or to put a plan together. As much as my heart is beating wildly as we head back to the compound, I try to rest against Ryker with my eyes closed. I'll be useless without my strength, and the knock to the head is causing me more problems than I expected.

Ryker presses his lips to my forehead, and I flutter my eyelids open to see we're close to the compound. I can imagine Emmett and Shift are going crazy waiting, but Ryker was right to make the call that they couldn't meet us at the diner. They would have acted before we got there, and we don't truly know what we're up against from this stupid fucking man, so it's better to face it together as a unit rather than divided.

My body aches as I push off Ryker to sit up, but I shake it off. Night has fallen and this could either be to our advantage or it could bite us in the ass, but it doesn't change the fact that we're about to go to war. Darkness surrounds us, apart from the lights coming from the main building, as we slow to a stop in the driveway.

Shift is standing with his hands tucked into his pockets, Maggie murmuring into his ear as Emmett paces back and forth. Needing to check on him, I step from the vehicle and rush to him as quickly as I can. It's slow going, my brain trying to move me quicker than my body can withstand.

"Snowflake," he breathes, taking me in. He catches me as I launch myself at him, and his warmth wraps around me like a second skin, heating my soul. "What the fuck happened to you?"

"None of the blood is mine. I just have a really bad headache," I explain, and he lowers me back to my feet slowly, running his hand over my head delicately.

"There's blood all over your fucking chin. What happened?"

I grimace, wiping at the dried stain. "I may have accidentally, on purpose, bitten the bottom of Kincaid's right ear off."

I'm not sure if he's going to be sick at the thought or not, but Axel steps up to my side and interrupts.

"That's my fucking girl," he declares with a wide smile, and I remember that he bit Gray's ear.

"Nope, it's not the same. I bit the enemy, you bit my

blondie." I wag my finger at him, but it doesn't wipe the grin from his lips.

"Are you heading out?" Everyone whips their head to the man peeking through the double doors. I don't know his name, he's part of Graham's crew.

"In a minute, yes," Emmett states, uncertainty thickening his tone as the door swings open further and seven or eight men clamber out.

"Do you need some extra men?"

There seems to be something I'm completely missing with everyone, but I don't really have time to ask. "With Declan gone, Graham is already heading home. We refuse to stick with a club that operates like that. If you'll have us, even just for tonight, we'll assist with whatever you need."

It almost feels too good to be true. If this guy seemed shady at any other time, I would be calling bullshit, but the way Emmett nods in acceptance says he believes him.

"We can discuss things further tomorrow, but for tonight, you can ride," Ryker states, cutting the distance to shake each of their hands.

"Are we ready to go now?" Shift asks, jaw tense as he approaches, and my heart breaks for him. It feels like this morning was an eternity ago, but it wasn't. We've been on a wild goose chase ever since, and this man right here had to spend his time pretending like he wasn't madly in love with my best friend for god knows however long they've been keeping it a secret. Now she's in danger.

"Yes," Maggie answers, rushing down the steps as she straightens her leather jacket. The look on her face begs anyone not to question her involvement, and to my surprise, no one speaks a word about it as we all shuffle into the waiting vehicles.

Ryker organizes the prospects to divide between protecting the club and coming to the diner with us. but I don't hear him properly as I'm bundled in Gray's lap this time so there's enough space for us in the vehicle.

Axel doesn't fuck around getting us moving as soon as we're all seated, we're heading off into the dead of night again. Gray's hands draw circles on my thigh, while Emmett is squished up against us to my left, and he trails his finger over my palm.

Despite the storm that still continues to brew in front of us, I feel calm right now with my men close. Thankfully, the town roads are pretty quiet, and the diner light shines like a beacon in the distance, before we roll to a stop at the back of the parking lot.

Taking a deep breath before I step out of the vehicle, I squeeze Gray's hands as the wind whips around me. If the adrenaline wasn't keeping my bones warm, I'm sure I would shiver. Rows of bikes line up beside the three packed SUVs.

I take a step around the back of the vehicle to get to

Ryker, when a whistle sounds, short and sharp from the tree line to my left. At the noise, my men instantly appear around me, while the prospects stand guard by Maggie at the other SUV. When a man steps out from behind the big oak tree, Ryker's shoulders seem to relax as he steps toward him.

"Paisley, isn't it a bit beneath you to be hiding in bushes?" Ryker muses, but his tone is tight.

"There are Brutes lining the exterior of the diner, protecting Hartman inside," he explains, making my eyebrows quirk in surprise. He clearly knows why we're here, but how?

"Of course there is," Gray grunts, swiping a hand down his face as he sighs.

"What has you out here, P?" Axel asks, lighting up two cigarettes and handing one off to the man, who accepts it with a nod.

"Delia."

"Why?" Emmett asks, folding his arms over his chest defensively, but Paisley doesn't take him on.

"She called us in."

"What for?" Ryker asks, interrupting his VP from trying to push this guy, but again, he seems completely unfazed by their approach. They're either always like this with him or he just doesn't care.

He takes a deep pull of his cigarette, the ember burning

bright in the otherwise dimly lit area. "Boots on the ground for you. And before you ask me why again, it's because I'm soft as shit on that woman and she fucking knows it." Well, that really shouldn't be surprising. If I've learned anything since I've arrived at the Ruthless Brothers MC, it's that we do crazy stupid shit for love. "Besides, I can see from here that the girl he has with him is nowhere near as acclimated to this way of life in comparison to this little lady here," he states, pointing at me.

Any other time, I would fake innocence, but I'm literally covered in dried blood and none of it is mine. So there's no point even trying to argue it. True or not. I step out from between my men, and he squints his eyes, tilting his head to the side as he stares at me. "You have a familiar face."

Uhh… okay?

"What's your club?" I ask, irritation starting to flood through my veins with the fact that we're out here chatting and not helping Emily.

"Iron Scorpions."

It sounds familiar, and his name isn't all that common either, but I still feel like I've heard it before. "It sounds familiar, but right now, my best friend is in danger and that needs all of my attention," I offer, giving him a tight smile. I take a step back, hoping to get everyone else moving, but he isn't done questioning me yet.

"Is that why you're covered in blood?"

I glance over my shoulder at him. "Yeah."

"I'm nervous to ask but whose blood is it?" he replies with a smirk, and I shrug.

"It's Kincaid's."

The ember from his smoke makes it possible to see his eyebrows raise in surprise at my words. "As in the Devil's Brutes?"

I nod once, before turning back around and marching toward the diner. Catching him up to speed isn't on my agenda. Not when a flash of blonde hair and a familiar button nose is visible in the left corner of the diner.

"Scarlett," Shift hollers, the urgency clear in his tone, but I keep going.

That motherfucker has Emily, and he's sitting in Ryker's usual booth. That can't be a coincidence. It's all mind games with these assholes.

"It's better if I go in first alone, you know, since I don't wear a cut and I'm not even a little bit intimidating." Axel rolls his eyes, and I smirk.

Brushing past one of Graham's men, I unhook the gun from his hip before he even realizes it's gone. I don't slow my pace as I check it over, making sure it's loaded and knocking the safety off. I'm done with the bullshit rules that no one else follows, and I'm tired as shit. So I'm walking in there, getting my best friend, and passing the fuck out.

I manage to tuck it into the waistband of my pants before I reach the steps up to the diner, fully aware of the two Devil's Brutes standing on either side of the glass.

They both shuffle to block the door, sneers on their lips as a little red dot appears on both of their chests. "Lay a fucking finger on her and we will happily take the shots," Axel bites. I'm sure they're going to move to the side, but the guy on the right grins, slowly reaching out to press the tip of his finger against my shoulder.

"You wouldn't—"

He doesn't get to finish his sentence as the echo of the shot rings around us and the foolish Brute drops to the ground. Dead.

"Do you want to try your luck too?" I ask, grinning wickedly at the other Brute who is now gaping at his friend in shock.

"I'm good," he mumbles, clearing his throat as he steps to the side, but the sound of a bullet rings out and another body drops to the floor in a heap of limbs. Looking over my shoulder, I eye Axel, who shrugs.

"I didn't like his choice of leather."

Shaking my head at his antics, I step inside, taking a deep breath as I realize every single person in here, bar two, are wearing Devil's Brutes' cuts. They're watching me like a hawk, but despite two of their men dropping outside, no one immediately rushes me.

The two in here without a cut are sitting in the booth I'm after.

"Scarlett," Emily breathes, thick tears in her eyes. She looks roughed up, but at first glance, there's nothing too concerning.

"Come any closer and I kill her," Hartman bites, waving a gun in the air as I shake my head at him.

"That's not how it works, remember? This is neutral ground, isn't it? Axel can take his shot out there, but in here, everything changes," I say sweetly, dropping down into the booth beside Emily.

I want to reach out to her, bundle her in my arms and squeeze her tight, but that can only happen once the threat is taken care of.

Hartman snarls as the little bell over the door chimes.

"I'm not going to lie to you, Hartman, I can't for the life of me figure out how you piece together in all of this," I muse, tucking a loose tendril of hair behind my ear like my entire head isn't a fucking mess of unruly ends.

"That's none of your business," he grunts, body tense as if he's ready to pounce across the table at me.

Tilting my head to the side, I smile. "Was it drugs? Gambling? What…... what debt did you have to repay?"

His eyes widen as I mention gambling, giving this motherfucker away. As long as it's only a debt owed, then there's definitely no further use for him. Local law enforcement or not, he's done.

"Shut the fuck up, you stupid whore," he grinds out, pissing me off even more. I hate the use of that word as a slur. If I want to be a whore, I fucking will be.

When I slip out the handgun from my waistband, he can't see what I'm doing but the movement makes him skittish. The man's an idiot. He may be wielding a weapon, but it's still got the safety on so his reaction won't be fast enough. Smiling, I poise the gun in my hand.

"What the fuck are you doing?"

"What, me? I'm just a whore, right? Nothing to worry about."

His mouth opens. A response on the tip of his tongue, but he doesn't get a chance to say it as I pull the trigger. The shot rings out, his eyes widening and skin paling as Emily jumps in surprise beside me. His gun clatters to the table, his hands dropping beneath the table as he glances down in surprise.

"The thing about us whores, Hartman, is we're excellent at locating cock. We don't even need to look, we just find it." I grin, loving the glare on his face as he looks back at me. I commit it to memory as I lift my gun above the table and take a second shot, hitting him square in the chest. His body goes lax, and as expected, chaos kicks off around us.

Throwing myself at Emily, I push her down on the red leather seat beneath us, lying on top of her as a shield as the sound of guns firing, glass shattering, and disaster echoes around us. When a good ten seconds pass and no more shots ring out, I push up just enough to see across the room.

Blood paints the walls, the floor, everything, right down to the sundae glasses on the far wall. One man stands in the middle of the room, shoulders rising harshly with every breath until his gaze settles on mine.

"Are you okay, Sweet Cheeks?"

I nod. "Are you?"

"Yeah." I smile at him, when a bang sounds from outside. "For the love of all mercy, Scarlett. Sit your ass in that booth with Emily and don't come out. Okay?"

I don't even bother to look at the chaos, trusting him and giving him what he needs right now. "Go," I breathe, nodding in agreement. "I'll be right here waiting for you."

The bell above the door chimes again and he's gone. Glancing down at Emily, I startle when I see tears streaking down her face as she silently sobs.

"Hey, what's wrong?"

She shakes her head quickly, swiping at her wet cheeks. "Thank you." Her voice cracks, and I hug her tight.

Her hands squeeze around my neck, clinging to me as she cries and I hold her firm, like this is all that matters in the world, like there isn't a riot happening outside. When her cries turn to hiccups, I slowly lean back and she releases her hold.

"You girls want a drink?" Delia asks from behind the messy counter like it's not a freaking bloodbath in here.

I look down at Emily, and she nods. Shuffling out of the booth, I offer her my hand and lift her so she's sitting again. "Can I have a hot chocolate please, Delia?" she asks, and our savior for the night nods, getting to work.

"You look like a coffee kind of girl. Extra strong or extra sweet?"

"Can I go for both?"

She grins and gets the coffee machine going. It's a miracle how it's survived the hail of gunfire, but the coffee Gods would allow nothing else.

The door opens again, and I whip around to see Maggie sauntering in with a relieved smile on her face as she looks at Emily. She walks around the dead bodies littering the floor like they're invisible, making this entire thing even more surreal.

"Oh, I was hoping to join you as I could do with a coffee myself," Maggie grumbles, glaring at Hartman's dead body like it'll make him get up and move. Grabbing his arm, I angle him and shove him from the booth, letting him drop unceremoniously to the floor, and Maggie beams. "Thanks, Doll."

She doesn't take his side of the booth, though, she shuffles into Emily's side and holds her tight.

A tray is placed on the table beside me with our drinks and a handful of rags. Without a word, Delia cleans the blood from the seat and slides in.

My gaze finally drifts outside, daring to look at the chaos unraveling there while I stay in here. The lighting doesn't help, but I quickly spot the outlines of my Viking, blondie, Mr. President, and my grumpy asshole. I squint, making sure I catch a glimpse of Shift too, and I spy him by the window a little further down.

"Ladies, the next time we have a catch up, let's leave the bloodshed at home. What do you say?" Delia asks with a smirk, lifting a mug between us, and we all clink ours against hers before taking a sip.

The noise outside dies down and the doors to the diner swing open. Tension finally drains from my veins as the Ruthless Brothers stroll in, Graham and Paisley's men along with them. The crowd looks thinner by a man or two, but otherwise we're looking strong.

Emily clambers from her seat, making Maggie chuckle as she leaps over her. Emmett and Shift are shoulder barging each other to get down the aisle first when Emmett huffs. "I swear to fucking God, Emily. If you run to him first, I'm going to shoot him."

My eyes bug out of my head as my best friend freezes

with fear.

"What the fuck, Emmett?" I hiss, instantly pissed at him.

Emmett rolls his eyes like I'm the one being unreasonable. "Please, before he was all 'the woman I love', like that trumps that she's my fucking sister. I've known her longer. I win. I mean, don't get me wrong, I'm not against whatever shit the two of you have going on, but don't make this a challenge because I'll fucking win."

Well, that leaves me fucking speechless.

Emily gives in and launches herself at her brother and he catches her in a bear hug. The pair of them cling to one another as the rest of us watch. Love pours from them, swirling in the air and wrapping us all up tight.

"You're pushing it now, Emmett," Shift grunts from behind him. It doesn't help that their embrace is blocking the walkway for everyone, but that doesn't seem to matter to him.

"Good."

Emily giggles, patting at her brother's chest to put her down, and the second he does, she is swept up into Shift's arms. Thankfully, he's a little more considerate and manages to create enough space for everyone to get past him while he holds her tight.

I'm on my feet before I even realize I'm moving. The room still sways slightly, and I'm sure it's the concussion

I'm contending with, but I don't complain as Gray comes to a stop before me and tilts my chin up.

"Missed me?" he murmurs, pressing a featherlight kiss to my lips, and I hum.

"Always," I breathe as he shuffles into the booth beside Delia.

Ryker's next, exhaustion dimming his eyes as blood stains his clothes and skin. He cups my cheek, and I lean into his touch as he kisses my forehead. "You are the most ruthless woman I have ever met. We'll forever not be worthy of you, but I'll spend a lifetime proving to you that there's nowhere else you should be."

My heart races at his words, warming my soul as he follows after Gray like he didn't just say some of the sweetest damn things to me.

"I can't follow those words," Emmett grumbles, pressing his lips to mine. "But tonight, I'll top his bullshit with my tongue." He grins, making everyone shuffle even tighter into the booth as he takes a spot on the end.

Axel's head hangs low, blood coating his hair as he smiles at me. His arms band around my waist, hoisting me into the air as he tucks his nose into the crook of my neck and inhales.

I tentatively wrap my arms around his neck, and he pulls me in even tighter. My eyes start to drift closed until I spy Maggie gaping at us in shock.

"I hope you know you're paying for all of this mess," Delia grumbles, and Axel slowly lowers me back to the ground. He spins me and pulls my back to his chest, resting his forehead on my shoulder.

"Of course, and I'll be settling everyone's bills," Ryker adds, nodding toward Paisley who isn't shy of the blood stains covering him too.

A comfortable silence descends over the table as Shift and Emily step closer, while the other men mumble among themselves.

"What now?" Maggie asks, eyes still fixed on where Axel is touching me. The amazement on her face is enough to make pride ripple through my veins.

"Now we just be," Gray states, like it's as simple as that. "No more bullshit, just love," he adds, winking at me.

That sounds like perfection and a little surreal too, but with no prominent threat in sight, I'll take it. The five of us, the extended group of people I care for and love, and the club. That's all I need and want.

A weight shifts from my shoulders as I look around at the group, a chuckle from Emily lightening my heart.

My childhood may have been stripped of all that is kind in this world, leaving me broken, bruised, and alone. But I have a future with the Ruthless Brothers, one where I'm loved and part of a family. Now, I can make peace with my pain, knowing everyone who hurt me is gone.

Life is no longer about survival; it's about living, and loving, and feeling. A luxury I've never had with the numbness that's always coated me.

I vow to forever be brave, forever be loved, and forever cherish my every breath.

RUTHLESS BROTHERS MC

EPILOGUE

Axel

"Welcome to the shit show that's the Ruthless Brothers MC," Gray cheers, lifting his beer bottle in the air, and the four new prospects copy him. A buzz zaps through the air, making me grin despite my usual icy exterior.

It feels like we're on cloud nine, dancing with victory, toying with hope, and basking in the bright rays of the sun.

Four months have passed since we brought the Devil's Brutes to their end, and it's been the best four months of my life. The club is getting stronger and stronger. No more looking over our shoulder, no more fucking fools thinking we owe them anything, and no more drama either.

It's not going to stay like this forever, there's always

someone thinking they're the next big dog barking for the top spot. Let them, I'll enjoy putting them back in their place.

I chug my beer with everyone else around the table in Church before Ryker hits the gavel against the wood. People slowly start to disperse, until only Ryker, Gray, Emmett, and I remain. Shift shuts the door behind him, knowing we'll want a minute of privacy to ourselves, and I sink back in my seat.

"We're going to have to start building another fucking addition at this rate," Emmett muses. Ever since Graham left, his men have stayed. We patched them in two weeks ago, and now another round of prospects have joined our ranks. Thankfully, most of them have somewhere to stay in town, but he's right. An addition may be necessary.

"Don't let Maggie get wind of that, she'll have us decked out and organized for the next six months," Ryker says with a chuckle. She is keeping us in top shape as always, but she's finally starting to let her hair down and enjoy a life away from the club. Watching Gray go and pick her up at four o'clock in the morning because she's completely drunk with Delia is amusing as hell.

"Speaking of women, Scarlett and Emily should be back from campus now," Emmett states, glancing down at his watch, and I quickly jump to my feet before him. He instantly glares in my direction, but since I'm closer to the door, I've got more of a chance than the rest of them.

Flipping him the bird as I grin, I rush out of Church in search of the woman that has been consuming my mind all day. I love the fact that she's fully invested in getting her degree. This time taking courses that are better suited to her, but I still wish I could spend twenty-four hours a day with her, seven days a week.

I step into the bar area, the atmosphere alive with members and what was the Ruthless Bitches, who are newly named the Ruthless Babes, thanks to Scarlett and Emily's influence. The music is thumping and everyone is having a good time. Moving toward the bar where Maggie is handing out bottles of beer, I brace my arms on the wooden top and wait for her to see me.

She serves two more people before her eyes settle on me and she smiles. "She's outside in the yard and has asked for me to send you out there when you are done with the new guys," she says, and I nod.

Moving around the bar, I don't give her a moment to process what's coming before I wrap my arms around her and pin her to my chest. She freezes, shocked at the touch before her arms slowly wrap around me. Her shoulders shake, a gasp echoing in my ear as I rock us slightly from side to side.

I've been building up to this moment, practicing with Scarlett and pushing my boundaries to let in those that love me wholeheartedly, past the grumpy exterior and into the vulnerable side of me. Besides Scarlett, Maggie is the only woman I wanted to be able to have a connection with. She's been a mother to me, the woman I could have only dreamed of as a child, and I need to know she feels that.

Slowly leaning back, I look at her to see tears tracking down her cheeks and a wobbly bottom lip. I smile softly at her, which makes her glare as she swats at my chest. "Do not make me cry like that, you big goof," she grumbles, and I take a step back.

Not wanting to make the moment awkward, I wink and spin toward the door. Taking purposeful strides in search of my woman, I shove open the double doors to find myself face-to-face with Scarlett.

"Hey." Something flickers in her eyes that I can't quite decipher.

"What's wrong?" I grunt, my mood slipping as the need to put an end to whatever is affecting her takes over.

"Oh, nothing. Nothing's wrong, there's just some people here... that are asking for you." Her words make me freeze, my eyebrows knitting in confusion as she points over her shoulder. "There are three men and a woman sitting on the bench to my left. The guys are dressed in expensive suits, but they look far from official. While the woman is dressed casually. I haven't seen them before," she explains, but it doesn't make me feel any better.

There's no point delaying the inevitable, so I lace my fingers with Scarlett's and pull her along with me. As I approach the picnic bench, my gaze casts over the three guys in suits, before I settle on the woman. Her shoulder-length blonde hair shines in the late afternoon sun, her bright red lips making her look more like a boss-ass bitch than a whore, and her small frame might make her look dainty, but her eyes and her posture tell me she's poised for an attack.

As we near, she looks up at me and gulps harshly. Before I can say anything, she rises to her feet, rubbing her hands down her jeans as she peers up at me. "Hi, you must be Axel."

"And you are?"

She smiles at me like I'm not being rude, but the way Scarlett grips my hand tells me I most definitely am.

"My name is Wren."

"And…"

The guys' gazes start to narrow, clearly not appreciating my tone with her. "I believe we had the same father." Her words rock my core, freezing me in place as I play them on repeat. Footsteps sound from behind me, and I glance over my shoulder to see Ryker, Gray, and Emmett slowly making their way toward us.

I wet my bottom lip as I turn back around, trying to figure out what the fuck I say back to that, but my mind catches on a single word she said.

"Had?"

"Yeah. He's dead." She shrugs as if she's not sad about it, and I huff at the irony between us. "I killed him. If anything, I did you a favor. But sorry about that, I guess," she rattles out, placing her hands on her hips as my brothers come to a stop beside Scarlett and I.

"You... killed our father?" I repeat, tasting the weight of the words on my tongue and she nods.

"Yeah. For real, he was an asshole though, I swear."

I purse my lips, glancing at Scarlett who nods for me to reply.

Fuck.

"So... you're saying you're my sister?"

"Right," she agrees, and it feels awkward as fuck.

Am I supposed to feel something for her immediately? Am I supposed to confirm this in case she's talking bullshit? Hell, I don't fucking know.

"I killed my mom," I blurt, watching her eyes widen for a beat. "She was a cunt. Maybe they're together now, getting their punishments in hell."

"Is this some weird kind of bonding session or something?" Gray murmurs from behind me, and one of the guys with Wren bites back a laugh.

"I don't fucking know, but they sound as fucked as each other," Emmett replies like we can't fucking hear him.

Fucker.

"They're so alike a DNA test isn't even required. I'm telling you, we don't need to call Maury about this," Gray whispers.

Glaring over my shoulder at him, I sigh, before looking back at the woman who is supposed to be my sister. "Why are you here?"

She clears her throat, bracing a hand on the shoulder of the guy closest to her, like she needs to gain strength from him. "I've known about you for almost a year, but I was too scared to come find you."

"Why now?" I push, intrigued.

"I was wondering if I was related to a single soul that was worth half an ounce of the blood I've been surrounded by since I was born. I wondered if there were good people out there with the same blood as me, or if I was the best of a bad bunch," she rambles, and the guy beside her strokes her leg calmingly.

"He's good people," Scarlett announces with a nod, and Wren smiles, her shoulders relaxing as if she needed someone to say that.

"That's good to hear," she mutters. "Well, I'm staying in town for a few days. If you decide you'd like to chat, here's my number." She extends a small piece of paper in my direction, and I slowly take it from her, nodding as she offers one final smile and turns to leave, guys in tow.

I stand frozen in place until they're through the gates and off the property. "How do you feel?" Scarlett asks, concern flickering in her eyes and I shrug.

I lean in close, whispering in her ear, and her cheeks grow pinker with every word I say.

"I meant about your sister."

I roll my eyes. "She's in town for a few days. I'm not handling that shit right now when I've fucking missed you, Reaper." I cock a brow at her, and she shakes her head at me.

"I've only been gone for a few hours." She cocks a brow at me like I'm being ridiculous, but I don't give a shit.

"So, are you in or not?"

"Fuck yeah, I'm in."

"Fuck, Axel. She looks beautiful," Emmett murmurs in awe as he stares at the stunning woman roped up on my bed. It runs around her thighs, up her chest, and down her arms without actually binding them. Her touch is like electricity zapping through my veins and now one of my many addictions when it comes to her.

"Please tell me we're sharing," Gray pleads, coming to a stop beside me as he grins at her, and she beams a sultry smile back at him.

"She's going to be our good girl and offer a piece of herself to each of us. Aren't you, Reaper?"

"Yeah," she rasps in response, and Ryker tosses his cut over the back of the chair and strips down, the rest of us following suit once I've made sure the door is locked.

I hold back, excited as they run their hands all over her. The soft layer of oil coating her skin makes each of them groan. Wait until they realize I've fully prepped her... mouth, ass, and pussy.

Emmett draws a line down her spine, all the way to her ass, and realization dawns on his face, but I'm already shaking my head at him. "You will ruin her ass for everyone that ever follows after you. Attempt that in your own time, not mine," I grumble, making Scarlett chuckle, but he quickly lies down on my bed and lifts her over him.

She teases her core over his cock, and when he tests the tip of his cock, she welcomes him in. His eyes roll to the back of his head as she takes him as far as possible, the pair of them groaning in sync with one another.

Gray crouches behind her, peppering kisses over the backs of her thighs and the globes of her ass, before pressing a finger inside her second hole. "Holy fuck, has he already stretched you out?" he asks, breathless from the thought of it.

"Find out, Gray," I murmur, stroking a hand down

my cock as I watch him line his cock up with her ass and slowly sink all the way home.

"My mouth, Ryker, fuck my mouth," she begs, tits bouncing, as both Emmett and Gray find their rhythm.

Climbing onto the bed beside Ryker, I nudge my cock at Gray's cheek, and he moans. "It's like fucking Christmas," he gasps, flicking his tongue over the edge of my cock as he thrusts into Scarlett at the same time.

I hold still, letting him find some kind of rhythm, and Ryker claims Scarlett's mouth. This is never going to get old, there's always going to be some combination for us to try, and I'm going to be just as addicted to it as the time before.

I may not be filling her myself, but preparing her, and watching her get so much pleasure from the three of them is all I need. The sound of skin slapping against skin, combined with needy groans, and Scarlett's cries is my own slice of heaven.

Fucking Gray's mouth, I watch in awe as Scarlett falls apart at their touch repeatedly, hitting her fourth orgasm before mine finally starts to creep up my spine. When there's no stopping it, I slip from Gray's lips and release my load all over Scarlett's back, just like she asked me to earlier. A roar rips from my throat, ecstasy claiming me, and a domino effect cascades around the room as everyone finds their release.

Sprawling out on the bed with our woman between us, spent and filled with ecstasy, I sigh with contentment.

No matter what the world holds outside of these four walls, we always have each other in here. I owe everything to Scarlett. She helped me find a level of peace with the demons I was struggling to battle alone.

She's ruthless, rebellious, but most of all, she's my Reaper.

AFTERWORDS

Wow, just wow.

This was an epic rollercoaster of an experience. Writing this book has been a healing process. There's a reason this book came now, and not when I first thought of Scarlett and her men in 2021. I wasn't quite ready to heal yet, I'm still on the journey now, but these characters will forever hold a special place in my heart.

It was hard to write at times, hard to find the right words to convey what I wanted, and yet it's somehow my shortest series based on word count, while somehow being so paramount to my being.

The writing ability it has given me when approaching Falling Shadows, after releasing so much of my dark cloud, has been life changing. Which has me even more excited for you to dive into the Silvercrest Academy series at the end of the month.

Thank you for being here and accepting every inch of my soul.

THANK YOU

Michael 'the hot man' husband. Thank you for experiencing this journey with me, being my biggest supporter, and unwavering pillar of support and comfort. I know I say it all the time, but I fucking love you. Thank you to the babies for always being on hand with hugs, cuddles, and high fives. You make our world so much sweeter.

Thank you to my Queen Bee's; Tanya, Nicole, and Jen. Somehow you manage to keep me sane. I didn't know that was possible haha

A million thank yous to my beta's; Monica, Michelle, Keira, Kerrie, Marisa, and Krystal! You rock! We cranked the spice up on this one and you still went all Oliver Twist and asked for more hahaha Your comments gave me life!

Kirsty. Thank you for holding my hand and being a breathing space of understanding. Imagine if I tried to function without you haha

Laura and Katie. Thank you for all of the pretty men. We're not worthy of your awesomeness.

Sarah, Sam, and Sloane, the final touches are down to you two ladies, and I am eternally grateful for what you have to offer.

ABOUT KC KEAN

KC Kean began her writing journey in 2020 amidst the pandemic and homeschooling... yay! After reading all of the steam, from fade to black, to steamy reads, MM, and reverse harem, she decided to immerse herself in her own worlds too.

When KC isn't hiding away in the writing cave, she is playing Dreamlight Valley, enjoying the limited UK sunshine with her husband, children, and furbabies, or collecting vinyls like it's a competition.

ALSO BY KC KEAN

Ruthless Brothers MC

(Reverse Harem MC Romance)

Ruthless Rage

Ruthless Rebel

Ruthless Riot

Featherstone Academy

(Reverse Harem Contemporary Romance)

My Bloodline

Your Bloodline

Our Bloodline

Red

Freedom

Redemption

All-Star Series

(Reverse Harem Contemporary Romance)

Toxic Creek

Tainted Creek

Twisted Creek

(Standalone MF)

Burn to Ash

Emerson U Series
(Reverse Harem Contemporary Romance)
Watch Me Fall
Watch Me Rise
Watch Me Reign

Saints Academy
(Reverse Harem Paranormal Romance)
Reckless Souls
Damaged Souls
Vicious Souls
Fearless Souls
Heartless Souls

Silvercrest Academy
(Reverse Harem Paranormal Romance)
Falling Shadows

Made in United States
North Haven, CT
06 December 2024

61739354R00250